THE
LAST
MAPMAKER

THE LAST MAPMAKER

CHRISTINA
SOONTORNVAT

CANDLEWICK PRESS

Text copyright © 2022 by Christina Soontornvat
Map illustration copyright © 2022 by Christina Chung

First edition 2022

Library of Congress Catalog Card Number 2021947153
ISBN 978-1-5362-0495-7

22 23 24 25 26 27 LBM 10 9 8 7 6 5 4 3 2 1

Printed in Melrose Park, IL, USA

This book was typeset in Bembo.

Candlewick Press
99 Dover Street
Somerville, Massachusetts 02144

www.candlewick.com

For Tom,
my compass

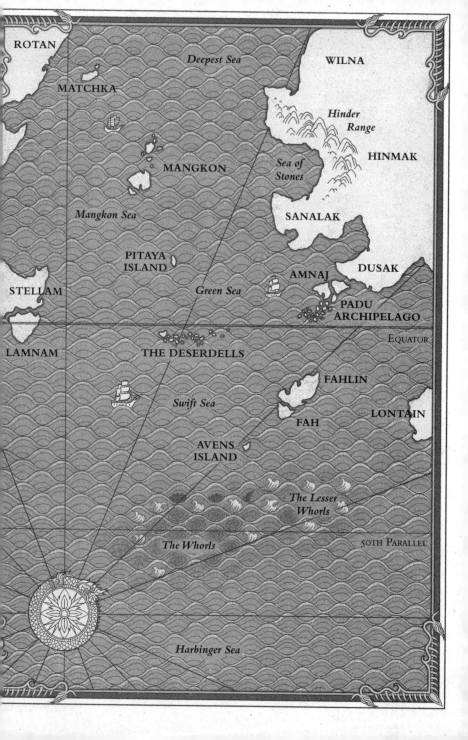

CHAPTER ONE
A Golden Morning

I must have looked like all the other Assistants standing in line for breakfast that morning at the Three Onions Café. We all wore the same starched white shirts, gray trousers, and stiff black cotton aprons with deep pockets. The Assistant's uniform was meant to put each of us on the same level, making us equals for the one year we would spend in service.

What a joke.

We may have worn the same clothes, but it was still clear as glass where we stood. We knew without asking who among us had carriages and who had to walk, whose mothers held important positions on this or that council, which of us had maids and which ones had to clean out their own bed pots. No one ever said anything, but we knew.

I lingered at the back of the line, doing my impression of the shy girl: feet tilted inward, head tipped down, looking like someone who had nothing to add to the conversation. You could learn more about people if they didn't think you were worth talking to, and I had a whole list of other details I needed to pay close attention to if I was going to play along with them.

Hair: combed free of lice and braided lovingly by my "mother" (or even better—my "maid"). Fingernails: cleaned out and filed. Shoes: the right kind, purchased from the right shop, shined, and with nothing icky sticking to the soles. Spine: held straight, as if I were proud of where I came from and had a bright future to look forward to.

Grumble!

I coughed to mask the sound of my growling stomach. A full belly was the one thing I couldn't fake, and coming to the Three Onions in the morning only made the grumbling worse. The steam in the wood-paneled restaurant smelled of fresh oysters, chopped garlic, and green herbs. It took real effort not to stick out my tongue and lick the air.

Something felt different from other mornings, though. The kids in line were chattier than usual. A tall Assistant leaned her elbow on the counter while the others pressed in close, hanging on her words. I called her Tippy because of the way she tipped her head back to look down at the rest of us. I didn't know much about her except that she worked for a Master Pastry Chef near the temple square. Tippy had always been popular and pretty, but that morning, she was glowing.

She laughed and smoothed her long braid over her shoulder. The light from the café windows bounced off something golden and shiny at her wrist.

So that was it. A lineal.

A pang of jealousy worked its way into my empty stomach. She must have turned thirteen the day before.

The other Assistants pushed in closer to gape at Tippy's gold bracelet. "Hold it up so we can all see!" said one of them. "Oh, it's so pretty!"

The others oohed and aahed as Tippy held up her wrist and gave the bracelet a little jangle.

"How many links is that—five?" asked another girl, unable to hide the envy in her voice. That spring, she had been the first among us to get her lineal. She touched it now self-consciously: four golden loops hanging from a brooch pinned to her blouse.

Tippy answered, a little too loudly, "Actually, it's seven."

Everyone murmured and pressed in closer to count the golden rings of her bracelet for themselves. Each link in a lineal represented one generation of ancestors—ancestors whose names you knew, ones you were proud to claim.

In my mind, I let out a snort. With a background that fine, what was she doing as a baker's Assistant?

Suddenly, I realized that all the eyes in the café had turned to me.

Tripe! At least I *thought* I'd snorted in my mind.

Tippy narrowed her eyes at me. "You, at the back of the line. What's your name?"

"Order forty-nine!" shouted a shrill voice behind the counter.

Thank the heavens!

I squeezed past the girls to get to the counter, then bowed to Mrs. Noom and took the container of porridge from her. "Thank you, ma'am," I said in the meekest version of my shy-girl voice. "I had better be going. I'm already late!"

I could feel the other Assistants' eyes on me as I passed. I knew they were sizing me up. They couldn't look down their noses at me until they figured out which rung of the ladder I stood on.

And what if they knew the truth—that I wasn't even on the ladder? That in a few months, when I turned thirteen, there wouldn't be so much as a cake crumb, let alone a lineal celebration? I had no proud family line, no noble ancestors. There was exactly one link to my past, and it certainly wasn't made of gold.

If they knew the truth, they would think I was nothing.

And who could blame them?

CHAPTER TWO

The Master Mapmaker

S team billowed behind me as I burst out the café
door. It had rained the night before, and the sky
still shimmered like a sardine's belly. Before heading up
the street, I stopped to say good morning to the café
owner's mother. She was in her usual spot on the side
porch of the café, but instead of sitting in her chair, she
stood leaning on her cane, her wrinkled face turned
out to sea.

"Good morning, Grandmother Noom," I said
softly. She couldn't see anymore, but the woman could
hear like a fox. I put my hand over hers, touching the
dark-green lines of faded tattoos that snaked up her
wrist and disappeared into her sleeve.

Grandmother Noom had been a merchant sailor
when she was younger. I liked to imagine her as a pirate.

"Can you smell the sea from here, Grandmother?" I asked.

"I can always smell 'er," she said without turning her head to me. "Do you hear them?"

"Hear what?"

"The hammers ringin' down in the harbor," she said in a hoarse whisper.

I listened but couldn't make out anything over the sound of people talking in the café and greeting one another on the street.

Grandmother turned her eyes to me, looking past my face. "They're readyin' the boats," she whispered. "I can hear 'em hammerin' the copper to the hulls. We're goin' to war again."

I patted her papery hand. I'd only ever known her to be sharp as a tack. Maybe her age was finally catching up to her. "I'm sorry. I have to go or I'll be late." I helped her back to her chair and bowed even though I knew she couldn't see it.

I crossed the street and headed uphill toward the Paper District. I turned onto Plumeria Lane, holding the porridge steady as I climbed the narrow stone steps. Up I went, past the bookshop, the paper-maker, the calligrapher, the other bookshop, and the art dealer.

All along the way, tidy shopkeepers in tidy aprons were busy sweeping the front steps of their stores. This had to be the cleanest street in the city of An Lung. The only thing allowed to litter the ground here were the pink-and-white blossoms of the plumeria trees that hung over the shop windows.

In a place this serene, how could anyone believe we were going back to war? After two decades of fighting every neighbor in striking distance, the Kingdom of Mangkon was bigger and stronger than ever. We finally had peace. We had security. It meant I actually had a good job for once.

At the top of the hill, the Temple of Nine Islands loomed over the street. The monks had come back from their morning walk by now, and they began ringing the temple bells, deep and slow. I was still early for work, but my feet skipped every other step until I finally reached the shop. Over the front window, a cotton banner swayed gently in the morning breeze. The words painted on the cloth read *Paiyoon Wongyai, Master Mapmaker.*

I twisted my key in the front door and closed it softly behind me. As I slipped off my shoes, I breathed in deep. For a brief moment, the smell of the shop filled me up and erased my hunger. It was the smell of crisp new sheets of paper (stacked by me), day-old ink (mixed by me), freshly washed wood floors (scrubbed by me), and tangy brass instruments (polished by me). My heart beat a little faster as I pulled open the shades. This was my favorite part of the day.

Golden sunlight spilled into the shop, illuminating the framed maps that covered the walls from floor to ceiling. Master Paiyoon had been the Master Mapmaker of the Mangkon Royal Navy for more than twenty years—the entire duration of the Longest War.

He had sailed all over the known world, charting more of it than anyone in Mangkon: the sheer cliffs of the Hinder Range, the puzzle-piece islands of the Padu Archipelago, the ice-clogged shores of Wilna, and tiny, distant Matchka.

Paiyoon was the last mapmaker of his kind still working in An Lung. He used old-fashioned mapmaking techniques, drawing coastlines as intricate as a lace collar. This meant that he worked slowly, but in the end, each map was exquisite enough to hang in a museum.

Some people in An Lung said, *That man would draw the pebbles on the beach if he had a pen fine enough*. Others said, *The spirits must have blessed him with the gift of far sight*. And still others said (in frightened whispers), *Stay away from that old Paiyoon. Everyone knows he sold*

his soul to a demon in exchange for his mapmaking talent.
I liked that one the best.

The shop door creaked open behind me. I set down the breakfast porridge and bowed as the Master Mapmaker walked in.

"Blast it, Sai, you are always early!" He scowled at me worse than if I had been late. His arms were full of papers, and I rushed to help him before they all scattered to the floor. "Windows, windows!" he chided me. "You keep this place too stuffy!"

Master Paiyoon slipped off his jacket and tossed it to me. He shuffled, belly out, to the counter at the back of the shop while I cracked the windows. I heard him groan as he bent to reach the lower cabinets. Not exactly the image of someone who made bargains with demons. I still hadn't figured out how old Paiyoon was, but his slow shuffle and his snow-white ponytail put him at least in his seventies.

I joined him at the counter, where he had poured the porridge into two ceramic bowls. He didn't thank me for getting it, just handed me my portion. I started to take a sip.

"No, no!" Paiyoon interrupted. "You can't eat it like that. Here." He reached for the spicy vinegar and ladled two big scoops into my bowl. "Now. Eat."

"Yes, sir."

I was used to his scolding by now, but when I first started my Assistantship, I was sure I was about to be fired every five minutes. It had taken me all these months to realize that no matter how much Paiyoon grumbled at me, my job was probably safe.

Seven months ago, when the Peace Declaration was signed, Paiyoon did what every shop owner in An Lung did: finally hired someone to help out. After so many years of having to go without, the whole city was in a rush to get back to normal business. I had been working for one of the shrimp stalls in the Goldhope Harbor Market and had just dropped off a delivery on the other end of Plumeria Lane.

As I passed Paiyoon's shop, a teenage boy burst out the front door, his clothes covered with ink and his face full of terror. Paiyoon chased the boy away, shouting that he had ruined two months of hard work with his sloppiness. Then the mapmaker had bellowed into the street, "Doesn't *anyone* around here know how to use a blasted ink pen?"

I raised my hand. I was hired on the spot.

Paiyoon must have been desperate. Usually Assistantships were arranged by family connections. If he hadn't been in such a hurry to hire someone, my job would have gone to one of those stuck-up kids I stood in line with at the café every morning. I knew how lucky I was, but I was still ready to bolt if Paiyoon ever started asking too many questions.

So far he hadn't asked me any questions about my life at all. He always paid me on time. And even though he was as grumpy as an itchy old cat, he was never cruel. It was the best job I'd ever had.

I raised the steaming bowl to my lips and took a slow sip. The porridge was mushroomy, oniony, and fishy. And, yes, I had to admit that it was better with the spicy vinegar. If demons really did bargain for souls, I would have sold mine to eat that porridge every day.

Master Paiyoon slurped his portion down and wiped his fluffy mustache with his handkerchief before reaching into his waistcoat pocket.

"Too much work to do and never enough time to do it," he grumbled as he shuffled to his desk. He said this so often that I considered it his morning prayer.

He brought out a polished gold disk and, with a quick snap of his fingers, flicked open the latch. He swiveled the glass lens out from its case, held it up to the light of the window, and began his morning ritual of cleaning it. The glass had a faint golden tint to it, and in the sunlight it glowed like a shard of amber.

This was Paiyoon's eyeglass, his most important tool. He used it to magnify the tiny pen strokes on his map paper, but it could also be used to see far into the distance. I'd always wanted to look through it, but I hadn't gotten up the courage to ask.

Paiyoon's lineal—a long chain of squarish gold links—ran from the eyeglass case to a clip on his waistcoat: a much more impressive way of wearing it than a dinky bracelet, in my opinion. I had never gotten close enough to count the links, but there had to be at least a dozen.

Normally, he would launch right into giving me orders for the day, but this morning he stared out the window as he cleaned the eyeglass over and over. I grabbed my notebook and pencil and walked closer to his desk.

"Ahem, Master Paiyoon, shall we go over the daily schedule? There was another delivery of boxes yesterday, but they're so light, I think they must be empty. Should I send them back?"

"Hmm, what? Oh, yes, just put them in the closet and I'll deal with them later."

"You still have to finish writing your lecture for the University. We have that order for the Koh Tang maps. And the naval secretary has asked if you can finish the new chart of Hinmak by September."

One result of winning a war meant that all the conquered places got new names, which was a pretty good deal for someone in the mapmaking business.

Paiyoon curled his lip as if he'd gotten a whiff of bad fish. "Hmmph. Waste of time. They'll just have to change the names back again after the next war."

"Um, yes, sir. And I guess you do have a lot of work on your list already." I tapped my pencil against my notebook. "Maybe you should focus on writing that lecture and I could work on making the copies of your map of Koh Tang?"

Master Paiyoon suddenly swiveled to look at me. His eyes, which had stared blankly out the window a moment ago, were now focused very keenly on my face. "Make copies of *my* map? Do you think you could?"

I had traced copies of other people's charts for him before—simple things that were beneath the Master's skills, like a chart of the fishing channel in Pristine Bay or a road map of some backwater province. But even though I had been working for him for six months, I had never been trusted to re-create one of Paiyoon's precious maps.

"I only thought . . . I was just trying to help, sir."

Paiyoon stared at me the same way he had stared out the window—as if he were trying to see past the

14

horizon. He picked up his pen and held it out to me. "Show me."

I looked down at the pen and then back at his face. He was acting so strangely. Was this some kind of test? The first rule of being an Assistant is humility. An Assistant must never boast that they can do the work of their Master. I swallowed my pride and cast my eyes down at my shoes.

"I'm sorry, sir. I don't know what I was thinking. Of course that's far beyond my skills."

Paiyoon's bushy white eyebrows furrowed to meet in one line. He opened his mouth to speak, but before he could get out a word, our doorbell jingled.

He shooed me toward the front. "That's the post. I'm expecting something, Sai. Quickly, quickly, to the door!"

Relieved not to be in trouble, I hurried to the front of the shop. I swung open the door and nodded to the delivery girl before taking the mail from her. There was just one letter. I could tell from the thickness of the paper that it was from someone important.

Master Paiyoon sliced through the envelope with his penknife. I started clearing away our breakfast, keeping my eyes on his face as he read the letter to himself. As he scanned the paper, deep wrinkles set into his forehead.

"What does it say, sir?"

Paiyoon looked up as if he'd forgotten I was there. "What? Oh, nothing, nothing. Just an invitation to some frilly luncheon at the naval academy, that's all." He waved the letter back and forth as though it wasn't important, but the wrinkles in his forehead stayed put.

He pointed to the counter behind me. "Back to work with you," he said gruffly. "We've both wasted enough of the morning."

As I set to work washing out the inkwells from the day before, I snuck a glance at old Paiyoon. He sat back in his chair, flicking the eyeglass in and out of its gold case, staring at the drawer where he had placed the envelope.

That letter was no luncheon invitation. Paiyoon might have been the Master Mapmaker, but when it came to lying, I was the expert.

CHAPTER THREE

The Prize

It was Friday, payday, so I shut the door to Master Paiyoon's shop with money weighing down my apron pocket. I walked down Plumeria Lane and lingered for a while around the bakeries at the bottom of the hill, looking into the shop windows and imagining blowing my entire week's pay on one box of doughy egg cakes wrapped in jasmine-scented paper. It would almost be worth it.

The sun had begun to set, which usually made everyone in the Paper District hurry: hurry to close up shop, hurry to put out the lamps, hurry to lock the door so they could hurry home to other people hurrying home to meet them.

But this evening was different. Instead of packing up their stores and rushing off to their families and hot

dinners, people milled around, huddling together and whispering. I walked as close as possible to listen in, but I could catch only snatches of conversation:

"... a huge waste of money if you ask me!"

"But you can't put a price tag on glory ..."

"You mark my words: one of those ships is looking for the Sunderlands. And when they find them, Mangkon will be the envy of the world."

Sunderlands?

What in the world was everyone talking about? I could buy a newspaper and find out, but I hated the thought of parting with even a half-lek of my wages. Instead, I headed west, away from the proper lanes of the Paper District and closer to Goldhope Harbor. Here, restaurants and food carts lined the waterfront, which was always crowded now that the War was over.

I ducked around the back of a stall that sold roasted duck legs. Greasy wads of newspaper filled the trash bin in the alley. I picked through it until I could find a front page of the *Mangkon Times* that wasn't completely soaked in duck fat. I shook it clean and read as I walked on.

HER ROYAL MAJESTY Queen
Siripatra announces the Expedition Prize.

a venture to extend the boundaries and glory of the Kingdom of Mangkon. The Queen has commissioned Her Royal Navy's finest ships for the expeditions. Captained by the heroes of the Longest War, these ships shall sail for all corners of the globe to claim new lands in Her name. Her Royal Majesty has directed four of Her best captains to set their sights for the Deepest Sea in the NORTH, the lands EAST of the Hinder Range, WEST past Rotan, and to break the fiftieth parallel in the SOUTH. Each captain who returns with a map of their discoveries shall be awarded a purse of 100,000 leks.

One hundred thousand leks! My head swam at the number. Mangkon must have done better in the War than I thought. I knew the names of the destinations from the maps hanging in our shop. Master Paiyoon had charted those places, but only barely. It was as if the Queen were sending her ships out to the very borders of his maps and ordering them to peek past the edges of the paper.

But there was no mention in the newspaper of the Sunderlands, despite what the people in the street were saying. And why would there be? That place was a myth. I combed through my memory for the few scraps of stories I had heard about it.

It was a continent floating on the back of a giant whale deep in the southern seas.

Or was it a group of islands, rooted to the ocean floor like a mangore tree?

It was covered in icy mountains.

Or was it smothered by steamy jungle?

Home to spirits.

Home to dragons.

That last one was the story that everyone knew, because it was the story of Mangkon itself. Long ago, dragons swam along the shores of the Nine Islands. We were a landbound people back then, with no knowledge of the sea. The dragons took pity on us and taught us how to make boats and ride the waves. They herded sardines right into our fishermen's nets. Soon our people began to thrive, and there weren't enough fish in our seas to feed a growing kingdom and a pod of giant sea serpents.

It was time for the dragons to move on. Before they departed, they left us one final gift: a golden egg. When it hatched, out popped a baby girl who grew up to become the first Queen of Mangkon. As for the dragons, they all swam down south and found a new home: the Sunderlands. No one had ever seen these lands, but they must have been a paradise, because the dragons never came back. Sailors even called the fiftieth parallel the Dragon Line, because no one had crossed it except the great serpents of old.

There were some folks who actually believed those stories, who swore they could show you the cave where their great-great-granddad had found a giant nest full of dragon eggshells. But most respectable people knew it was all just myths and bedtime stories. That made it even more surprising to hear anyone on proper Plumeria Lane talking about the Sunderlands seriously. Maybe more people believed in bedtime stories than I knew.

I was so lost in thoughts of dragons and ships and queens that I hadn't realized the sun had nearly sunk and I had left the streets of downtown An Lung far behind me. I tossed the newspaper into the gutter, then gave my head a shake to clear it. I had reached the Western Gate of our city. Beyond this point, the streetlamps thinned and the roads became muddy footpaths. I stopped to stare up at the gateway, just as I did every evening.

In the center of the gateway's arch was a wooden carving of a coiled dragon. Its slender body formed a perfect circle, and it held its tail clamped in its own jaws. That same symbol was engraved on all our coins and delicately stamped onto each link in every lineal in the nation.

The image graced our flag as well, which also included our kingdom's motto: *The Tail Is the Teeth*.

That one little sentence held a book's worth of meaning. It meant that the end was connected to the beginning. It meant that where you ended up depended on where you started. It meant that each person was one link in a lineal that went around and around in a never-ending circle, just like the dragon with its tail in its mouth.

Good little Mangkon children were taught to say the royal motto whenever we walked through one of our city's gates, as a reminder that we are the living links to our past.

I stared up at the wooden dragon, my lips shut tight. And then I walked into the darkness, heading for home.

CHAPTER FOUR

The Fens

Past the Western Gate, the solid streets of An Lung became mud, and then even the mud disappeared, melting into the marshy waterways of the Fens. The only way to get across the swamp was either by boat or along the floating bamboo walkways that snaked through the tall reedy grass.

The bamboo bridge swayed from side to side as I jogged across it. My ears pricked up and my eyes scanned my surroundings. I held one fist around the coins in my pocket so they wouldn't jingle. I needed to hurry and get out of my nice clothes.

The Fens were what was left of the marshland at the mouth of the River Hama. Way back before that mythical queen popped out of her golden egg, this was where Mangkon began. Centuries ago, it was probably

a nice place to start a civilization. Our people built their homes on rafts that drifted among the reeds and lotus blossoms. They let their babies nap in floating baskets tied to lily pads while they fished for paper-skin shrimp.

No one let babies float in the water now unless they didn't want them back. Once we dammed the River Hama to bring fresh water into the city, the Fens became too salty for anything but the mangore trees. The people beat them back with machetes and hammers every year, but while we slept, they crept toward us on their roots. Every kid who grew up in the Fens was told to stay out of the water or the mangores would pull them under and drink their blood.

One benefit of those creepy stories was that no one was going to go poking their noses around mangore roots looking for money.

I followed my usual route along the maze of creaky walkways. It was still early enough in the evening that I didn't see anyone other than the odd fisherman wrestling with his trap of slurpy eels. But you never knew who you might run into in the Fens, so I hurried on until I got to the old mangore whose roots held my hiding spot.

After checking over my shoulder, I slipped off my shoes and tucked them into my apron. I climbed off the walkway and onto the roots, clutching them with my toes. Ugly scars crossed the tree's thick trunk, making it easy to grip. On the far side of the tree, I was hidden from sight. A deep crevice in the trunk held a rice sack where I kept my regular clothes.

Getting changed was the tricky part. The mangore had thick, sturdy roots, but one slip and I'd end up in the black water.

It was nearly dark now, so I worked by feel to change out of my stiff clothes and into my tattered pants and tunic. As I folded up my Assistant's uniform and put the clothes away, I cringed to think about how much money I could get if I sold it. But it was out of the question. I couldn't make money in the first place unless I dressed the part.

I braced my shoulder against the mangore, reached my hand deep into the crevice, and pulled out the square candy tin that held my money. I let it bounce in my palm. It was deliciously heavy, but even after half a year of saving, still not heavy enough.

This had been a one-of-a-kind year. As twelve-year-olds, all Assistants in An Lung were on equal footing (or at least we pretended to be). But the little differences in our status—the type of shoes we wore, the number of sweets we could buy at the candy shop—would soon give way to the glaringly obvious ones as we began turning thirteen and starting school.

The wealthy among us would go to private conservatories. Middle-class kids would go to public academies. I couldn't afford either one. Some schools gave scholarships to good families who fell on hard times. But of course that required a lineal as proof that you were a worthy investment.

How long would Master Paiyoon let me keep working in his shop? I couldn't pretend to keep being twelve forever. He'd eventually ask me why I hadn't started school, or why I didn't have my lineal yet. I wouldn't be able to lie about my situation much longer. And then people would start to whisper. *The Master Mapmaker has a Fens rat as his Assistant?* It would be too embarrassing for him. Too embarrassing for me.

Without Paiyoon, without a diploma, and with no lineal to help dazzle my way through a job interview, the best I could hope for was to go back to the Harbor Market and deliver shrimp for the rest of my life.

I shook my head to banish the thought, swishing my hair hard enough that my braid slapped my eyes. The money in my tin couldn't get me into school, but I had started to believe it might at least get me out of the Fens. Ferryboats left the harbor all the time for the other eight islands. I could buy a ticket to snowy Koh Tang, or Koh Soolin, where I could get a job on a pretty little farm, somewhere no one knew me. Good luck had shone on me with my Assistantship; maybe it would shine on me again.

The last light in the sky was fading. Time to stop daydreaming. I counted out fifteen leks from my wages and put the rest in the tin before sliding it back into place.

The sky was black by the time I tiptoed back to the walkways and made my way to Down Island, the Fens' one plot of solid land. Once, I'd heard the other Assistants say that people from the Fens smelled bad because Down Island used to be Mangkon's trash heap, but they were wrong. I had checked. I'd spent an entire Sunday down a back alley, digging a deep hole, and all I ever found was dirt and water. Besides, I didn't smell bad.

Tall wooden buildings crowded one another for space, creating a warren of tight alleys. Doors on either side of me began to swing open, and I heard the usual sounds of the island waking up for the night: squid fishermen's boots thudding toward their boats, the clink of the bottle collectors' bags.

The thumping of piano keys meant I was nearing the Rooster Room. The glow from a fire lit up the bar's windows. Inside, customers howled the words to a popular drinking song. On the front steps, a group of men squatted around a dice game.

I walked a little closer, scanning their faces. But the person I was looking for wasn't there. A boy wearing a rumpled cap looked up and locked eyes with me. A jagged scar trailed from underneath the cap to the middle of his eyebrows. Startled, I took a step back, and the coins in my pocket clattered.

Mistake.

I turned and hurried away, hoping no one else had heard. But footsteps sounded behind me, matching my stride. I cut around a corner and slipped into a long alley. I counted a hundred paces, then glanced over my shoulder. The boy with the cap had turned the corner after me. He was just a kid, but almost twice my size, with broad, thick shoulders. He must have heard the jingle of money in my pocket. I was close to home now, but I didn't dare run.

I turned another corner, then quickly ducked into a doorway. As I flattened myself against the door, the boy passed by. I waited for him to disappear down the alley before stepping back out. I peered ahead into the alley but didn't see him.

Suddenly, I felt the darkness stir behind me. Before I could run, thick arms encircled my body. They pinned my biceps to my ribs, squeezing the air from my lungs.

"All your money. Now," demanded a gruff voice.

A surge of panic rolled through my stomach. My reflexes kicked in. I flapped my elbows like wings, forcing the boy's grip to slide up to my shoulders. Before he could tighten his hold on me, I dropped to a squat at his feet. I reached through my legs and grabbed his ankle. I sat back against his leg *hard*, throwing all my weight onto his kneecap. He cried out as he lost his balance and crashed to the ground.

I was already into a sprint when I heard a familiar hoarse laugh behind me.

"Ha-ha! Just like I showed ya!" Coughs and more rough laughter rose from the dirt. "That's how a small girl brings a big man down! You do that move better 'n me, Sai-girl!"

I whirled around. The blood still pumped in my ears, and it took me a second to find my words. It wasn't the boy after all.

"Mud," I said, panting. "I should've known that was you."

The man rubbed his leg as he called into the shadows. "Hear that, Catfish? The girl oughta be thanking me for teaching her to protect herself, but I don't even get a hello. How's that for manners?"

A small man in a tattered jacket stepped out from behind a pile of crates. He clucked his tongue. "Kids today are spoiled as old pumpkins. It's a real disgracement."

An acid taste rose in my mouth when I saw Catfish. I knew why he was here. I almost turned around and walked away from them. But now my adrenaline was gone and I felt completely drained. I needed to sit down. Wearily, I followed Mud and Catfish up a wooden staircase to the second floor of our building. Halfway up, I patted my hip. I gasped and reached into my pocket. It was empty.

Mud turned to me, laughing. He held out a hand full of coins and winked. "Still got my touch. Let's get home, Sai."

CHAPTER FIVE

New Business

"Home" was a one-room apartment in the oldest section of Down Island. A single lantern cast wavering shadows onto the yellow papered walls. Catfish settled himself at our table in the corner, grinning with his awful teeth. Mud limped to his seat and pulled out a chair for me. I wondered if I'd hurt his bad leg during our tussle in the street. Well, if I had, that was his fault, not mine.

He spread out the coins he'd picked from my pocket. Normally, payday put him in a good mood. I'd usually get a couple nights of him cheerful and chatty, at least until the money I gave him ran out. But tonight he eyed me suspiciously.

"Where were you last night?" he asked. "And don't tell me you came home late, 'cause I was here and you never showed up."

I swallowed my surprise. The night before, I'd snuck back into Master Paiyoon's shop after closing and slept under my desk. I'd done it specifically because I knew there was a kickboxing match in the Fens. Mud never missed those, and afterward he usually stayed at the bar till dawn.

"Me and the other shrimp girls snatched some fireworks from the docks," I said. "We stayed out all night setting them off."

Mud grunted approvingly. Still, his red-rimmed eyes searched mine. I held his gaze but wondered how much he suspected. It would take only one visit to the Harbor Market and a little questioning to find out I had left that job months ago. Lucky for me, Mud's injured leg and criminal record kept him out of all the respectable sections of An Lung. He rarely ventured farther than the Rooster Room these days.

I wish I could say that Mud was my stepfather, or an uncle, or anyone else besides what he really was. But you only had to look at us together to know that wasn't true. I was my father's spitting image, down to the inky-black flecks in our brown eyes. Only our hands were different. Mud had big, blocky fists—not what you'd expect from someone who could pick your pocket clean before you drew a breath. I must have inherited my slender fingers from my mother.

Mud stacked the coins and counted them again. "You're wasting yourself working that shrimp job. You could get something better. Something that pays decent."

"Don't scold the child," said Catfish. He smiled at me and patted the top of my hand. His yellow teeth overlapped one another like a fanned-out deck of cards. "Your current employment won't be of no consequence much longer, my dear Sai. The three of us shall soon be sitting in the lap of luxury. We've got us a plan, envisaged by your father and to be carried out by my good self."

Mud rolled his eyes at Catfish's flowery language. "It's a job. Best one I've come up with in a long time. Show her."

Catfish opened the brass buttons of his jacket and rummaged inside one of the pockets. He still wore his Navy uniform proudly, even though he'd spent most of the War locked up for selling rations on the shadow market. He pulled out a packet of crumpled documents and handed me a scrap of newspaper. It was an obituary notice. Apparently, a Navy captain had passed away last week one city over, in An Song. From the list of titles and properties, he must have been rich as a lord.

Catfish pointed down to the paper. "This captain was a true hero. Fought in the Battle of One Hundred Ships. Every officer who survived that battle donated their armor to the Mangkon War Museum."

"So what?" I said.

"So," said Mud, "his armor's still in the museum. Now the War's over, Navy battle armor brings in a real nice price on the shadow market. One of the captain's close family friends really should go to the museum and bring such a valuable heirloom home."

Catfish licked his jutting teeth and put both hands over his heart. "That's where I come in. Yes, indeed, I was a true bosom friend of the dearly departed captain." He pretended to wipe a tear from the corner of his eye. "The least I could do for my dead compatriarch is to fetch up his armor and carry it home to his wife and children."

I rolled my eyes. "And who in their right mind would believe a story like that?"

"That's where *you* come in," said Mud. "Catfish is goin' to show up at the museum with a letter from his dear old naval friend that gives permission for Catfish to take the armor home to An Song."

And now we came to it. A forgery job.

Catfish was beaming. "When Mud came up with this plan, I said to him, Mud, this is pure perfection. Your daughter's the greatest forgery artist the Fens has ever known."

An artist? That was going a little far. I had helped Mud and Catfish with dozens of schemes over the years, writing hot checks or forging letters to our landlords from fake aunts who promised so sweetly to pay our rent if we could just keep on living there. But this job was much bigger than anything I had done before. Impersonating a decorated Navy officer to steal a valuable heirloom? My palms were sweating at the thought of it.

"Where's the sample?" I asked Catfish.

"Sample?"

I bugged my eyes out, exasperated. "The sample of the captain's handwriting. The thing I'm supposed to forge."

Catfish scratched his head with one fingernail. "Well, now, it turns out that a handwriting sample has been a little complicating to acquire." Mud made a low growling sound in his throat. Catfish quickly added, "But it don't matter! The museum don't know what the captain's handwriting looks like. You just need to write 'em a letter that's nice and fancy, use the words fancy people like to use."

Relief ran through me. I sat back in my chair. "I'm sorry, but I can't do it. I can't write a letter like that out of thin air."

Mud's nostrils flared. "What was the point of sending you to that teacher if you can't even write a simple letter?"

The Fens had one school, and it was shut down more than it was open. The kids who did learn to read and write had patchwork educations. When I was nine, Mud had paid an old widow who lived at the edge of Down Island to tutor me. She was supposed to teach me all the subjects, but the only thing I remember was writing. The old lady was obsessed with penmanship and made me copy row after row of letters for hours. If I didn't copy them perfectly, she'd pinch the top of my hand with her yellow fingernails. I was so relieved when Mud couldn't afford to send me to her anymore. But in our short time together, I had developed flawless script and could copy anyone's letters.

I had also learned that Mangkon's strict social rules extended even to handwriting.

"It's not going to work," I explained to Mud. "Rich people like that captain would use a very formal alphabet for something like this. It's not the same way as normal people write. I could copy it if I had a sample, but it's too complicated to just make it up."

"Can't be that different," said Catfish. "Just words on paper. Make it look proper and no one will know."

I snorted, thinking of the Assistants I waited in line with every morning, who knew from one glance at your hair ribbons whether you belonged or not. "Trust me: it won't work."

Catfish tried to put on a sweet smile, but it just made him look slimier. "Sai-Sai, come on, now. I've been here for you since you was a little girl, and now I need your help. You wouldn't want to cheat your old uncle out of his share of eight hundred leks, would you?"

Eight *hundred* leks! Was that really what someone would pay for a rusted suit of metal? I looked at Mud, who was drumming his fingers nervously on his thigh. My father was not a nervous sort of man. Something wasn't right. I never liked any of Mud's plans, but I liked this one least of all.

"Please, Sai-Sai?" Catfish mewed. "Just one itty-bitty letter?"

Mud would never force me to do this job. I could always tell him no.

But I wouldn't, and he knew it.

"Fine. I'll try," I said.

Catfish clapped his hands. "That's our girl! And I can get you a letter to copy. I got a lady friend in the post office, and I'll just—"

"No, thanks," I said. Knowing Catfish, he'd pick the wrong thing *and* get caught in the process. "I'll figure something out on my own."

Mud was looking at me, and the relief on his face gave me a hint at why he had been so grim. He needed this money badly. He probably had debts, as always. "How long will it take?" he asked.

"I'll need a couple days."

"Perfect—two days it is!" said Catfish. "That's great, ain't it, Mud?"

"Great," he said flatly.

Catfish licked his lips as he made for the door. "Excellent. All right, chum, shall we raise a glass to commemorize this new line of business? Come along—the Rooster Room beckons!"

Mud scooped up my coins from the table and slid them into his pocket. He lingered in the doorway without meeting my eyes. "Just this one job, Sai. Then we'll have enough to get back on our feet again. You'll see. Things'll change."

I didn't answer, and he left without shutting the door.

I waited until they were gone, then I flopped down on my pallet on the floor and stared up at our water-stained ceiling. It hovered low over my face, and the walls were close enough that I could smell the mildewed paper.

Just this one job. How long had I been hearing that? But Mud was right about one thing. Things were going to change.

The Tail Is the Teeth.

I had heard those words all my life. They meant that no matter how hard you tried, you couldn't escape who you were or where you came from. But they couldn't be true. I wouldn't let them be true.

I would find a way to leave it all behind, even if it meant I had to bite off my own tail to do it.

CHAPTER SIX

Expedition Fever

I needed a letter.

I spent the weekend sneaking by mailboxes and swiping whatever I could find inside. It was no good, though. The types of houses whose mailboxes might contain what I was looking for were locked behind high copper gates or guarded by snooty doormen. If only I could have gotten close, I could have taken what I needed. The city was certainly distracted enough that no one would have noticed.

All of An Lung had caught Expedition Fever. Old Grandmother Noom had been wrong about us going to war, but she had been right about the hammers. Even all the way in the Fens, you could hear them clanging in the harbor as they converted the kingdom's warships to vessels of exploration. Though it

was the weekend, when businesses should be closed, door chimes jingled nonstop as messengers delivered official royal orders for this or that. Bankers gleefully drew up loans, and accountants even more gleefully calculated the taxes. Everyone was in a rush, hurrying to get the ships ready and loaded in two weeks—in time for the Queen's birthday, the day she'd send her ships out across the globe.

Time was running out for me, too. Sweat soaked the back of my shirt as I tromped through the city, searching for a mailbox I hadn't tried yet. The August heat had arrived overnight, evaporating all the rain that had seeped into the ground during the previous months, making the streets steam like boiled prawns.

Mud was home when I got there Sunday night.

"Did you find one?" he asked before I could even get through the door.

"Not yet," I grumbled, heading straight to my mat in the corner of the room.

"It's all right—you will," he said with forced cheerfulness. "If you need more time, just say the word. Catfish is itching to go, but he can wait a little longer."

I flopped onto my mat without a reply.

Mud scooted a chair closer. He cleared his throat. "Listen, Sai, I know you don't like doing this. I don't like asking you to do it. But this won't be like other times. It's enough money to make a difference. With four hundred leks, we could move out of here. We could get a nice place." He smiled a half-smile. "Your birthday's coming soon." I looked up at him, and his smile spread to his eyes, crinkling them at the corners. "Don't you worry, I didn't forget. You'll be thirteen this year. With this kind of money, I could get you a lineal."

I felt my eyebrows lift.

"That's right," he went on. "And I wouldn't just get one link, either. I'd get you a whole bracelet. I know a guy. He makes them in his blacksmith shop, and they look perfectly real. He even does the royal stamp and everything."

I dug my fingers into my mat. Of course Mud "knew a guy." The punishment for buying a fake lineal was prison, but that didn't bother him. What was I expecting? That he'd save up for a real one? Take me downtown to the Hall of Records to get it stamped by the Lineage Council? They'd probably laugh in our faces, anyway.

"I don't *want* a lineal," I said.

Mud's face fell, leaving only the scrap of a smile on his lips. "I know. They're stupid. I hate 'em. But still, every kid in Mangkon needs one if they're gonna get ahead—"

"I don't need a lineal," I spat. I knew I should hold my tongue, but I was fuming—from my frustration, from the heat, from our tiny, cramped room. "I won't need one because I plan on being a lowlife con just like my father!"

Mud shot to his feet, fists tight at his side. I stayed exactly where I was. I wasn't afraid of him. I'd seen him get in fights before, but I knew he would never lay a finger on me.

Every muscle in his body tensed, then sagged again. He rubbed his leg, and his face became a stony block I couldn't read. "I know what you think of me, Sai. You think you're so much better than me. Well, maybe you're right. But I'm still a part of everythin' you are, like it or not."

He limped to the door. The walls of the room shook when he slammed it behind him.

I balled my hands and pressed them to my temples. I was so angry, my eyes were blurry. I hated our horrid stinking room. I hated slimy Catfish. I hated Mud and his never-ending crooked plans.

I had to get out of there. If I stayed, there would always be a new scheme, and I would always get dragged down into it. Even if Mud and Catfish got lucky and one of their cons worked, it wouldn't last. We could live in a palace and there would always be something rotting in the corner.

I would finish this job and then I'd be out. I shut my eyes and let out a long, slow breath. I had spent the weekend looking for a letter from a stranger to copy, but it wasn't working. Maybe I had known all along that it wouldn't work, and I just didn't want to admit that I only had one real option. If I was going to forge a letter, there was one place to get it.

I would have to go to the shop.

CHAPTER SEVEN
An Honest Start

Monday morning, I slipped out of the apartment long before dawn, tiptoeing past Mud, who lay snoring near the door, fully dressed with his shoes on. He and Catfish must have had a big night at the Rooster Room.

As I jogged down the bamboo walkways, the Fens were sleepy and still, with a thin mist hanging over the black water. Something shiny slapped the surface, startling me and nearly making me slip.

Calm down—it's just an eel.

But I couldn't shake that jumpy feeling as I changed into my Assistant's uniform. I tried to tell myself that I was still anxious after being followed by that boy the other night, but I knew that wasn't the only reason.

I hurried into An Lung, taking the shortcut along the hill that overlooked Goldhope Harbor. Sunlight

had started to seep over the horizon, and I could see the four ships down below, clustered like a herd of fat-bellied seals. Workers were already busy down on the docks, hammering, painting, hoisting, racing to make them ready on time.

I was breathless by the time I got to the shop and lit the lamp on Master Paiyoon's desk. All night I had been thinking of the letter that had come on Friday, the one that had seemed to disturb Paiyoon so much. I hadn't seen the return address, but I remembered the thick paper of the envelope and the formal seal. It might even have been sent from someone in the Navy, which would have been the perfect thing to copy for Mud's plan. But when I slid open the desk drawer, there was no envelope inside.

I was almost relieved. I had given it my very best shot, and it just hadn't worked out. But then I saw a piece of paper tucked beneath the sketches on the desk. It was a letter written by Master Paiyoon. He must have started it on Friday and not mailed it yet.

I held up the letter and scanned it. He had written in the very formal, swooping script that upper-class Mangkon people used only for special occasions. I stood staring at the letter, biting my lip. There was no way around it. This was exactly what I needed.

I took Paiyoon's letter to my own desk and pulled out a fresh sheet of paper. My plan was to make a quick copy that I could take home to use as a model for Catfish's fake letter for the museum. I would worry about what to say later.

I soon lost myself in the work. The contents of the letter were boring: it was basically a long-winded thank-you to some old admiral. But Master Paiyoon had a beautiful script that made even the boring words interesting. Each character was like a work of art in itself. As much as I hated helping Mud with his schemes, I did love the actual forgery. Watching my hand form words that weren't mine made me feel like I was someone else, and there was nothing better than being someone else.

My first copy was good, but I wanted to do it a second time to make sure I got the characters perfect. I had the hang of Paiyoon's looping style now, and I loved the feeling of my pen making the strokes. I was enjoying myself—too much, as it turned out.

The bells in the Temple of Nine Islands gonged the hour. Seven o'clock.

Breakfast!

I needed to fly if I was going to make it to the Three Onions Café and back before Paiyoon arrived.

47

Hurriedly, I began cleaning up, but my inkpot tipped over, and a stream of jet-black ink dribbled off the edge of my desk and onto the floor. I grabbed a rag and was still wiping up the spill when I heard the key click in the front door.

When Paiyoon saw me, his jaw dropped. "Sai? What in the world are you . . . ? Blast it, girl! You are always here so early!"

I stood up and tried to hide the desk with my body. "I'm so sorry, sir . . . I just, well, I thought I would drop off my things before going to get breakfast..."

He hung up his coat and set down his leather satchel. "I was sure I would beat you here this morning," he grumbled. "I'd swear you slept in the shop if I didn't know better." His hands moved over the surface of his desk, searching for something and not finding it. He looked up at me. "What is that you're working on?"

My heart plummeted to my knees as he shuffled toward my desk. I couldn't think, let alone make my mouth form words. I had no choice but to step aside and let him see.

He picked up his letter off my desk. His eyes grew wide when he saw my copy. He picked it up too and held both letters side by side. "You did this?" he asked.

I could hear the shock and accusation in his voice, and it made me want to crawl into a hole. "I . . . I have been trying to improve my handwriting, sir. I wanted to be ready for school when I start, and . . . I think your script is so nice, and . . ."

It was the worst lie I had ever told—so obviously untrue that I couldn't even finish it.

Master Paiyoon seemed not to have heard me. "Unbelievable," he murmured, flipping the pages back and forth. "I cannot tell these two apart. I don't even know which is my own." He lowered the papers and spun around to face me. "How long have you known how to do this?"

"I've . . . always had a talent for copying things, sir."

Paiyoon's eyebrows pressed together, and he eyed me as he had on Friday, as if I were a window he was trying to see through. "I have never seen anyone who is able to do this so flawlessly. Can you only copy script?"

I swallowed. "If I have something to follow I can copy anything almost exactly."

Not almost, I thought. *Exactly.*

Paiyoon did something strange then. Without looking away from me, he took the golden eyeglass from his pocket and held it up between us. I'd never seen him use it to look at a person before. His eyeball seemed enormous magnified through the pale glass. It might have made me laugh if I hadn't been so worried, and if he hadn't stared at me so seriously, his eye roving over me like a blackbird's.

Paiyoon lowered the eyeglass and nodded, as if he'd found something he had been searching for.

He pulled out the stool at my desk and pointed to it. "Sit."

This was it. End of my job. End of Mud's scheme. Maybe Paiyoon would even call the police on me. I should have started for the door, but I was too ashamed to move.

Paiyoon pulled a stool next to mine and sat. He let out a deep breath and crossed his arms over his chest. Wonderful. Not only was I about to get fired, I was going to get a lecture to go with it.

But Paiyoon had no lecture for me. His usual gruffness had softened slightly, and he seemed tired more than angry. "Sai, I am about to leave on a long journey. Have you heard of the fiftieth parallel?"

I looked up at him. "The Dragon Line?"

Paiyoon waved his fingers in front of his face and rolled his eyes. "Not the bedtime stories. I mean the actual place." He reached into his pocket and pulled out a small piece of clipped newspaper. It was the announcement about the Expedition Prize from the article in the *Mangkon Times* that I had read a few days before.

Suddenly, everything clicked. The Expedition Prize, the reason empty packing boxes kept arriving at the shop, the mysterious envelope, and the thank-you letter to the admiral in the Navy. Mangkon was getting ready to send boats out to map the world. Of course the country's most celebrated mapmaker would be on board one of them. What a convenient time to fire his Assistant.

"You were given a place on the southbound expedition," I said flatly. "Congratulations, sir."

His eyes cut from the newspaper to me. "Wrong," he said with a huff. "I wasn't asked to join the expedition. Quite the opposite, in fact."

He stood up and started pacing in front of me. His mouth opened to speak and then snapped shut again. Finally, he sat down with a weary sigh. For the life of me, I had no idea where this conversation was going.

"The Queen's Council thinks I'm too old," he said quietly. "I'm past my prime, and this expedition will be all about youth. The heroes of the War are captaining the ships. You should see the crews—hardly more than toddling babies. The captain of the west-going ship still wears her hair in pigtails! I had to pull every string, call up every old friend. I did everything short of begging on my knees to ask for a position on that southbound ship."

I could not imagine my cantankerous employer begging for anything, much less on his knees. "And they granted you a place?"

He raised one eyebrow and nodded. "They did. Finally. And now I find myself in a terrible situation. Because you see, they are right, Sai. I am too old."

He picked up a pen from my desk and began to draw a line on a sheet of paper. His fingers trembled. He set his mouth tight and gripped the pen, concentrating. It only made the shaking worse. The line snaked in a zigzag.

I looked from the wobbly line on the paper to the perfect maps lining the walls. "But your work . . . the maps . . ."

Paiyoon set his pen down and rubbed his fingers with his other hand. "The tremor began almost a year ago, before you started working for me. I take injections each morning to calm the shaking. I thought I could bring enough to last the entire voyage, but my doctor neglected to inform me that they expire. The first week out at sea and I'll be wobbling too hard to hold a pen. The point of the expedition is to make a map. I can't make one if I can't even draw a straight line." He leaned back on the stool and looked squarely into my eyes. "But perhaps fortune has thrown me one last coin. Given what I have seen here, I think you could fill in for what I lack. I could teach you everything. I'll help you take all the readings, make all the measurements. I'll check all your work. You would only have to draw and write for me. And you can even do it in my handwriting. No one will know."

My brain felt full of seawater. Was I really hearing him right? "I . . . I . . ."

A worried look spread across Paiyoon's face. He shook his head apologetically. "Oh, my goodness, what was I thinking? I can't ask you to lie for me. You're just a child."

"How long is the journey, sir?"

Master Paiyoon frowned. "We may be gone for a year. More if we get waylaid for some reason. Oh, blast, this was a foolish idea. This is far too dangerous to even bring up."

A year away from Mud and Catfish. A year away from the Fens. I had been saving my money for a ticket away from my life, and here was a free ride.

"You'll be starting school soon, and your parents would never agree to it," Paiyoon continued. "Forget I ever mentioned it."

"Oh, but they would, sir!" I blurted out. "I know they would. It would bring so much honor to the family to have me be a part of such an important mission."

"You'll be thirteen soon, right?" said Paiyoon. "You'll miss your lineal ceremony, all those important family moments . . ."

"My family would understand. We can delay the ceremony until I get back. This is for the glory of our kingdom, after all."

Paiyoon snorted and scowled at the newspaper article. "The kingdom is drowning in glory as it is. But you are right. This mission is vitally important." He looked at me, and the weariness in his voice was gone. His eyes were bright and fiery, and in that moment it seemed ridiculous that anyone would claim he was too old for anything. "This expedition is too precious to leave to anyone else. I have to be the mapper on that ship, but I can't do it without help. You have been with me for months, Sai—longer than anyone else. You're a hard worker and honest. I need someone I can trust."

I could count the compliments Paiyoon had given me up to then on one hand, and guilt pricked my stomach to hear him call me honest. "I won't let you down, sir. It would be an honor to serve by your side."

Paiyoon eyed me gravely. "Sai, everyone in An Lung is treating this expedition like it's all for fun. But the truth is that it could get dangerous. There's a small chance we won't come back."

That's exactly what I was betting on. I wasn't coming back. Ever. A ship on an expedition would stop at ports along the way out and on its return. I could pick the one farthest from Mangkon, step off with my money tin tucked under my arm, and not look back once.

"I'm willing to take that risk, sir."

Paiyoon tapped the pocket where he kept his eyeglass. "Very well, but I want to speak with your parents about it, and there is a ship's contract they'll have to sign since you're underage. Ask them to come with you tomorrow."

"About that." I cleared my throat. "It's difficult for my father to come all the way up Plumeria Lane. What with his back injury and all."

"Hmm, yes, well, I suppose I could go to your—"

"And the wounds." I rubbed two fingers down my throat. "In his neck. Ever since he came home from the War, it makes conversation awkward, sir. I don't think either of my parents will have a problem with me going. But you could write them a letter to be sure."

"Fine." Paiyoon opened his desk drawer and took out a sheet of paper with his name stamped at the top. Luckily, he didn't give people one-tenth the thought he devoted to maps. "But I'm going to disclose all the risks to them in my letter." He wagged his finger at me. "I won't have us setting sail under any deception."

"Of course not, sir. None at all."

CHAPTER EIGHT

A Forgotten Key

Now that I knew I'd be leaving An Lung, I had no stomach for helping with the armor-stealing con. So what if we lost the apartment? Or couldn't afford supper? I would be a thousand miles away, fattening up on ship's rations. I worried how I would tell Mud that I wouldn't do it, but then it turned out that I didn't have to. Catfish had gotten caught pretending to be a monk gathering donations for a new temple. He'd had to run from the police with his monk's robes hiked up around his knees, and now he would have to lie low for at least a month. He was lucky not to be in jail, though he was probably more afraid of facing Mud's temper than the police.

Mud's schemes had fallen through before, but I had never seen him this upset about it. He must have needed the money even more than I thought. Normally, that would have made me nervous. We'd been kicked out of apartments before for not making the rent. But that wasn't my problem anymore. I would never again have to worry about whether or not Mud could take care of us. From now on, I would take care of myself. I just had to hang on until our ship set sail.

The Friday before the Queen's birthday and our departure, Paiyoon closed the shop for the last time. He had to attend to his house and make his personal preparations for our long absence. We agreed that I would meet him on Monday morning in the harbor. Our ship was called the *Prosperity*, which was just one more sign of my good luck.

"We cast off at nine," said Paiyoon. "Plan to be there early so there's no chance you'll miss it. And take this." He gave me a handful of coins. "It's your pay for this week, plus a bit extra for your parents to ease the sting of your being gone."

"Thank you, sir," I said, dropping the coins into my apron pocket. Paiyoon would be covering my room and all my meals on board the *Prosperity*, which would cut into the wages I'd be paid upon our return. But that was fine, because I didn't plan on lasting that long anyway.

"I'll be there by dawn on our departure day, sir."

Two and a half days until we set sail. What in the world was I going to do with myself? I wished I could still go in to work just to make the time go faster, but the shop would be boarded up over the weekend. With no other ideas, I headed back to my hiding place in the Fens and changed into my old clothes for the last time.

Before I left, I pulled out the wool cap and double-woven cloak I had bought in the Harbor Market. It cost way too much, but Paiyoon had told me it could get cold on the deck of a ship. I smiled, imagining myself standing on the deck of the *Prosperity*, warm in my cloak while a cool sea breeze blew into the sails. I hid the cloak again and headed for home.

In my mind I still stood on the deck of our ship when I walked into our apartment. The door slammed shut behind me. I whirled around to see Mud, his nostrils flared and his mouth pinched in anger.

"I guess you think I'm just a fool, don't you?" he growled.

"What are you talking about?"

Mud glowered and planted his feet in front of the door. "I knew you were acting funny. I went down to the Harbor Market and asked for you at the shrimp stand. They said you left the job months ago! Now tell me where you really been!"

My stomach twisted. Of all the times for Mud to uncover my lies, why did it have to be now? I was stupid to have come home at all. I reached into my trouser pocket and pulled out my wages.

"Here's two weeks' pay. Just leave me alone."

Mud lit up at the sight of the coins, and I knew he was only thinking of the Rooster Room. Good. Let him go. As soon as he was gone, I'd slip out and never come back. I'd sleep on the streets if I had to.

"Two weeks' pay? All of a sudden you've got more money than a banker?" He grabbed the coins off my palm, and a few of them clattered dully onto the floor. "Hey, now, what's this?"

My stomach dropped as Mud picked up the small brass key. In my daydreaming I had forgotten to leave the key to Paiyoon's shop in my hiding place.

"Are you holding out on me, Sai?" said Mud, twisting the key in the light. "If you've got yourself a little treasure box to pick from, you should tell me."

I grabbed for the key, but he held it out of reach. "Give that back!" I shouted. "I don't pick from a treasure box. I earned those wages. Where I get them is my business."

Veins popped out on Mud's neck as he shouted, "Tell me where this key is from right now!" He stepped back from me, breathing hard. After a long pause, he rubbed his temples and slowed his breath. "Listen, Sai," he said more calmly, "I'm sorry for shouting. You just tell me where to go and I'll do all the work."

"Yeah. I know what that means."

"I need the money," he said slowly. "Really need it. You understand me?"

I understood, but I didn't want to know the details. Maybe he owed money to some Down Island gambler. A frightened look flickered in his eyes, one I had never seen on him before.

A part of me felt sorry for him. Why not just tell him the truth? Once the *Prosperity* set sail, no one would be watching the shop. And I had no doubt that Mud would do a clean job of it. Besides, I'd be long gone by then.

But something held me back. I thought about the precious maps hanging on the walls. They'd fetch a fortune on the shadow market. Not to mention all the other expensive equipment. Stealing a letter from Paiyoon was one thing, but setting up a robbery of everything he owned was something else entirely.

I backed away from Mud. "I can't tell you. I won't tell you."

"Fine," spat Mud. He dragged his rickety chair in front of the door and sat down. He tapped the shop key against his thigh. "But you're not leaving this room till you tell me what this key unlocks. I can wait. I got all the time in the world."

CHAPTER NINE

Departure Day

I felt sure that if I just waited long enough, Mud would have to leave our apartment at some point before the *Prosperity* set sail on Monday. I tried to put on a bored, careless attitude, while inside, my pulse ticked like the gears of a clock.

But Mud didn't leave. He sat in his chair in front of the door continuously. He'd pulled our little table in front of him, and for hours the slap of cards was the only thing I heard as he played solitaire. Twice each day there was a knock on the door, and Mud went into the hallway and came back with food. Was Catfish bringing it? Or someone else? There was no way to know.

Mud gave me water and half of what he had to eat, but I could barely touch the food. I felt sick. With each passing hour, I became less and less sure that I'd find

a way to get out of that room and make it onto the *Prosperity* on time.

Mud broke up the hours by telling me I could have this or that special treat if I told him what the key unlocked. He made scores of empty promises: We'd leave the Fens. We'd find a place in the country. He'd get a real job, maybe buy a small farm. Things would be different.

I'd heard it all before. I kept my mouth shut.

But the long hours of waiting frayed my nerves. I had strange waking dreams. Staring at Mud in his chair, I suddenly saw myself sitting there instead. It was me flipping the cards over and coughing hoarsely. Then I would disappear and it would be Mud again.

I nearly gave in to him several times but always stopped short. I still held out hope for some chance to escape.

Darkness fell on Sunday evening and that chance still hadn't come. I could tell Mud's leg was bothering him more than usual. He rubbed it constantly. Whoever was bringing him provisions dropped off a dinner of fried eggs and rice. This time they also left a tall brown bottle.

"Here you go, Sai," said Mud, sliding me the paper box of food. The smell of the fatty eggs made my stomach growl.

He set the bottle down in the corner of the room farthest from his chair. His eyes flicked back and forth from me to the corner. It was hot in our apartment, and sweat beaded on his forehead. "I'm sick of sitting here, aren't you?" he said. "Just got to tell me one little secret and we can both get out."

I gobbled up the omelet and shook my head.

"Fine," he spat. He stood up, sat back down, and then stood up again with a groan. He limped to the corner and grabbed the bottle, twisted off the cap, and then took a swig.

He nursed it all through the night, sipping it between card games. He started to tilt and sway in his chair. With a soaring feeling, I began to hope my chance had really come this time. With no windows and no clock, it was impossible to tell what time it was exactly, but from the noises outside, I knew it must be the middle of the night on Sunday. I curled up on my pallet and pretended to sleep.

I must have dozed off without meaning to. When I opened my eyes, everything was quiet. The candle flickered low. Mud lay sprawled on the floor between the table and the door.

Oh, for tripe's sake. Even in his drunken state he'd had the foresight to block my way. He snored steadily. I rose and tiptoed over to him. I touched his shoulder. He didn't move.

It was now or never. I scooped my hands under his armpits and dragged him backward. Mud was as heavy as a crate of melons, and I nearly fainted with the effort. I managed to get him far enough from the door to edge it open.

I sucked in my breath and squeezed out into the hallway. I tiptoed down the hall and to the stairwell, then bounded down the steps two at a time. At the bottom I flung open the door to the outside and blinked against the morning light. And then, behind me, I heard a roar.

Mud was awake.

I sprinted up the alley, knocking into two old women as I rounded the corner. I heard them sputter and curse at me, but I didn't turn. I fled past the Rooster Room, weaving my way around the sour-smelling customers staggering home.

Behind me, Mud's hoarse voice rang out. "SAI! GET BACK HERE!"

I swerved onto one of Down Island's many narrow streets. Behind a butcher's shop, I flew over the rail of a pigpen, stepping right on the backs of the sleeping hogs, and kept running. Mud's voice followed me down an alley. He knew these escape routes. He'd taught them to me himself.

But I knew places where he couldn't follow. I could hear the morning bells ringing from the temples at the edge of town. I had maybe thirty minutes to get to the harbor, and I still had something to do. I darted through the alleys, my feet slipping beneath me. I finally found what I was looking for. A wide alley blocked off at the end by a high wooden wall.

Halfway down the alley, I heard Mud call out behind me. "Got ya!"

He took his time to catch his breath as he limped toward me. "You don't got the strength to scale that wall," he puffed.

"No, I don't."

I ran straight for the wall and, at the last moment, slid onto my side. My feet punched through the rotten wood boards at the base of the wall, and I wriggled through the jagged opening. I'd found this secret hole months ago, never dreaming I'd have to use it to escape my own father.

Mud roared, but it was no good. He'd have to find his way around the alley, and by that time I'd be far away.

Even with my advantage, I raced down the walkways that spanned the Fens, not slowing until I got to my hiding place in the mangore tree. Panting, I pulled off my filthy shirt and pants and changed into my work clothes. I would be allotted some basic clothes for the expedition, but I couldn't show up at the harbor looking like a beggar or they wouldn't even let me on the ship. I slipped my new cloak around my shoulders and grabbed the tin of money.

I left the old clothes and didn't bother hiding them. I was never coming back. With the money jangling inside the tin, I took off running for the harbor.

Normally, carrying a can full of money would have made me nervous, but the streets were deserted. Everyone was down at the seaside to watch the ships depart. I was grateful for empty streets as I bolted through them. But then I came up to the top of the hill that looked down onto the harbor. Throngs of people stood crammed together, shoulder to shoulder. In the bay, the ships of the expedition were lined up like plump geese ready to take flight.

I stopped and tried to catch my breath. Sweat poured off me, drenching the heavy wool cloak.

I looked around. Was there a way for me to get to the water without going through the crowd? I turned, thinking I might backtrack, but then I saw Mud lumbering down the street behind me.

I ran from him, straight for the crowd, shouting, "Out of the way! Out of the way, please!"

No one budged. I tried to squeeze between them, but they shoved back, not willing to give up their prime views. I tried to elbow past a tall girl in an Assistant apron who elbowed me right back.

"Excuse me!" she said. "It's very rude to—wait a minute. Don't I know you?"

I turned to see Tippy glowering down at me. She held a large circular basket perched on her shoulder. Her lineal bracelet gleamed at her wrist.

"Oh . . . hello," I panted, looking over her shoulder for any sign of Mud. "Sorry about pushing you. I'm in a bit of a hurry . . ."

"Ha, good luck with that! I'm supposed to take these egg buns down to the Council members." She nodded up at the basket and shifted it on her shoulder. "But I'll be smothered by the crowd before I ever get there!"

I could hear Mud's voice behind me, bellowing above the din. He'd knock as many people out cold as

69

he'd have to in order to get to me. I had to get through this crowd.

"Here, let me deliver your basket for you," I said to Tippy. "I can slip through the crowd more easily than you can."

Tippy turned her nose up. "Thanks, but I don't want to get them dirty."

Even in my desperate hurry, I paused to reflect on how much I loathed her.

"Oh, well, if you're sure," I said, candy-sweet. "But just be careful flashing that lineal around out in the open. There's going to be a lot of pickpockets down near the action."

A horrified look crossed Tippy's face. She tried to hide her right hand in her pocket, but she couldn't hold the big basket without it.

"Well, if you promise not to crush any of the buns, I suppose I could let you take them," she said snottily.

I took the basket off her shoulder with a smile. "I'll treat them like precious jewels."

I balanced the basket on my head and started shoving my way through the throng. For a moment, I felt guilty for what I was about to do.

The moment passed.

"Hurrah for the expeditions!" I shouted. "Free egg buns by the Queen's decree! Hurrah!"

I reached into the basket and grabbed a handful of the golden pastries. I tossed them in the air to my right. Instantly, the crowd turned and surged for the buns before they could fall onto the ground. I threw more. People scrambled to catch them, leaving just enough room for me to rush forward.

I went on tossing the buns until they were gone, then dropped the basket. I was only a few yards from the pier now. I squeezed under and around the rows of war veterans in their faded uniforms. Near the water, the ancient Council members stood on a makeshift stage, solemn as funeral goers. They could probably use an egg bun about now, the poor things. The Queen herself must have been watching from some high perch, protected from having to mingle with the ordinary people below.

Finally, I pushed past the crowd and emerged into the open. The breeze off the harbor blew my hair back. I tilted my face to the sky. I felt dizzy. The enormous hulk of the *Prosperity* loomed high over me, its towering masts grasping for the clouds. The ship's copper-plated hull had been polished so smooth that it reflected the faces of the crowd behind me. Overhead, flags rippled impatiently.

I ran for the gangplank leading up to the ship. My foot was inches from the plank when two uniformed women stepped in front of me. My face nearly smashed into the brass buttons of the first woman's coat.

"Just where do you think you're going, young lady?" she said.

"I'm supposed to be on the *Prosperity*, ma'am. My name should be on the crew list."

"Bit late, aren't you?" said the second officer. She pointed to a man in a dark-blue uniform near the bandstand, holding a sheaf of papers under his arm. "You'll have to speak with him. He's got the list."

I started in that direction when fingers closed around my shoulders. "There you are, child," Mud wheezed, his sour breath close to my ear. "Thought I lost you."

"Let go!" I tried to kick at his shins, but he kept out of range and held me tight.

The guards were distracted now, talking to someone in a black suit. They paid no attention as Mud dragged me away from the shadow of the *Prosperity*, back toward the pressing crowd.

We reached the ropes that held back the throng. I twisted around to face him. "Let me go, please! Mud, I'm begging you!"

He snorted. "And then what? You think they're gonna let you get on that ship?"

"They have to! I'm on the crew list!"

Mud's bloodshot eyes narrowed, confused. "That's not possible."

Over his shoulder, I could see the wharf officials saluting each other, folding up papers and putting them away. Any moment they'd take down the gangplank.

I managed to slip my hand into my pocket. I pulled out the money tin and pressed it to Mud's chest, keeping it covered so no one in the crowd could see.

"Here. That's one hundred ninety leks." The words burned in the back of my throat, but I forced them out, looking away so I wouldn't have to see my money in Mud's hands. "It's yours if you will just let me go!"

"One hundred ninety!" Mud whispered. He looked me up and down, noticing my nice work clothes for the first time. "Where'd you get that kind of money?"

The band started up, and a singer began crooning our national anthem. I felt like I could leap out of my skin. I had to force myself not to shout, not to cause a scene.

"I've been saving it for months. I earned it. Every coin. And you can have all of it if you'll let me go!"

Mud's eyes darted from the tin to my face. "You'd give me all this money just to let you get on that ship?"

"I'd give you the Queen's jewels if I had them! I'd give *anything* to get away from you! Can't you see that?"

Mud's face slackened. "Yeah," he whispered. "Yeah, I see it, Sai."

His grip on my shoulders loosened. I wasted no time. I bolted to the end of the gangplank, where the officer with the ship's manifest now stood.

My fingers trembling, I smoothed down my braid and steadied my voice. "My name is Sodsai Arawan, sir. I'm Assistant to the *Prosperity*'s mapmaker."

He rolled his eyes and checked the list in his hand. "All right. But get to it! They're shoving off."

The plank rattled beneath my feet as I hurried up and up. I kept my eyes forward. I had never been so high off the ground before. I finally reached the end and stumbled onto the deck of the *Prosperity*. The crew shoved the gangplank off and sealed the hull. In a blur of commotion, Master Paiyoon rushed over to me. He was a flurry of questions.

"Blast it, Sai, where have you been? I worried that you—"

He was cut short by the shouting of orders from the top deck. Sailors swirled around us, hurrying to fulfill the commands. The anchor chain clanged against the hull as the crew grunted to crank it up. Sheets of sailcloth billowed loose overhead, then snapped taut in the wind. The deck surged beneath my feet, and I clutched Paiyoon's arm to keep from falling over.

He led me to the rail, where I could see all the citizens of An Lung waving us farewell. I looked down at the people crowding the docks below, shrinking as we sailed away from them. Everyone in the harbor cheered and shouted, jumping in the air.

Everyone except for one man, who stood clutching a small metal tin, his eyes on his feet.

CHAPTER TEN

New Friends and Old

I clutched the edges of my hammock, trying to ignore the rocking of the ship. My queasy stomach slung side to side while my thoughts sloshed around inside my head. What had I done? I kept seeing my money tin—half a year of my life—clutched in Mud's big hands.

Now, with nothing in my pockets, I couldn't leave the ship at some random port. I had bought myself a year of freedom, but I was stuck with the *Prosperity*, and when she returned to An Lung, she'd take me back with her, back to Mud, back to the Fens, with just a few leks to show for it. I didn't know what made me feel worse: my pathetic situation or the seasickness. I cracked open one eyelid and the room whirled.

Definitely the seasickness.

I'd never felt this bad before. We'd been at sea for four days, but I hadn't been able to leave my room. If our whole journey was going to be like this, I wished they would just throw me over the side now.

My door swung open, and Master Paiyoon popped his head inside the room.

"Still chucking up?" he asked cheerfully.

He'd brought me some cabbagey-smelling broth, and he set the bowl down on top of a trunk.

"I don't have anything left in me to chuck," I croaked, though the smell of the broth was making me rethink that.

"Staying down below will only make it worse," said Paiyoon. "It's better to get up on deck and set your eyes on the horizon. Smell the fresh salt air."

I didn't want to smell anything. Ever. Paiyoon didn't seem like he had been seasick at all. In fact, I'd never seen him this chipper.

"Well, come up when you can. There are some people I want you to meet."

"Yes, sir," I mumbled as he went out the door.

I stayed swaying in my hammock until I couldn't stand the smell of the soup any longer. Maybe bringing it to me was part of Paiyoon's plan to get me out of my room. I sat up and swung my legs over the side of my hammock. The ship pitched, tossing me out and onto my stomach on the floor.

I picked myself up and staggered out the door into the dark hallway. The *Prosperity* was one of our Navy's biggest battleships, built at the height of the War to carry seventy-two cannons. Back then, the lower decks would have been gun decks—long, open spaces where the sailors slept in hammocks strung between the cannons. The new renovations had divided the first of these decks into a warren of smaller rooms: the galley, the doctor's surgery, the carpenters' quarters, and my tiny room, which must have been some sort of converted closet. The crew slept one deck beneath me.

To my left, a shaft of bright light shone down the companionway, the name for the staircase that led to the main deck above. I put my hands out to steady myself, but as I reached the bottom of the stairs, a body barreled down the steps, knocking me backward.

"Watch yourself!"

The voice was young, but the silhouette towering over me belonged to a big, balding man.

A sailor with her hair tied back in a bun stomped down the steps toward us. "Grebe!" she shouted at the bald man. "Lieutenant wants us up the mizzen top." Her eyes swung to me. "Who are you?"

"I work for Paiyoon, the mapmaker. Do you know where I can find him?"

"Quarterdeck," she barked. "Let's go, Grebe!"

I waited till the two of them had gone up, then climbed the stairs and stepped out onto the main deck. Squinting against the blinding sunshine, I nearly got knocked off my feet again when a sailor bumped into me. I stammered out an apology, but he had already moved on. All around me, the main deck swarmed with bodies. Sailors scurried around each other, pulling ropes and tying them off. Another group furiously scrubbed the deck boards with white stones.

I shuffled around the rowboats stored at the center of the main deck, holding on to them for balance. Thwacking and cooing sounds came from inside. I peered over the rim of one of the boats and found it packed with chickens in wire cages. A rooster spotted me with its scale-crusted eye, and I lurched back as it lunged at its cage, talons out.

"Hope we eat you first," I muttered.

My eyes traveled up the towering mainmast. Reams of sailcloth crowded out the sky. The amount of rope strung across the ship seemed enough to wrap all the way around the globe. I caught confused glimpses of the parts of the ship I had tried to learn from old

Grandmother Noom before I left: stays and tackle, shrouds and ratlines.

Up above the top edge of the sails, sailors ran barefoot along ropes the way children might skip along the sidewalk. They were so high, they looked like little dolls. If any of them lost their balance, they'd fall more than a hundred feet before hitting the deck. The thought nearly made me throw up again.

I made my way toward the rear of the ship—the stern, where the quarterdeck and top deck rose like cake tiers above all the commotion of the main deck below. I tried not to get trampled by any sailors as I climbed the stairs.

I stepped onto the quarterdeck and gasped, salt air stinging my throat. In every direction, there was only sea and sky, both a shade of bright, glittering blue. I had never seen anything so beautiful.

I could have stood there for an hour without moving, drinking in all that blue, but Paiyoon spotted me and waved me over. He stood near the ship's shrine, speaking with a man and a woman who were clearly not sailors. They looked completely out of place, dressed like nobles in silk trousers and embroidered jackets.

I bowed to greet Master Paiyoon and then bowed to the shrine, touching my thumbs to my forehead.

Paiyoon chuckled at me. "So the caterpillar has finally emerged from her cocoon!" Being at sea seemed to agree with the old mapmaker. He'd left his coat down below, and he stood with his hands in his pockets, sleeves rolled up to his elbows. I knew he did this to hide his trembling hands, but it made him look like a sailor, right at home on the sea.

"Friends, allow me to introduce Sodsai Arawan, my Assistant. Sai, this is Mr. Lark, our ship's naturalist . . ."

I bowed, and Mr. Lark nodded back at me like a bobbing bird, jangling the lineal chain pinned to his collar. "A pleasure to meet you! A real pleasure!" he said excitedly.

Paiyoon explained, "Mr. Lark is collecting specimens of interesting plants and insects to bring back to court."

"For the Queen's new museum," said the energetic man. "I hope to fill an entire wing with rare discoveries!" He bent at the waist to look right at my face. "But say, now, you're quite young to be so far from home, aren't you?"

Master Paiyoon patted my shoulder. "Sai is just shy of thirteen. She's delaying her lineal ceremony so that she can accompany me on this trip."

"Splendid!" squawked Lark. "Good girl!"

"And this is our ship's surgeon, Dr. Pinching," said Paiyoon.

The hollow-cheeked woman standing beside Lark was as grim as he was bubbly.

"It's an honor to meet you, Doctor," I said, bowing to her.

"You won't think it's such an honor if you ever need her services," said Paiyoon with a laugh.

The doctor didn't seem to find this very funny. "Boil all your water and keep your wounds clean," she said gravely.

Paiyoon smiled and shook his head at her. "Dr. Pinching, you've grown too used to wartime conditions. If our expedition goes as smoothly as planned, you should be able to put your feet up and relax."

Lark leaned in and whispered, "Speaking of *smooth*"—he snickered and nodded toward the stairs—"here comes Miss Rian Prasomsap."

A young woman dressed in a black jacket and trousers was climbing the steps toward us. She seemed upper-class, with both her suit and her short hair cut in the latest fashion, but the lineal pinned to her jacket was only five links long. Unlike Lark and Pinching, who looked sweaty and stifled in their silk clothes, this woman moved easily among the sailors, as if she'd spent all her life on ships.

She bowed respectfully to Paiyoon as she approached us. "Good morning to you all," she said with a friendly smile, but she didn't stay to chat. Her hair swishing at her chin, she strode up the next set of stairs to the top deck.

Dr. Pinching lifted her nose in the air. "And what exactly will *her* duties be on board?"

Mr. Lark lifted his nose even higher. "Duties? Ha! She looks like a society peacock to me, nothing more. I'm sure she has no credentials whatsoever."

This was funny coming from Lark, who was dressed more like a preening peacock than anyone. He was starting to remind me of Tippy.

"Now, now, Lark, it's too early in the day to forget our manners," Paiyoon said out loud before leaning in and whispering to me: "That 'peacock' is the reason you made it on board the ship at all. Miss Rian is friends with our captain, and the ship's departure was held up just for her. If she hadn't been running late, you would have been left behind!"

I tracked Rian as she strode up to a tall woman standing in the center of a swarm of officers on the top deck. My stomach did a little flip. Even if the woman's uniform hadn't been decorated with a dozen medals and ribbons, I would have guessed who she was.

Captain Anchalee Sangra, the Tiger of the Sea. No other captain who had sailed during the War had sunk more enemy ships than Sangra. She was revered all over Mangkon for her bravery, even more so because she could have easily gotten out of serving altogether. She was the Queen's great-niece and could have taken a much safer position until the War was over. I looked for her lineal, but she either wasn't wearing it or kept it out of sight.

Rian and Sangra bent their heads together to exchange words. They addressed each other without bowing, like old friends.

Master Paiyoon put his hand on my shoulder. "Come along, Sai. If you're feeling better, we've got work to do."

Paiyoon led the way down the stairs. "My cabin is tucked underneath the quarterdeck. The door to reach it is here, off the main," he said. "Come on. Whoever loaded the crates from the shop must have been tipping back the wine bottle. It will take us all day to sort out that mess!"

As I followed Paiyoon, I looked across the ship to see Grebe, the bald sailor who'd knocked me over, climbing down a rope as nimbly as a monkey. He jumped the last yard to the deck and stood up.

That's when I realized that he wasn't a grown man at all, but a boy not much older than me. In the darkness belowdecks, I had thought he was balding, but in the sunlight I saw that the front section of his hair was missing, as if it had been ripped away. A thick, jagged scar ran across his forehead, from his crown to his eyebrows.

My stomach lurched as I placed him. The last time I had seen him he was wearing a cap, but I knew without a doubt that he was the same boy who had followed me that night in the Fens.

Before he could turn toward me, I pretended to look out to sea. My heart pounded.

What if he placed me too?

The Fishermen's Maps

My seasickness had faded by the next day, but I kept pretending to hack up my guts so I could stay in my room as much as possible. I did feel sick, but not from the sea.

What if that boy, Grebe, recognized me? That night when he followed me in the Fens, it had been dark already, and I'd been dressed in my worn-out clothes. Surely I'd looked like any other kid from Down Island.

But what if he did put it together and told someone? If anyone found out who I really was, Paiyoon would be humiliated. He'd know I'd been lying to him about my family—about *everything*—and he might even ship me back to An Lung at the next port. Not only did I have no future to look forward to after our journey's end; now my very place on the expedition was in danger.

So I tried to avoid Grebe, which wasn't an easy feat on a crowded ship, even one as big as the *Prosperity*. The sailors worked in six-hour shifts they called watches. Captain Sangra kept a portion of her crew constantly manning the sails or rinsing the lines, while the rest slept in their hammocks. When officers rang the bell, they would switch. I tried to never be up on deck during Grebe's watch, though my training with Paiyoon meant I couldn't always avoid it.

The only places I felt safely hidden were my own room and Paiyoon's. Luckily, the old man had plenty of work for me to do in his cabin.

"No, no, don't put that there!" Paiyoon shouted at me. "That box is full of ships' logs! Very important, and they will get ruined from the salt spray coming in from the window."

"Yes, sir," I grunted, moving the box from one corner of the tiny room to the other.

"Not there either! Oh, blast it, Sai, do I have to do everything myself?"

The Master Mapmaker was in a mood. Whoever had loaded his crates onto the ship had jumbled them all up, and he was afraid that some of his more precious items were missing.

Master Paiyoon's cabin was one of the nicer bedrooms on the ship, which meant that it was about the size of a large closet. A very luxurious closet, though, with teak walls and furniture polished to a shine. The bed was built right against the ship's hull, with a cabinet beneath for storage. A narrow desk and bench took up the corner, with built-in bookshelves overhead. It was a very efficient use of space, but we were still crammed in like dumplings in a basket.

"Oof!" I set the box down among a half dozen others. "Well, sir, you won't run out of reading material on this voyage, that's for sure."

"You talk as if I've brought along novels," grumbled Paiyoon as he began opening the box. "These crates are full of vitally important documents: every book, chart, ship's log, or captain's diary I could get my hands on that deals with anything south of the equator. And I'll need to read them all if I'm to help Captain Sangra decide what course to take in the southern seas."

"We don't already have a course plotted out, sir?"

Paiyoon scowled. "Course-setting takes time! No one ever seems to understand that. Our expedition left in such a hurry that I didn't have enough time to finalize it." He turned to wag his finger at me. "There's no telling what we'll find once we cross the fiftieth parallel: islands full of riches or leagues and leagues of empty ocean. It's up to me—and the captain, of course—to pick the best route and then get us home, and . . . ah! Finally, the one I've been looking for . . ."

Paiyoon bent to pick up a small wooden box that had been hidden behind the others. His hands shook, making the lid slide off. Several handkerchiefs spilled out and fluttered to the floor

I set down the crate I was carrying and rushed to help him. "Here, let me get those, sir."

I scooped up the handkerchiefs and started stacking them in my palm.

"No, no, give them to me!" Paiyoon shouted.

Startled, I stood up and held the little cloths out to him. "I'm sorry, sir. I was just trying to help."

His fingers trembled as he reached out to take them from me. He lowered his hands again and pressed them flat at his sides. "You are a help to me, Sai. Of course you are," he said softly.

I felt awkward and embarrassed for both of us and didn't know what to say. I tried to think of an excuse to leave, but Paiyoon shuffled to his desk and waved at me to follow. "Come, bring them here and we'll look at them together."

I pulled a large crate up next to his chair and gently

spread the handkerchiefs out in front of us. They were yellowing and old. Some of them had frayed or torn edges. When I looked closer, I realized that what I had thought was embroidery were actually faded lines scrawled onto the fabric with an ink pen.

"These handkerchiefs are pretty, sir," I said, bending over them.

"Not handkerchiefs. Maps." Paiyoon looked up at me from beneath his bushy eyebrows, his eyes gleaming bright and mischievous. I had to smile. Nothing cheered him up more than talking about maps.

"To be exact," he went on, "they are fishermen's maps. It's an old way of mapmaking, a lost art that few people in Mangkon remember. You draw them on silk, using a pen dipped in mottlefish ink so that it won't smudge. You can roll them up in your pocket or stitch them right onto the ship's sails. Even soaked with water, they wouldn't be damaged."

"Where did you get them, sir?"

"In the Harbor Market in An Lung. There's an old woman there who sells trinkets from all over the globe. She sells me these little charts cheaply; calls them 'chicken-scratch rags.'" Paiyoon grinned. "She has no idea that I would pay ten times her price. They may not be beautiful, but they are worth a fortune to me. We think we're so fancy with our expensive pens and paper, but this is how you make a map when you are sailing beyond the borders of the world."

I raised my eyebrows. "That far, sir?"

He nodded. "Fishermen chase fish. And fish go everywhere."

I looked down at the maps in awe. I had never considered that anyone else may have seen as much of the world as Paiyoon. I gently ran my finger along the fraying edge of one of the silks. "This one is beautiful, sir." The chart showed a cluster of islands with pretty little waves sketched in the bays. "That looks like the Padu Archipelago. But I can't understand the words written here."

Paiyoon nodded approvingly. "Yes, very good. And you can't read it because it's written in Pramong. The Pramong are a fishing people, and almost all the silk maps I have were made by them. They settled around the Padu Archipelago for a time. I can only make out a few words in their language. Mostly, I marvel at their drawings."

Most of the little charts were Pramong, but Paiyoon also had a couple from Mangkon, showing the nine islands and Rotan beyond. But it was the last map in the stack that caught my eye.

It was the smallest chart and seemed to be the oldest—I could barely make out the faded ink lines. There were no words on it at all, no scale or compass. The map showed a chain of islands that curled in a crescent shape. Each island along the chain was smaller than the one next to it, as if someone had sorted them neatly by size. But the best part of the map had nothing to do with geography: a long, elegant dragon snaked through the islands, its body undulating like waves around the shores.

"Oh, this one is my favorite," I said, picking it up carefully. "Do you think they drew this because they saw a dragon there?"

I had meant to make him laugh, but Paiyoon had turned serious. Lost in thought, he had taken out his eyeglass from his waistcoat and was looking down through the lens at the little faded map.

He glanced at me as if I had startled him. "Hmm? Ah, the dragon." He snapped his eyeglass back into its case. "That is one of the tricky things about sorting through any of these documents. You have to sift out the facts from the fantasies. Sailors have good eyes, but after so long at sea, they often see visions that aren't truly there, and they love making up stories. But these little maps can teach us a lot if we know how to look at them."

Master Paiyoon always kept up an invisible wall around himself, but for this brief moment I felt like he had let it come down. I wanted to ask him a hundred more questions, but I saw him rub his hands together. When he took a breath, he sighed as if the air itself were heavy. I could tell the old man was tired.

I yawned loudly. "Master Paiyoon, I'm sorry, but I'm feeling so tired. Do you mind if I take a little break?"

"Oh, yes, of course," he said, scooping up the fishermen's maps and placing them carefully in their box. "You should get up top and let the fresh air revive you."

"Yes, sir. Thank you, sir."

I left Paiyoon, hoping he might take a nap, and walked down the short, narrow hallway that led from his room to the main deck. I paused in the doorway before stepping out into the sunlight. I didn't want to risk bumping into Grebe if he was on watch. I didn't see him, but I did see Miss Rian leaving her room. She shut the door behind her and started for the stairs that led to the quarterdeck.

I opened the door a little farther so I could watch her glide up the steps, her black coattails fluttering behind her. She was so interesting. I'd never seen someone walk the way she did—regal as a lady but whistling like a schoolgirl. I took a step forward to try to get a better view of her face, but the wind whipped her short hair across her cheeks. I saw flashes of her eyes, her lips, her nose, but never all at once. I still didn't know exactly what she looked like.

A sudden smile spread over my face as I took the dark stairway down to my own room.

I had been inspired.

CHAPTER TWELVE

The Captain's Friend

"Blast it, Sai, what in the world have you done to your hair?"

I stood in the doorway to Paiyoon's cabin, patting the back of my newly exposed neck. "I . . . cut it, sir."

"I can see that!" he bellowed. "And now it's too short to tie back! The wind will constantly be thrashing it over your face when you're on deck."

I frowned, pretending that's not exactly what I had planned. "I'm sorry, sir. I didn't think of that. I was just worried about lice."

I ran my fingers through the blunt strands, still a little shocked that they stopped just under my chin. I had tried to copy Miss Rian's hairstyle, but with only a pair of work shears and no mirror, I was sure I hadn't succeeded. Oh, well. I didn't need it to look nice. I needed it to disguise me from Grebe.

"Yes, well, you'll soon learn which is more annoying," grumbled Paiyoon. "An itchy head or not being able to take a latitude reading." He reached into the drawer of his desk and pulled out his brass quadrant. "You can test out your foolishness now. Remember what I taught you?"

I nodded as I took the heavy piece of equipment from him. "Hold steady," I recited, "and sight the sun through the scope—"

"First!" he exclaimed. "What do you do first?"

I sighed. "Sorry. First, lower the shade over the lens so the sun doesn't burn my eyeball. Sight the sun and measure the angle using the scale on the side."

"And how do you keep still so you can take an accurate reading?"

I planted my feet in a wide stance the way he'd shown me the day before. "Keep loose in the knees. Let my hips sway with the ship."

"Hmph, yes. Now take three separate readings and come back and report them to me." He leaned back and pointed to the charts spread out in front of him. "Then we'll record it and let the captain know how much longer until our first stop at Pitaya Island. Go on or you'll miss high noon!"

I left him and climbed the stairs to the quarterdeck. I paused before taking the last step. It was Grebe's watch, and I was almost sure to run into him. A part of me still wanted to hide, but I needed to test out my new disguise.

I found a place to stand at the rail out of the way of the ever-busy crew. I held up the quadrant and began taking the first reading. Paiyoon was right about the hair. The breeze flicked it across my face, covering the scope lens and blocking my view of the sun. But with my face hidden, I also felt protected, as if I were in my own little bubble.

I steadied my feet to take the reading again. As the ship dipped down and rose back up, I rocked on my toes and swayed my hips so I wouldn't get knocked off balance.

"That's an interesting dance," said an amused voice behind me.

I whirled around to face a field of black silk and jet buttons.

Miss Rian pushed her own dark locks behind her ears, giving me a look at her face for the first time. Her skin was as smooth and pale as fresh butter in a jar. She smiled, and her dark eyes lifted at the corners. "I like the haircut."

I blushed as I bowed, embarrassed that it was so obvious I had copied her. "Oh, thank you. I was just . . .

worried about lice—not that I have lice! I just didn't want to get any, so . . ."

She nodded as if I weren't babbling on like a fool. "I think short hair suits you. And it's nice to make a change when you start something big and new, isn't it?"

I quit babbling and smiled back. "Yes, it is, miss."

"Please, call me Rian," she said warmly. "And I know that you're Sai. I heard you and Master Paiyoon talking in his cabin this morning. I wasn't trying to eavesdrop, but he wasn't exactly whispering."

I blushed again, realizing that she must have heard him scolding me for cutting my hair. I liked her even more now for complimenting it. "He can be a little grumpy sometimes. But he's a good man to work for."

"The very best, from what I hear." She leaned her elbow against the rail. The salt that had crusted there rubbed onto the black silk of her sleeve, but she didn't seem to care. "So tell me, what do you think about life aboard the *Prosperity* so far?"

I stumbled over my answer, then stumbled again as Rian asked me more polite questions. As we chatted, I tried to decide how old she was. She must have been near the captain's age, since they were friends, but she seemed much younger. With her bright eyes and the playful way her nose twitched when she was making a joke, she reminded me of the black kitten that lived behind Paiyoon's shop. She laughed easily, and it didn't take long before I was laughing along with her.

The sunlight glinted off her lineal brooch, drawing my eyes toward it. A chain of five links hung from the ends of a small gold bar that was pinned to her jacket.

She must have noticed me looking at it. "I really should take this thing off," she said. "It's probably tacky to be showing it off up here on deck. But it's fairly new, and I guess I'm still a little proud of it."

"It's new?" I asked. It was a strange thing for someone over the age of thirteen to say.

She nodded and ran her finger over the links. "This is a Lineal of Honor, given out by the Queen herself for 'acts of great bravery.'" She said the last part in a fancy accent. "Apparently, Her Majesty decided that nearly getting killed in battle is worth the same as five generations of good breeding."

I blinked, taking all this in. I had never heard of a Lineal of Honor, and it was just as much of a surprise to hear that Miss Rian had once served in battle. "You were in the War?"

She shrugged. "Not for long. My 'act of great bravery' landed me in the hospital. By the time I recovered, the fighting was nearly over. Here, do you want to see?" Rian turned to face away from me. She ran her hand up the back of her neck, lifting her hair. At the base of her skull, there was a patchy bald spot and a thick pink scar. "They had to shave my head to sew me back together. I looked like a monk for months!"

She laughed, but I was ashamed of myself for listening to Mr. Lark's gossip that first day on board. He had called her a peacock when really she was a war hero!

"If you don't mind me asking, miss, what did you do?"

Rian glanced up at the top deck, where Captain Sangra stood with her officers. "Got between a swinging saber and the Queen's great-niece."

I sucked in a breath and rubbed the back of my own skull. So that explained why Rian looked so at ease on the ship, and why she and the captain seemed so comfortable with each other. They had been through a war together, and Rian had saved Captain Sangra's life.

She turned to me and put her hand on my shoulder. "Uh-oh, I've upset you, haven't I? I'm sorry. This isn't exactly the stuff of pleasant conversation."

"Oh, no, it's not that." I tugged at a lock of my newly chopped hair. "It's just that . . . well, now I feel ashamed that I cut my hair like yours. When you had to do it because you were injured."

She laughed and her dark eyes danced. "Don't be silly! I'm absolutely flattered that you did. There's no shame in having good taste, which clearly you do."

I could feel a warmth spreading over me from where her hand still rested on my shoulder, but the feeling chilled as I glanced to the center of the quarterdeck. Grebe stood below the mizzenmast, holding a bucket and a brush. He was looking straight at us.

I dipped my head so my hair would fall back in front of my eyes. I hoped Miss Rian would turn away from him, but to my horror, she spoke to him directly.

"Doing well there, Grebe?" she called out.

He blinked, startled by the sound of his own name. "Er, yes, miss. Doin' well. Thanks."

"Good to hear it."

Grebe looked very uncomfortable, as if he wasn't supposed to be speaking with us while he was on watch. "Well . . . I better get on with it. Good day, miss." He bowed to Rian. When he lifted his head, he looked right at me.

I held my breath behind my hair but didn't turn my face away. I had to know for certain if he would recognize me. His eyes narrowed just slightly, and his brow furrowed, crinkling the scar on his forehead. But then he looked at Rian again, shook his head, and left to go about his duties.

I let my breath out, relieved for the moment.

Once Grebe had walked out of earshot, I turned back to Rian. "Do you know that boy, miss?"

She nodded. "I've been playing cards at night in the galley with the crew. Grebe plays dismally. Owes me a fortune already."

I knew the crew played cards. I could hear them from my room at night. But I couldn't imagine someone like Rian mingling belowdecks with the others, drinking their sour wine.

Rian must have noticed my confused look, because she added. "We don't actually play for high stakes. They're on sailors' pay after all. It's simply a way to keep up my card game and avoid boredom. And I like hearing their stories. Everyone scoffs at sailors' tales, but there's always something to learn from them if you know what to listen for."

I wanted to ask her more about Grebe, but before I could figure out how to phrase my question, we heard the bells ringing from the top deck above us.

Rian arched one thin eyebrow. "That's the all hands call."

"Is something wrong?"

"They usually don't ring the call otherwise." She smiled at me again. "I'm going back down to the main deck, but I do hope we get to speak again, little sister."

She winked and cupped a hand under her bob of thick hair, and then she left me, her jacket fluttering behind her like a cape.

CHAPTER THIRTEEN

The Sailor's Dishonor

Within seconds, the main deck of the *Prosperity* was packed shoulder to shoulder with the nearly one hundred members of our crew. Lark, Pinching, and Master Paiyoon climbed the stairs to the quarterdeck. They looked as confused as I felt.

Paiyoon joined me at the quarterdeck rail, looking down on the sailors below.

"Do you know what's going on, sir?" I asked him.

He looked behind him to the top deck. "No, but whatever it is, it can't be good."

Tall Captain Sangra strode down the top deck stairs flanked by her first and second lieutenants, with a half dozen junior officers following behind. She didn't glance our way as she continued down to the main deck.

The crew snapped to silent attention. Even our sails stilled, as if they didn't dare to flutter against Sangra's wishes. She stood with her chin high, surveying her crew coldly.

It was strange to think that she would have been the Lady Sangra if she hadn't joined the Navy, and her skin would be bone pale instead of deep golden brown. I could never imagine her dressed in the flowing silks of the royal court, with a servant holding an umbrella over her head. She looked so solid and unyielding that I wondered if she even needed battle armor.

"Bring up the thief," she called.

Concerned whispers passed among the crew as two of Sangra's officers stomped up the companion-way. Between them, they each held the arm of a sailor who wore her hair tied high in a bun on top of her head. I recognized her as the woman who had barked at Grebe and me on my first day out of my cabin. She had seemed so tough then—she looked much younger up here in the sunlight, with her head bowed fearfully.

In fact, now that the entire crew stood gathered together for the first time, I was struck by how young everyone was. Only a few of the sailors had gray hair. We had about a dozen "pups," the name given to sailors younger than sixteen. Some of them looked even younger than me, with wide eyes and still-chubby cheeks. Technically, Grebe was a pup too, though he stood as tall as the full-grown men.

The two officers guided the woman to the mainmast and released her arms. She sank to her knees in front of Captain Sangra, bowing her forehead to the deck.

Sangra didn't even look at her. When the captain spoke, she addressed the crew directly.

"My officers have discovered a thief on board. This sailor was caught stealing tools and medical supplies from our ship's hold with the intent to sell them when we stop in port at Pitaya Island." Sangra turned her gaze down at the woman. "Do you deny this?"

"No, Captain," the woman muttered miserably.

"Let me be perfectly clear," said Sangra, speaking to the entire crew. "If you were under the impression that this journey would be a jolly sailing holiday around the world, you were mistaken. This is a Mangkon Navy vessel, and we sail under orders of Her Majesty the Queen." The captain's voice grew louder and sharper with each word. "We are on a mission, which I intend to execute swiftly and without distraction. I will not tolerate any behavior that puts our mission—or our speedy return home—in jeopardy."

She turned to her first lieutenant. "You have the slate?"

The lieutenant nodded at the thin, gray slab in his hand. A loop of cord was strung through the top of it.

"The thief shall undergo the Sailor's Dishonor," announced Captain Sangra, "for a full day and night."

The woman with the bun winced, and several of the pups drew in their breath. I looked to Paiyoon for some hint of what this meant, but he didn't take his eyes off the scene below.

"Afterward, the thief shall remain locked in the brig and be discharged at our next port," said Sangra. She nodded to her lieutenant, then turned on her heel and strode back up to the top deck.

The first lieutenant held the slate in the crook of his arm and began scrawling something across the front with a stick of white chalk.

The sailor bowed her head and let the lieutenant loop the cord over her neck. The slate hung over her chest. The bright white letters spelled out the word *THIEF*.

The first lieutenant turned to address the solemn crew: "The thief will now stand in silence at the main-mast until noon tomorrow. No person is to give her food, water, or comfort during that time, nor speak to or acknowledge her in any way. From this moment on, she is no longer a member of this ship's crew."

And now I understood why the woman had winced. She would have to stand on her feet in the full heat of the sun for the rest of the sweltering afternoon. She would stay out all night and through the next morning, with nothing to eat or drink. All that time, her shame would be on full display.

There was a long moment of silence during which no one moved, and then the lieutenant barked, "Don't stand there gaping. Get back to work!"

As quickly as they had assembled, the crew scattered like a shoal of startled fish.

I turned to Master Paiyoon. "Is that sort of thing typical on board a ship, sir?"

"On a warship, yes. Technically, the captain was in her rights, but in a situation like this, discharging the sailor would have been enough." He put his hands on the railing and looked into the distance, muttering, "Oh, Anchalee, this isn't like you."

"Sir, what do you mean?"

"I have known Anchalee Sangra since she was a little girl hiding beneath the Queen's drawing table so she could listen in on cabinet meetings. Even then she was a leader, as commanding as an old admiral."

He moved closer to me and lowered his voice. "But this public humiliation was a mistake. Now the crew will be afraid of her, but they won't respect her. In fact, they may even grow to hate her. They are too young to have served beside her in the Longest War. They have no loyalty to her and no stomach for harsh discipline." He drummed his fingers on the wooden rail. "She should know all this. She seems distracted, and it makes me uneasy for the journey ahead."

Paiyoon sighed and turned back to me. "Did you take the readings I asked for?"

"I still need one more, sir."

"Come to my cabin when you're finished," he said, starting back down the stairs. "It would be nice to get some small scrap of work done before this day is over!"

I lingered at the rail, looking down at the sailor, who stood with her head still bowed. The crew swirled around her as they went about their work, avoiding her like a rock in a stream. *Dishonor* was the right word for her punishment, and she'd have to endure it for many hours longer.

Just as I was about to return to my own work, I caught a flash of black fluttering below. It was Miss Rian, striding gracefully across the deck. Like everyone else, she avoided meeting eyes with the disgraced sailor.

But as Rian passed the woman, she reached into her pocket and pulled out a chunk of bread. Quickly and discreetly, she handed it to the woman without breaking stride.

I looked around to see if anyone else had seen what I had just witnessed, but she had acted so swiftly that no one seemed to have noticed.

Rian kept walking on, as confidently as a cat along a fence.

CHAPTER FOURTEEN

Drifting

In the weeks after the Sailor's Dishonor, life on board the *Prosperity* settled into a serious, quiet rhythm. The late-night card games stopped, and there was less laughing and joking among the crew, even belowdecks. I could feel some unspoken tension among them, like a low, steady thrum.

We were crossing the tranquil Green Sea. Aside from the occasional dolphin or whale breaching the surface, the water was almost as calm as a lake. The wind barely filled our sails, and the air got stickier the farther south we went. The top of my nose burned and peeled, and my skin turned sala fruit brown. I would never fit in with the pale Assistants back in Mangkon now, but I almost didn't care. I was slowly becoming sea hardy, and I liked it.

The *Prosperity* may have been moving slowly, but Master Paiyoon worked as feverishly as ever. He had long ago used up all his medicine for his hand tremor, and he needed me to help him draw daily charts and write notes for the captain.

After Pitaya Island, we would head to Fahlin. From there, our southern course was still undecided. The final decision would be Sangra's, but she was depending on Paiyoon to advise her. Every day, we read through old ships' logs and studied other maps (which Paiyoon criticized ruthlessly) to try to piece together our own chart to give to Captain Sangra.

"For an expedition like this, it's very important to have a good, solid plan," Paiyoon kept saying. "Otherwise you can spend months flitting around from one empty patch of ocean to the next, or even get lost altogether."

"But how do you chart a course for somewhere no one has ever been, sir?"

"Ah, that's the thing," said Paiyoon, tapping the side of his nose. "Do you really think that in the entire history of time, no one has ever sailed where we are trying to go?"

I glanced at the box where he kept his tiny silk maps. "The Pramong. The fishermen. You told me they sailed beyond the borders of the world. Do you think they crossed the fiftieth parallel?"

"Possibly. Or others like them have. But of course it doesn't 'count' unless you hoist a Mangkon flag over your head when you do it," he said with a snort. He gestured to the bookshelves, where he kept all the documents and materials he'd brought from home. "Our task is to follow in the wake of those who sailed before us. We just have to figure out where they went—not an easy feat by any means."

I smiled at him. "This is fun, isn't it, Master Paiyoon?"

"It's work, Sai. Hard work, that's all." His mustache quirked from side to side, and I knew he was trying to hide his own smile.

Mapmaking with Master Paiyoon *was* fun, no matter what he pretended. In fact, I think I could have been genuinely happy with my life on the *Prosperity* if it hadn't been for two things.

The first was Grebe. Our work kept us apart mostly, but in the rare times when we were on deck together or crossing paths on the stairs, I had the feeling that he was watching me. He never spoke to me, and I never caught him looking directly at me. But I could *feel* his

113

stare, like a tiny spider crawling across the back of my collar.

Did he suspect that I was the same girl he had followed in the Fens? But if he did, then why hadn't he told anyone by now? I didn't like the idea that my fate was resting on whether this kid could put it all together. But until I could figure out a solution, there was nothing to do except stay out of his way.

The second thing that weighed on me was my future. No matter how hard I tried to put it out of my mind, I couldn't stop thinking about my inevitable return to An Lung. I racked my brain, but I couldn't come up with a new plan to avoid eventually going back to the Fens. For years, I had clung to the goal of leaving all that behind. With that goal out of reach, I was adrift.

I wished I could speak to Rian again. She had been so funny and kind when we chatted that day, and I longed for someone lighthearted to talk to. I daydreamed about us becoming friends, even though I told myself that was ridiculous. A decorated war hero, friends with a kid from the Fens? It sounded like a joke.

But was it so impossible? We had something in common, didn't we? Her family hadn't given her a lineal, either. I doubted she had a background as low as mine, but whatever her station was in life, she had risen above it. I longed to know how. I still clung to the hope that somehow I could do it, too.

I looked for her anytime I was on deck, but she was always in her room or with the captain. I didn't run into her again until we had arrived at our first stop in our voyage.

CHAPTER FIFTEEN

Pitaya Island

We'd been at sea for nearly a month when we finally glided into the bay of Pitaya Island. It was small—a little emerald bubble floating just above the equator. Technically, Pitaya belonged to Mangkon—one of our first victories in the Longest War—but it was the only island in the middle of the Green Sea, which made it a stopping point for anyone traveling between the western and eastern hemispheres. As a result, the tiny island was surrounded by ships. A rainbow of flags from dozens of nations fluttered from their masts.

A shelf of coral skirted the island all the way around, so to reach it, we had to drop anchor far offshore and launch the rowboats. While the crew unloaded the chicken coops to make room in the boats, I leaned

over the bulwark, watching speckled fish nibble our hull.

Behind me, I heard the slow click of expensive boots drawing closer. I knew it was Rian even before I turned around to bow.

"Good morning, miss," I said, trying not to sound too happy to see her again.

But she looked just as happy as I felt. "Good morning, Sai! Let me guess: You're looking forward to going ashore?"

I nodded. "I'd give three of my toes just to step on dry land."

She tossed her hair back and laughed. "I know the feeling! Speaking of toes, make sure you stay on yours when you get there. The markets of Pitaya Island are full of people who will try to scam you out of all your pocket money."

"Aren't you coming, too?"

Rian shrugged and shook her head. "We're not stopping for long, so I'd rather leave space in the boats for others more eager for the break. Such as your map-maker, for instance?"

She nodded to Paiyoon, who stood near the sailors lowering the rowboats. He tapped his eyeglass case impatiently, as if it were a pocket watch.

Rian leaned closer to me and whispered, "Why do you think he's in such a hurry to get ashore? Maybe he has an old girlfriend to see?"

We both giggled.

"Have fun, Sai," Rian said, patting my arm. "Tell me what you buy in the market. And don't let anyone swindle you!"

We bid our good-days, and I joined Paiyoon in line for a place on one of the rowboats. The disgraced sailor with the bun stood apart, flanked by two officers. Ever since her punishment, she had been kept in the brig, a cell down in the ship's hold. She looked pale and thin, and her clothes were filthy.

Captain Sangra stood at the head of the line, perfectly still and straight-backed as always. But from this close, I could see the muscles in her jaw bouncing, as if she were grinding her back teeth together. One finger rested on the bulwark, tapping out an impatient tempo. When the first rowboat was ready, she leaped down to take her seat.

What could she be so anxious about?

"All right, Sai, our turn," said Paiyoon, waving me toward the second rowboat. "Stay with me and follow my directions while we're here. This will be a quick trip, just long enough to take on fresh water, and I don't want you getting left behind."

I climbed into the boat after him, gripping the side as it rocked on its ropes. We weren't the only ones excited to leave the ship. As the rowboats raced one another to shore, the crew belted out sea chanteys that reminded me of the songs played on the Rooster Room's piano.

In the boat beside ours, Grebe's face beaded with sweat as he worked the oars. I'd give him this much: he was a strong sailor. The other rowers were all older, but it was thick-shouldered Grebe who set the pace, pulling his boat through the water with ease.

A fleet of stingrays glided under us as we neared the shore and the rickety shacks of Pitaya Town. The buildings were made from driftwood and old boat planks, held fast with rusted nails or lashings made of coconut fiber.

"The whole place looks like it would fall over if you sneezed on it," I said.

"It's sturdier than it looks," said Paiyoon. "Pitaya Island is full of surprises, as you'll soon find out. Your parents sent you with some spending money?"

"Of course, sir," I said, frowning to think of my empty pockets. "I promised to buy my mother a souvenir."

"You will have plenty of options," said Paiyoon. "Here we are!"

Our boat skidded up onto the beach, and I jumped out. As soon as my feet hit the sand, I fell over. I got back up, but it felt like I was still bobbing up and down on the sea. I reached out for Paiyoon's sleeve.

"Steady now!" Paiyoon laughed as he helped me to stand. "You've earned your sea legs, and they aren't so easy to get rid of. Just try to keep moving and keep your eyes distracted. It shouldn't be too difficult in a place like this."

The crew had rushed off to find their own distractions, and I followed Paiyoon through the sandy streets of the town. Open-front shanties sold everything from pearl-handled swords to tea infused with real gold. You could buy shot and powder in one store, then go next door for a foot massage. I'd always thought the markets in An Lung were lively, but they were nothing compared to this place.

People crowded the street and leaned out of windows overhead. I spied every shade of skin from the deepest brown to the palest pink, burned to red by the brutal sun. The customers and shop vendors shouted at one another, speaking in Mangkon and a jumble of other languages I didn't know.

Men and women bent over open fires or carts, selling fruit I'd never seen, making soups and stews right there in the street, and grilling every kind of meat imaginable skewered on sticks.

My stomach grumbled miserably, and not just from the smell of good food. This would've been the perfect place to jump ship on the return journey home if I still had my tin of money. My savings would have gone a long way here, and Mud wouldn't have found me in a thousand years.

Paiyoon pointed up and down the crowded lane. "You have a wander around these stalls and find your mother something nice. I have an errand to attend."

"No, it's all right, sir," I said, shoving my hands into my empty pockets. "She wouldn't go for these trinkets. I'll save my money for the next port."

I started to follow along beside him, but he stopped me with a firm hand on my shoulder. "You can't come to Pitaya and leave empty-handed. Here." He gave me three leks. "At least have a bite to eat. My treat. Try the roasted octopus. It's a local delicacy."

"Oh! Thank you, sir."

"Wait right there for me!" he called over his shoulder.

Clearly Paiyoon didn't want me to come with him wherever he was going. Curious, I followed him from a distance and watched him disappear through the doorway of a faded blue shack. From my lessons with him, I could tell the shop's sign was written in Pramong. I couldn't read the words, but the open palm painted on the window told me what sort of place it was. I smiled, shaking my head. No wonder he wanted to get rid of me. The logical Master Paiyoon was visiting a fortune-teller.

I left him to his superstitions and wound through the narrow streets, following the smells of roasting garlic and fried fat. Vendors waved this or that elixir or trinket in front of me as I passed.

"Limes and wort, to fight off scurvy," shouted one.

"Sell yer teeth, make some coin," called another. "Thirty leks fer the front 'uns, twenty-five fer the back!"

An old woman wearing a faded Mangkon Navy coat stepped into my path. "You're part of the *Prosperity* crew," she said in a rasping hiss. "You'll need one of these where you're going."

She dangled a cluster of necklaces in my face. The pendants—rounded triangles the size of a baby's hand—rattled against one another.

"Dragon scales," said the woman with a sneering smile. "Plucked straight out of the Harbinger Sea.

They'll trick the beasts into thinking you're one of their own."

"No, thank you . . ."

"Or maybe you'd fancy this instead." She reached into a pocket of her skirt and held up a thin disc of lemon-colored glass.

I stumbled back in shock. My first thought was that she had robbed Paiyoon and stolen his eyeglass. But that couldn't be possible. "Where did you get that?" I demanded.

She laughed, baring her rotten back teeth. "It's a dragon haw." She tapped her finger to the corner of her eye. "The beast's inner eyelid. Very rare. Very precious."

The woman held the glass between us, scanning me with her magnified eye. "They say a dragon haw shows you the true nature of a thing. Dragons can look through it, right to a man's very heart. Maybe you've got a sweetheart, hmm? You want to know if he loves you back? This eyelid will show you the truth when you look through it. I'm selling it cheap today. A discount just for you."

She held the lens out to me. I ran my thumb along the edge, entranced by how much it looked like the one in Paiyoon's case. It was as thin as an onion skin and glowed in the sunlight.

Suddenly, a giant of a man with no shirt on barreled past us down the alley. We both had to leap out of his way to keep from getting trampled. The woman's necklaces clattered onto the dirt, chipping at the edges. She shook her fist at him, shouting, "My dragon scales! You'll pay for that, you clod!"

"Dragon scales, my hind!" boomed the man. "Don't let her scam you, girlie. The woman's got the finest *turtle-shell* dragon scales you ever seen!"

He laughed as she cursed him, gathering up her wares. I took the opportunity to get away. A scam—of course it was. I laughed at myself for nearly believing she was selling actual dragon parts.

Even if she was, I had much more important things to spend my money on. I was determined to fill my belly before we left, and *not* with an octopus tentacle. I picked out a food stand selling golden rice with nuts and ginger cradled in bowls made from carved-out pineapples. The smell made my mouth water.

It was midday and dozens of other people were waiting in line for their lunches. I stood with them, trying to hold my ground and not get skipped. As I finally neared the front, I felt a slight flutter on my right side, just below my hip. Most people wouldn't have even noticed.

But most people didn't have a world-class pickpocket for a father.

I shot my hand into my pocket and grabbed a thin wrist. When I turned around, I twisted the rough-skinned hand in the opposite direction. There were my coins, right in the center of the palm.

A wiry boy with a mop of thick black hair grimaced at me from under the brim of a straw hat. *"Grummit,"* he whispered. "Let go of me, you soggy dangle of dog dung!"

I took back my coins but held tight to the boy's hand. "Not until you apologize for trying to steal from me," I said calmly.

A man standing beside me turned toward us. "Wot's goin' on here?" His eyes grew wide as he realized the situation for himself. "He's gone and picked your pocket, has he?"

"Tried, anyway," I said.

The boy jerked to get out of my grip, dropping his hat to the ground. "Let go of me, vulture turd!"

He seemed about my age, but I was bigger and I held him tight. The boy swung his foot straight into my shin, the kick landing right on the bone. I winced and let his wrist go, bending to clutch my leg.

The boy took off running. The man standing beside me pulled out a whistle and started tweeting it shrilly. Immediately, two men in dusty red uniforms pushed through the crowd, nearly tripping right over me as they ran after him.

There was more shouting from people on the sides of the street, a scuffle, and then the crowd parted to let the two men back through. They dragged the wiry boy between them by his arms.

They stopped in front of the man with the whistle, whom I guessed must also belong to this ragtag police force.

"This the one?" the police asked the whistle man.

"That's him." He pointed to where I knelt in the dirt, hugging my shin. "Tried to pick that one's pocket. Didn't he, child?"

I looked up and nodded.

"Come on, little rat," said one of the police to the boy. "It's the courthouse for you."

The boy kicked his legs so that they had to carry him with his feet off the ground. "Filthy *Ublesos! Mul sat!*" he shouted at them.

"Curse all you want, urchin," said the policeman. "That language won't sway the judge."

The boy turned and glared at me as they dragged him away. "You're a filthy snitch! I hope you rot in Agryssus for a thousand years. Snitch!"

The people around me helped me to my feet and let me go to the front of the line. I bought my pineapple rice and ate in a quiet corner of the street. I knew I should have been enjoying it, but it had no flavor on my tongue.

The word *snitch* had stung me hard. Mud had brought me up to believe that ratting someone out to the police was the lowest thing you could do. He'd gone to jail enough times to know that sending someone there was serious. And he'd never once given the police a tip to lessen his sentence—even if it meant his only daughter had to wait in the girls' home while he served out his time.

Loyalty, Sai. Even a dog knows how important it is.

I didn't owe that kid any loyalty. He would have robbed me clean and not felt bad about it. But I still didn't feel right about getting him in trouble. I didn't even want to think about what jail was like on that island.

When Paiyoon found me, he was in a hurry. "Ah, there you are! Did you eat?"

"I did, sir."

"Good. Let's get back to the *Prosperity* before they leave us!"

We hurried to the beach, where we met up with Captain Sangra and some of the crew, just boarding the last of the rowboats.

Sangra ran her finger inside her jacket collar to loosen it, revealing a flash of gold at her neck. I guessed that must be her lineal. Only members of the royal family were allowed to wear lineal necklaces. They were also the only ones who had enough links to circle their necks.

Sweat dripped from Sangra's temple, and she looked ill. Whatever she'd seen or eaten during her excursion to Pitaya hadn't been good. I wondered if she was about to throw up over the side.

Paiyoon, by contrast, was beaming. As we rowed back to the ship, he hummed softly to himself, looking fondly at the island. I wanted to laugh. Had he really visited a fortune-teller, or was Rian right, and he had seen an old girlfriend?

Our boat reached the *Prosperity*'s shadow, and the crew on board began to haul us back up to the deck. As they leaned over the side to pull us up, it became clear how they'd spent their pay on the island. Tortoiseshell

128

dragon scales swung from their necks, catching the last rays of the sun as it hurried away to light up the other side of the globe.

"Say goodbye to the peaceful waters of the Green Sea," said Paiyoon. "From here we head south, and our journey truly begins."

CHAPTER SIXTEEN

An Unlikely Partnership

The wind picked up once we left Pitaya Island, and we were across the equator within two weeks. We had left the calm turquoise waters behind us, and I took my wool cloak out of the trunk in my room for the first time. The cold, bleak days when I would need it still lay ahead of us, but we were barreling straight for that future.

With our ship sailing at speed, the crew was kept busy. The captain must have been busier, too, because I saw more of Rian. One afternoon, when I had finished taking the readings for Master Paiyoon, I spotted her standing on the forecastle deck, the small deck at the prow of the ship. When she saw me, she waved me over to join her.

I looked around as I climbed the steps. I had never come up to the forecastle, since the prow bobbed up

and down too much for me to take my readings. Wind whipped my face, and sails snapped high above me. The *Prosperity* was sailing at a fine clip now, caught up in the winds of the Swift Sea. The sunlight skipped off the sparkling water and danced in my eyes.

"Over here!" called Rian. She stood among stacks of extra sleeping hammocks. They formed two thick walls of canvas on either side of the forecastle. I slid in between the stacks with her, and the wind immediately calmed.

"There, that's better, isn't it?" asked Rian, her cheeks pink from the breeze. "Isn't this a nice, peaceful spot? Out of the way of the crew. You can look up and see the sky, and there's no wind to whip you to death with your own hair."

"It's perfect, miss."

She reached over and tapped my notebook. "What's that you're working on?"

"Same thing as always. Readings and observations for Master Paiyoon."

"Ah," she said, nodding. "And what is *he* working on?"

I sighed. "Same thing as always. Charting our southern course. We've been working on it nearly every day since we left An Lung."

She raised one dark eyebrow. "Oh? And where does he have us going?"

"Well, right now we're on our way to Fahlin, where we'll stock up on fresh water and food. At that point, Master Paiyoon thinks we should strike southeast for Lontain, then turn south to break the fiftieth parallel from there." The destinations were fresh in my memory because I had just sketched out the last part of the course for him this morning.

"And then?" asked Rian.

"And then Paiyoon thinks we could push straight south toward the pole. He thinks we'll find some volcanic islands and maybe even be able to map some sea ice."

"Mapping sea ice, hm?" She tucked her hair behind her ears and looked me in the eye. "Sai, has your mapmaker talked to you about the purpose of this expedition?"

"To cross the fiftieth parallel," I answered. "Then sail south and fill in the last blank spaces on the globe."

Rian tilted her head slightly. I had the feeling she was sizing me up, but for what I couldn't guess. "Yes, but fill them in with *what*, exactly?"

I paused. "I don't know what you mean."

Rian glanced to either side even though we were clearly alone. "Do you really think that if the Queen thought those blank spaces were just full of sea ice, she'd go to all this trouble to make a map of them?"

I hadn't given it much thought before. I'd assumed the Queen wanted to have a Mangkon ship be the one to cross the Dragon Line, just so no one else could claim it.

"Well," I said, "the announcement in the *Mangkon Times*—"

"Didn't print the Queen's entire statement." Rian let that sink in for a moment before going on. "They only printed the first part. Would you like to see the whole thing?"

She reached into her jacket pocket and pulled out a half sheet of paper with a blue wax seal at the bottom, stamped with the Queen's dragon symbol. "This was sent to Anchalee—the captain, I mean. She shared it with me."

The first of the announcement was exactly what I'd read in the newspaper, about the Queen sending her ships out to north, east, west, and south. But Rian was right. There was one more paragraph that the newspaper hadn't printed.

TO MARK MANGKON'S new Era of Discovery, it is her Royal Majesty's express wish to confirm or refute, for once and for all, the existence of a Great Southern Continent, and to claim it in the name of Mangkon if found. The captain of any Mangkon ship returning bearing accurate geographical knowledge of this continent shall be awarded an additional purse of 50,000 leks. The ship's crew shall be rewarded for their Act of Great Bravery.

"A southern continent?" I repeated curiously.

"You may have heard of it by a different name," said Rian. "The Sunderlands."

"The Sunderlands!" I laughed. "But that's just a children's story."

Rian folded the paper and returned it to her pocket. "That sort of reaction is likely why Her Majesty told the newspaper not to print her entire statement. Queens generally hate being laughed at."

"I'm sorry. I didn't mean to be disrespectful. But you're saying that the Queen is offering a reward for discovering a magical land? An entire continent that no one has ever seen before? You have to admit that it sounds, well . . . kind of wild."

But though Rian kept her smile, she clearly wasn't joking. "It is wild, I can't deny that," she said. "And that's why it's been kept secret from almost everyone on board."

"Does Master Paiyoon know?"

Rian nodded.

I bit my lip. "Oh. I wonder why he didn't tell me about it."

"Probably because he thinks it's a bunch of nonsense. At least that's what he told our captain." Rian fluttered her lips. "Not that she needed much convincing."

"Master Paiyoon is a logical type of person," I said. "He doesn't believe in myths and legends, at least not that I can tell." *Though he did visit a fortune-teller*, I thought.

"But every myth is based on reality, isn't it?" Rian pressed on. "If the Great Southern Continent was just a story, why would our queen send out her best ship and her greatest warrior to find it? There must be some reason to believe it's out there."

"But Captain Sangra doesn't want to go looking for it?"

Rian frowned and shook her head. "No. And it doesn't help that the legends say that the Sunderlands lie in the middle of the Harbinger Sea."

I had heard of the Harbinger Sea—everyone had. Those words were scrawled across a hazy patch of blank space on the bottom of the globe in our shop. Some people said that it was the boundary between the human world and the world of spirits. According to legend, no human was allowed to cross it, and any ship that tried was doomed.

"Is the captain afraid it's too dangerous?" I asked.

"Anchalee isn't afraid of anything," said Rian. "She says that she doesn't want to risk sailing through the Harbinger Sea, but I know that's not the real reason. After all, we're on board the best ship that Mangkon has ever built! The *Prosperity* survived the worst battles of the War; I think it could handle a few miles of rough seas, don't you?"

"Then why not go for it?"

Rian sighed and leaned back against the canvas. "My old friend is battle weary, Sai. She's been at sea for nearly twenty years, and now that the War is over, she wants to go home. I understand, of course. Anchalee has a cushy hero's life to go back to. She doesn't have a good reason for taking a risk to go in search of a wild, wonderful thing like the Sunderlands. Not like the rest of us."

I blinked at her. "The rest of us?"

She shook her head at me and smiled. "Didn't you read that last part? The Queen has decided that finding the Sunderlands is an 'act of great bravery.' Don't you remember what that means?"

My stomach flipped somersaults as I looked at Rian's gleaming lineal. An act of great bravery. A Lineal of Honor.

"But . . . the Queen wouldn't give a lineal to *every* person on the ship. Would she?"

"She won't have to. The officers and ship's staff like Paiyoon and you already have them." Rian glanced down at my wrists. "Or at least you will have yours soon, anyway? When you turn thirteen?"

I swallowed and nodded.

She went on. "The Queen will give all of us a choice between a lineal and a purse of money: two thousand leks. The crew will almost all take the cash. I nearly took it myself when I was offered it. But I knew that if I ever wanted to walk the halls of Mangkon society, I would need a key to open the door." She tapped her glimmering brooch. "But you see, Sai, the captain doesn't have to worry about any of that. She's got more money than she knows what to do with and a lineal a yard long. I love my friend, but she doesn't understand what it's like for the rest of us."

My thoughts were a tangle in my brain. Suddenly, one thought fought its way through the snarl. It was actually the type of question Mud would ask: *What's in it for you?*

I looked up at her. "You already have a lineal too, Miss Rian."

She turned her eyes from me and picked at the seam of her jacket. "Yes, a Lineal of Honor. Which I received for getting knocked in the back of the head. Not much honor in that, is there?" she said bitterly. "Don't get me wrong. I'm proud of serving my country and proud that I saved my friend's life. But I want to *do* something with my own. Something real and something big."

Clouds sped past the sun overhead, and the bright light flitted across Rian's face. She kept her cool composure, but underneath all that polish was a restlessness I hadn't noticed before.

"You know what they say in Mangkon," said Rian. "*The Tail Is the Teeth*. The past is your future. Well, I refuse to let that be true. My past is nothing. And

I refuse to be nothing. I'm going to make my own future, and I don't care what I have to risk to do it."

Her words shot straight through me. They were words I had only dared to think to myself. I had never heard someone say them out loud before.

Rian continued. "Listen, Sai. The Queen's proclamation says that she'll award that prize to *any* Mangkon crew. The Queen wants the globe filled in, but she doesn't care who does it—as long as they do it in her name. When we left An Lung, there were a half dozen more ships being outfitted to go exploring. The *Prosperity* has a head start, and the Queen's great-niece is our captain, but if we don't take advantage of it, someone else will come along and do the job for us."

The sea was smooth, but I felt off balance. "But what can we do? How can we have a hope of finding the Sunderlands—if they even exist?"

"They exist—I know it," said Rian, her gaze steady. "And it's up to us to make sure the *Prosperity* finds them. I'll keep working on Anchalee. She's stubborn, but I know that she respects your mapmaker—"

"He's stubborn, too."

Rian smiled. "But he respects *you*. I've seen it. Talk to him and see if you can get him to at least be open-minded about searching for the Sunderlands. If he sets us on a promising course, I know the captain will follow it. But if we sail into the southern seas with no bigger goals than mapping sea ice, then we'll go home empty-handed for sure."

I straightened my shoulders. "I'm not sure that I can convince Master Paiyoon of anything, but I'm willing to try."

Rian beamed. "I swear to you that it will be worth it. From now on, you and I are on the same team." She held out her hand to me. "Are we partners?"

I shook it and smiled. "Partners."

When I returned to my room, my mind whirred with thoughts of lineals, money, and maps. If I hadn't seen the Queen's proclamation with my own eyes, I wouldn't have believed it. The Sunderlands. I never would have dreamed that I'd be on board a ship that might be searching for that mythical place.

And then there was the reward.

Two thousand leks was a fortune, but without even thinking, I knew what my choice would be. A lineal of my own. And one with five links! If I had that, maybe I could keep working for Master Paiyoon, or use it to get a scholarship, or get another job elsewhere in the

Nine Islands. More than that, a lineal was a key, just as Rian had said. One that would open all sorts of doors for me and let me hold my head high wherever I went. It would be like starting life over as a completely different person. And I would never, ever need to return home to Mud.

One worrying thought kept barging its way in past the other shimmery ones: Why hadn't Master Paiyoon said anything about this part of the expedition? Was it because he didn't believe the Sunderlands were real? Or was it because he didn't trust me to keep it a secret?

I lay in my hammock, trying to make sense of everything I had just learned, but I was distracted by the scratching sounds from the wall behind my head. I stood up fast, tumbling out of my hammock onto the floor.

Rats! Ever since we left Pitaya Island, they had been skittering around in the storage closet on the other side of my room. I felt like I could hear their disgusting little claws inside my skull.

I grabbed my shoe and went into the hallway. Slowly, I opened the door to the storage closet, letting the dim light from the hall shine into the small room. I held the top of my shoe, ready to strike, and moved farther inside. At the back of the closet, several large sacks of grain leaned against one another. I stepped closer to them and peered over the top.

All at once, an angry face rose to meet mine. Before I could react, I'd been punched squarely in the stomach.

Someone clawed their way over the grain sacks and pushed me aside. I spun around in time to see a set of scrawny limbs and a lash of dark hair escape through the doorway and out into the hall.

It was the boy who'd tried to pick my pocket on Pitaya Island.

CHAPTER SEVENTEEN

Rats and Tuna

The boy had somehow managed to steal himself a sailor's deck shirt and trousers, but there was no mistaking that mop of black hair. I sprinted up after him onto the main deck and spun around in both directions, searching for a sign of him.

If someone caught him, they'd take him straight to Captain Sangra. Stowaways weren't tolerated on a Mangkon ship. He was lucky it was lunchtime and most of the crew was down below, save the lookouts up in the crow's nest, their eyes trained on the horizon.

I searched the entire main deck before climbing the quarterdeck stairs. I had nearly given up when I caught a flash of movement between large piles of coiled rope and nets on the starboard side. I hurried to the rope coils and found the boy crouched like a mongoose ready to strike.

When he saw me, he held up both fists in front of his face.

"Stay back, goat turd, or I'll break your nose this time," he hissed.

"Go on and try," I whispered back. "They'll catch you and you'll be thrown in the brig!"

"Wouldn't that just make you smile, you squealer," he said. "It's 'cause of you I'm here at all."

"It's not my fault the police caught you! You were the one who—"

The sound of whistling made me stop. I looked back and saw Mr. Lark coming up the quarterdeck steps toward us.

"Get down!" I whispered.

The boy flattened himself to the deck boards behind a large pile of rope. I put my hands on my hips and looked up, pretending to take note of the clouds.

"Afternoon, young Sai!" said Lark, striding toward me. "How lucky I found you. Today you have the privilege of helping me launch my collection net."

"Absolutely! Great fun!" I tried to make myself as animated as possible to keep Lark's attention on me.

Luckily, Lark was the least observant man I'd ever met. He took a step within inches of the boy's legs and didn't notice him, then reached down and grabbed a large net.

"Yesterday I caught a new species of tuna," he said brightly. "I believe I'll name it after myself."

I helped him haul the rope net across the quarterdeck toward the starboard rail. "Did you, really? How fascinating, sir."

"Yes, these nets are quite good for catching fast swimmers." Lark struggled to drag the heavy netting to the edge of the deck.

The quarterdeck was enclosed by a wall of thick planks. There were square holes in the planking, spaced at regular intervals all along both sides of the ship. These were the gunports, where the quarterdeck cannons had been placed during the War.

"Help me, Sai," grunted Lark as he heaved the net to one of the gunports. "Now . . . push it through with me . . . That's it."

I helped him shove the net out through the hole.

"There," he said, wiping his hands on his pants. "Now I'll just watch over it and see what we turn up."

"Let me watch it for you, sir. I have the next hour free, and I'm delightfully excited to see what you discover next."

Lark smiled proudly. "You have all the makings of a naturalist, Sai. Come get me and I'll get someone to help you haul it in."

I watched him walk away, letting out a big exhale when he disappeared down the stairs. Near my feet, the rope attached to Lark's collection net zipped along the deck boards as the net was dragged farther behind the ship.

My eyes followed the snaking rope to the coil the boy crouched behind.

Tripe.

I hurried over to him and tried to get him out of the way. "Careful! Look, you're—"

"Stay back!"

He jerked away from me and stood up. Hand loops had been tied at regular intervals along the rope, and when he stepped back, he put his foot inside one of the loops. At that moment, the rope pulled taut and yanked his feet out from under him.

The boy clawed at the smooth boards as the net dragged him toward the cannon hole. I scrambled after him, reaching out for his hands, but I slipped. I grabbed the rope, but it was moving too fast. It burned my palms as it ran through them.

He'll stop at the deck wall. He'll stop and I'll grab him.

But the boy was so thin, and the weight of the net so heavy, that it pulled him straight through the gunport and off the ship.

He had gone overboard.

CHAPTER EIGHTEEN

An Impressive Catch

I ran to the gunport and stuck my head out. With a lurch in my stomach, I searched the water for the boy's body. Then, straight below me, I heard a yelp. The boy hung upside down, still caught by the single loop of rope around his ankle. He dangled against the side of the ship, knocking against the hull.

Oh, holy, holy TRIPE.

"Hold on!" I called to him.

I had to help him fast. If he twisted the wrong way, he would come loose and fall into the water. I grabbed the rope and yanked as hard as I could. It was no use. The net alone weighed at least a hundred pounds. But if I asked anyone to help me, the boy would be found out.

I looked down again. He hung just outside the windows of the living quarters at the stern of the ship. With the ship's cross-section in my mind, I counted

the windows. I was realizing that I just might be able to save him, when behind me, a voice said, "Sai, what on earth are you doing?"

I spun around and found Paiyoon watching me with concern.

"Oh, dear, you aren't seasick again, are you?" he asked.

I puffed out my cheeks and clutched my stomach. "Yes! Yes, I am, sir. Terribly sick."

He took a step back. "I hope Cook didn't let the food spoil again." He glanced at the top deck, where Captain Sangra stood looking out at sea like a noble statue. "I'm off to have a word with Sangra. Have you noticed she's been acting strangely since we left Pitaya Island?"

It took all my willpower not to check on the boy still dangling upside down over the side. "No, sir, I haven't noticed."

"Hmm, well, perhaps it's nothing, but in my experience it's bad luck to have a moody captain." Paiyoon turned back to me. "You'd better lie down, Sai. You look terrible."

"Yes, sir," I said.

I waited for Paiyoon to start climbing up to the top deck, then I shot down the stairway to the main deck and yanked open the door that led to his room.

149

If I'd counted right, the boy hung outside the window of either this cabin or Dr. Pinching's. Thankfully, I saw him through the glass, scrabbling to get his hands on the rope above.

I shut the door behind me and dragged a chair to the window, knocking boxes and stacks of papers off the desk. I reached up and unlatched the glass, swinging it open. It slammed against the boy's forehead.

"*Ow!* Watch it, you *vingo!*"

I leaned out the window and grabbed him by the elbows. He wrapped his arms around mine.

"Just don't let go, whatever you do," I told him.

Gripping him as tight as I could, I twisted his body to loosen his ankle from the loop of rope above. The rope untangled, and his legs dropped straight down, nearly yanking me out the window with him. It was a miracle we both didn't end up in the sea. He cursed the entire time I hauled him through the window into Master Paiyoon's room.

Together we collapsed onto the floor. It took a long minute for me to catch my breath enough to be able to stand up and shut the window. My hands trembled as I closed the latch.

"That was unbelievably close," I said, sitting down on the chair.

The boy was a tangle of limbs on the floor. He sat rubbing his ankle where the rope had scraped up a bloody rash on his gold-brown skin.

"That looks bad," I said, stepping closer. "Let me see."

He slid away from me. "Stay back, pox-breath."

"I just saved you from a watery grave. You might be a little thankful."

"Don't be so proud of yourself," he said, glaring hatefully at me. "I know how to swim."

"Across the *ocean*? Then, please, go ahead and jump out the window. Don't let me stop you."

He looked down at his ankle again. "What's it matter? I'm good as dead now anyway. And the captain'll flog me first before throwing me over."

I didn't think Sangra would whip a child, but it was still hard to imagine our strict captain tolerating a stowaway. The best he could hope for was to be thrown in the brig and then dumped in jail at the next port. I rubbed my stomach, which still ached from where he had punched me. Oh, why couldn't I have just sat in my hammock in peace and left the "rats" alone?

Finally I said, "Listen. I won't turn you in."

The boy jerked his face up at me. "What?"

"I said I won't turn you in to the captain. We'll stop at Fahlin, and you can get off there. We'll pretend this whole thing never happened."

"Fahlin!" A look of dread flashed over his face. "This ship's not going to Mangkon?"

"Keep your voice down!" I whispered, glancing at the door. "It's going back there eventually. But we're crossing half the globe first."

The boy rubbed his bleeding ankle and didn't say anything.

I took a deep breath and let it out. "Listen, I think we can avoid having you punished—which I'd rather not see, to be honest. But we've got to go now. And you can't hide in that closet. Our cook would find you at some point. You need to hide somewhere no one ever goes, like the hold."

The boy shivered. "Down in the ship's bowels? I'll go mad down there."

"I'll bring you food and water. Look, you've got no other options. And I won't help you if you're just going to get us both caught."

He nodded slowly. "Fine."

"What's your name?"

He frowned like he wasn't going to tell, then blurted out, "Bo."

I offered my hand to help him up. "I'm Sai. Come on, we can take the back way down below. Quick, help me clean this up before Master Paiyoon gets back."

Bo dragged the chair back to the desk, and I gathered up the papers off the floor. As I set them back into place, a single page slipped out from the stack and fluttered to my feet. I bent to pick it up. The same word was written on the paper over and over, in Paiyoon's hand:

Alang   *Alang*   *Alang*

I didn't know what it meant, but the way the word was repeated gave me a strange, unsettled feeling under my rib cage.

"What're you waiting for?" whispered Bo, already at the door. "Let's go!"

I tucked Paiyoon's note back into the stack of papers and led Bo out of the room.

Perfect. Just perfect, I thought as we crept toward the ladder to the hold.

I could now add "harboring a stowaway" to my long list of accomplishments.

CHAPTER NINETEEN

Secrets in the Dark

Our ship's hold was not a nice place. All the supplies not needed daily on deck got stored there: extra sails, food and fresh-water rations, wine, timbers, and carpenters' tools. Nasty bilge water collected and sloshed around in the bottom. It was dark, echoing, and cold.

And then there was the smell.

"It stinks like the bloody bowels of the devil down here!"

The light from my lantern shone on Bo's face.

"Shhh!" I hissed, closing the hatch behind me. "You're supposed to wait for me to come down and give you the signal, not peek your head out where someone can see!"

I handed Bo the lamp and the food I'd brought before descending the ladder. I pinched my nose shut, but I could still taste the bilge-flavored air with every

breath. We'd chosen a hiding spot for Bo near the stern where the extra sails were stored. It was drier there and farthest from the supplies the crew would come looking for. Bo had made a nest for himself out of sailcloth and tarps behind some large crates so he'd be hidden from sight if someone did come down.

"You've got no idea what it's like down here," said Bo. "It's depressing. And dark as the inside of a dog's—"

"Yes, I know," I interrupted. "You've told me."

Bo rolled his eyes. "Sorry, didn't mean to offend your dainty ears."

"You might try saying thank you instead. It's a big risk bringing you this food, you know. Not to mention it's food I should be eating myself."

I had been hiding him for four days. It wasn't easy to get away from my navigation duties and sneak belowdecks without anyone seeing me. Not only did I have to bring Bo food and water, but I had to carry his night bucket up top and empty it over the side. The first time I did it, I nearly gave up and turned us both in. Anything would be better than tending to this ungrateful, curse-slinging brat.

"Hold on . . ." I sniffed and caught a whiff of something smoky mixed in with the bilge. "Have you been lighting *candles*?"

"No . . ."

I swung the lantern over Bo's nest and spotted two large yellow drops of candle wax. "You have! Are you out of your mind? Do you want to start a fire down here?"

"Actually, yeah, I *was* going out of my mind in the dark all alone," he spat back. "And you don't need to worry about a fire. I think I know how to handle a stupid candle."

"Well, you can't do it anymore," I growled. "I know it's not ideal down here, but you just have to last a few more weeks. We'll be in Fahlin by then and you can get off there."

Bo had already half-devoured the bean curd and gravy I had given him. "That's Mangkon territory, right?" he asked.

"Yes, they surrendered near the start of the War. I'm sure you'll find lots of fools who'll let you pick their pockets." I picked up the stubby candle remains. "Where did you get this, anyway?"

Bo licked around the rim of his food bowl. "Now, don't go getting upset . . ."

"Please tell me you didn't leave the hold . . ."

"I was like a ghost. No one saw me . . ."

156

"Please tell me you didn't go into . . ."

". . . definitely not that skinny *widge* with all the jars in his room."

"You snuck into Lark's cabin? You idiot!"

Bo picked a piece of food out of his teeth with his pinky fingernail. "The man sleeps as heavy as potato curry."

"Ugh, you are hopeless!" I threw down the candle stub and grabbed my lantern to start climbing up the ladder.

He got to his feet. "Wait—are you coming back?"

"Why should I?" I said bitterly. "You're not worth risking my neck for."

"Knew I shouldn't have trusted you," he called after me. "Knew you'd treat me like I was nothing, like I was a nobody."

I stopped, one hand on the ladder. Suddenly, I could see myself standing in line at the café, praying the other Assistants didn't notice my dirty shoes. I turned, letting the light from my lamp shine onto his face. "I don't think you're a nobody."

He stared back at me, looking as defiant as the day he tried to pick my pocket.

I let out a sigh. "Really, that's not what I think. If I did, I wouldn't have helped you at all."

He softened. "Sorry for sneaking out. I just wanted to breathe air that didn't smell full of wet farts for one minute, that's all."

I laughed. "Do you know that you've got a fouler mouth than anyone I've ever met?"

He grinned, revealing a deep dimple in his left cheek. "Bet that's not saying much, Lady Sai."

It was saying a lot. Not even Mud's lowlife friends cursed as much as Bo. Bo spoke perfect Mangkon, but with an accent I couldn't place and *r*'s that rolled off his tongue. He also seemed to know how to swear in every language on earth.

I glanced around the dank hold. It truly was a wretched place. I didn't want to be there for five more minutes, and Bo had existed like this for days. "Just try to hold on a little longer, all right? I'll see if I can figure out a way for you to get out of here."

I climbed up the ladder, leaving him behind in the darkness.

As I replaced the hatch over the door into the hold, I heard voices echoing around the corner in the narrow passageway ahead. I froze and listened.

". . . you'll shut yer mouth, then . . ."

". . . but the Harbinger Sea . . ."

My ears pricked to attention. These weren't the voices of adult sailors. They were pups. Why were they talking about the Harbinger Sea? Curious, I lowered the tin cover over my lantern and edged forward in the darkness.

I recognized Grebe's voice: "And if you know what's good for you, you won't say another word about it," he hissed.

"Please don't do this!" begged a small voice in reply.

I started to round the corner but hesitated. I hated to come face-to-face with Grebe in such tight quarters.

There was a scuffle of feet, and then the small voice squealed, "Don't hurt me!"

I lunged around the corner and pulled the cover off my lantern. "Stop it!"

Grebe and another boy much smaller than him squinted against the sudden flood of light. I recognized the small boy as one of the youngest pups in the crew, maybe even younger than me. Everyone called him Dumpling because of the way his hair twirled to a point on his head.

"Did he hurt you?" I asked.

Dumpling shook his head, looking more afraid of me than of Grebe. "No, miss. We were just talking. That's all."

Grebe's shock at seeing me turned into a sneer. "That's right. Just having a nice chat. What are you doing down here?"

I let my hair fall over my cheeks as I reached into my apron pocket and pulled out a set of paintbrushes, which I had been carrying around in case I had to explain myself. "Paiyoon had me come down and get these out of his storage trunk. When I was coming out of the hold, I heard voices." I looked at Grebe from behind my fringe of hair. "It sounded like a pretty big argument. Something about the Harbinger Sea?"

Dumpling's lower lip quivered as his eyes went between Grebe and me, and then words tumbled out of him in one big gush. "Please, miss, tell your Master Mapmaker not to take us there! We can't cross it—it's not right! The spirits will be angry. They'll send the Slake after us!"

Grebe snorted and rolled his eyes. "Here we go again."

"What are you talking about?" I asked.

"The Slake!" Dumpling's eyes were wide as tea cakes. "She's the queen of the dragons, and she guards the Sunderlands, devouring any ships that wander near. If we try to cross the Harbinger Sea, she'll come for us!"

160

I would have laughed if he hadn't looked so close to tears. "But aren't dragons supposed to be good luck?" I said.

Dumpling shook his head. "Not if you disrespect 'em. Please, miss, you've got to tell your master to steer us clear of there. We mustn't look for the Sunderlands. We must leave that place be!"

This last part seemed to infuriate Grebe. He shook his fist at Dumpling's face. "You'll shut up about that or someone is gonna make you shut up. I already told you it's a done deal. We're looking, and if you know what's good for you, you'll pray we find it. I'm not giving up my chance at two thousand leks because of your stupid ideas."

Poor Dumpling was near tears. "What good is a pouch full of money if you're dead in the belly of a dragon?"

"Hold on!" I said to Dumpling. "How did you hear about all this?"

Grebe answered for him. "Everyone always thinks us sailors don't know what's going on. But we got our own eyes and ears." He glowered at me. "Sometimes we know more than anyone else does."

"You can't let him take us there," Dumpling begged me. "The Harbinger Sea is where we'll all meet our deaths!"

I nearly told Dumpling to shut up myself. His sniveling was unbearable. "Please stop worrying," I told him. "I haven't heard Master Paiyoon even mention the Harbinger Sea or the Sunderlands."

Dumpling broke into a relieved smile. "Yes, miss! Oh, thank you, miss, thank you!" He slunk sideways away from Grebe, then ran up the corridor, his feet padding on the wood like a toddler's.

Grebe watched him go but didn't follow. He turned his face to mine. This time I kept my chin up and returned his stare. We were too close for a haircut to hide me now.

He tilted his head. "There's something I been meaning to—"

"Do you know something strange?" I blurted out. "I have this feeling I've seen you somewhere before. But for the life of me I can't imagine where the two of us would have crossed paths."

Grebe held his mouth half-open, confused.

I went on, doing my best to copy Tippy's upper-class accent. "Ah, I have it!" I snapped my fingers and smiled. "Have you ever been to the Goldhope Harbor Market?"

"Um, yeah . . ." said Grebe, because anyone in An Lung with a pulse had been there.

162

"Yes, that's where it was. My governess took me there once, and you bumped into her and knocked all the packages out of her hands."

"Your . . . governess?"

I waved my fingers forgivingly. "You didn't even notice or stop to help, but it wasn't your fault. She's such a tiny thing! It was the last time she took me to the market, though. Don't worry; it's all water under the bridge now. But, yes, that's where it was. I'd remember you anywhere." I touched my fingers to my hairline and glanced at his scar.

I held my breath along with my chipper smile as I waited for his reaction. He stared back at me, and I could see the doubt working into the wrinkles of his forehead. What was more likely: that he remembered my fresh-scrubbed Assistant's face from the Harbor Market? Or from the grimy alleys of the Fens?

Finally, he gave me a curt, apologetic bow. He mumbled something I didn't hear, then turned and pounded up the steps.

I waited until he was gone, then let out a huge breath and leaned against the wall, swaying with the tilt of the ship as the boards groaned around me. I said a silent thank-you to Tippy for teaching me how to be a spoiled brat.

I should have known that snobbery would be a better disguise than a haircut. I would have to remember to play up the spoiled manners and accent whenever Grebe was around.

The funny thing was that he and I were actually on the same side in a way. We were both eager to go looking for the Sunderlands. In fact, it sounded like the secret of the prize was blown and the crew had found out about it. If the rest of the sailors were as keen as Grebe to go and make their fortunes, then Captain Sangra and Paiyoon were outnumbered.

Well, they did have Dumpling. But that kid was ridiculous, going on about a dragon queen. What had he called it—the Slake? Who could take him seriously? I wanted to talk to Rian about all of this, but I knew what she'd tell me. Our only hope was to convince Master Paiyoon that the Sunderlands were worth searching for.

It was up to me. And I needed to get to work.

CHAPTER TWENTY

A Clear Picture

The next morning, I was determined to speak with Paiyoon about the Sunderlands no matter what. The past few days, either he had been too grumpy or I had been too busy with Bo to bring it up. But I didn't want to wait any longer.

It wouldn't be easy. He was in one of his busy working moods, when I could barely get a word in edgewise.

"Come on, come on now, don't drag," Paiyoon huffed as he led me up to the quarterdeck from his room. "We are coming to the Deserdells, a day I have been waiting for since we left An Lung. Today, your mapmaking education truly begins!"

I followed, lugging a heavy box full of clanking brass equipment. A few hundred yards out, a cluster of

scrubby islands bobbed on top of the water like enormous moss-covered turtles.

"The Deserdells are the perfect size for you to start sketching," said Paiyoon, reaching into the box for a scope and a sheet of paper. "Anything larger can be overwhelming at first—so many things to record. Here, take the scope and focus on that island with the bay."

I planted my feet and bent my knees as Paiyoon had taught me. Luckily for my cheekbones, the sea was calm. I didn't need any more bruises from banging the scope into my face.

I held the instrument up and scanned the water until the first island came into view. "Oh . . . all right . . . I see it! Now I just have to dial the focus . . . a bit more . . . there! Master Paiyoon, I have it!"

I glanced over and saw him smiling proudly.

"Good. Now keep it in sight and take this pen. Here, I'll hold the paper steady for you. Good. Now just sketch what you see. Try to get the whole bay and the coastline . . ."

I took a deep breath and started to draw. Even with Paiyoon holding my paper, I felt like a street juggler, clutching the scope in one hand and the pen in the other, all while estimating distances, keeping everything to scale, and sketching the major features on the island.

Paiyoon was surprisingly patient. "Try not to look back and forth to your paper so often. You'll make yourself dizzy. Keep your eyes on the island. It helps if you don't pick your pen up from the page at all."

I tried that. But when I looked down at my sketch, I frowned. It was a complete mess. "Master Paiyoon, I'm afraid this isn't at all what it's supposed to look like."

Paiyoon gently took the scope from me and placed it back in the box at his feet. "That is your problem. You are worried about what it's *supposed* to look like. A mapmaker has to look for what's really there, not what they expect to see."

"But when I try that, I can't—"

"Nonsense," he said firmly. "You just need to know what it feels like to get it right."

To my surprise, he reached into his pocket, took out his eyeglass, and handed it to me.

I had never held it before. The gold case took up my whole palm, and yet it weighed much less than I'd expected. Paiyoon reached over, and with trembling fingers, he showed me how to click open the case and swivel the glass out.

He nodded to the island. "Look through the lens and tell me what you see."

167

I held the glass up to my eye, grateful that Paiyoon had kept the lineal chain connected to his jacket so I didn't have to worry about dropping it overboard. It took me a moment to figure out how to hold the lens to get the island in focus. The glass had a slight golden tint to it, as if someone had swirled in a drop of honey when it was made. But it didn't distort my view. If anything, the gold hue made all the features of the island stand out from one another. I felt like I could see everything, all at once, the way it truly was.

"What do you see?" Paiyoon asked.

"Everything, sir! I see now where I made my mistake. The bay doesn't keep curving around. It actually runs straight for about a hundred yards and—"

Paiyoon pressed the pen back into my hand. "Don't talk. Draw."

I imagined that my fingers and eyes were connected. Instead of concentrating on making my lines perfect, I let my pen track my gaze as I took in every jutting rock and stretch of beach. It actually wasn't so different from forging a signature.

When I was finished, I held up my paper. My lines were a bit messy, but it looked just like what I had seen through the glass. I had drawn a map of the bay.

Paiyoon beamed. "There! It's not so hard, is it? You just needed a little taste of success."

I couldn't stop smiling. This was the first time I'd made a map of my own instead of copying someone else's. It felt like I had just performed a magic spell.

"This eyeglass works wonders, sir. Where did you get it?"

Paiyoon smiled wistfully. "My grandfather gave it to me when I graduated school, just as his grand-father had given it to him."

I rubbed the edge of the thin glass with my thumb. That wall that Paiyoon usually kept up around himself had come down completely, and it made me feel less guarded, too. I found myself telling him all about the old woman on Pitaya Island, her dragon scales, and the "haw" she had tried to sell me.

Once I finished my story, Paiyoon stared at me for a long moment. And then he threw his head back and laughed a great, booming belly laugh. "A dragon eyelid? Does this mean my ancestors wrestled a dragon to the death?"

I laughed along with him. "Isn't it funny, sir? The woman told me that if you looked through it . . ."

I don't know what came over me then—maybe I thought it would add to the joke. I held the eyeglass

up between us and peered at Paiyoon through the lens. His smile faded and he suddenly looked uncomfortable. Through the glass, he seemed . . . different. I told myself it was just the yellow hue of the material, but I knew that wasn't the reason.

I was struck by the strange feeling that I was looking at someone with a secret. His eyes had that fiery determination to them that I had noticed back in the shop when he was telling me how important this expedition was. But his eyes didn't match the rest of him. He held his hands behind his back, as though he were hiding something.

"Well? What do you see?" he asked with a nervous lilt to his voice.

I lowered the lens and blinked. He seemed back to his usual self.

I handed the gold case to him with a smile. "Nothing out of the ordinary. No offense, sir."

This was my chance. "Master Paiyoon, have you finalized our southern course yet?"

He nodded, winding his lineal chain around and around the eyeglass case. "I believe I have. We should reach Fahlin in a little over three weeks, and then we can strike south. I'd like us to sail southeast for Lontain so that we can avoid getting bogged down in the Whorls, and then we can break the fiftieth parallel from there. If we have enough warm weather left before winter hits, we can map the extent of the sea ice near the pole. That would be quite a feat. Something no one has ever done."

I cleared my throat softly. "You don't think we'll find anything more interesting? Another large island like Fah or Fahlin, maybe? Or even a whole continent?"

Paiyoon raised his bushy eyebrows and looked at me over the tip of his nose. "A continent? Sai, what are you trying to get at?"

I kept my eyes out at the horizon. "Oh, nothing, sir. Just that I know that, well, some people say that the Sunderlands—"

"Bah, is that what this is about?" he said gruffly. "That foolish proclamation about the Sunderlands?"

"Well, surely the Queen wouldn't offer a reward unless—"

"Queens are always offering ridiculous things! It's the very definition of being a queen!" He narrowed his eyes at me. "How did you hear about that, anyway?"

I swallowed, not wanting to say that it was Rian who told me. "Back in An Lung, I heard some people talking about—"

"And when these people talk about the Sunderlands, do you know where they say it lies?"

I nodded. "In the Harbinger Sea."

"Right in the middle of it!" boomed Paiyoon, throwing up his hands. "Now, isn't that convenient? That this mystical hidden continent that no one has ever seen just so happens to be located in the center of an uncrossable ocean?"

"Have you ever sailed there, Master Paiyoon?" I asked.

"Right to its edge, never through," said Paiyoon grimly. "It was one of the few times in my life I've prepared myself to die." He raised one arm, sweeping it over the ocean. "Waves like mountains. Endless rows upon rows of them, each one ready to swallow us whole." He lifted one eyebrow at me. "And is that where you propose we take this ship and all its crew? To go looking for a myth?"

The bell rang and the next watch of sailors began swirling to their places. Whatever trust Paiyoon and I had built up over the past hour had vanished, and he had put that wall back up.

"Sir, I wasn't suggesting that we put anyone in danger."

Paiyoon glanced at the crew and lowered his voice. "I know you weren't. But we have to be very careful about what we say, Sai. The Harbinger Sea has a dreadful reputation among sailors. The last thing the captain wants is to stoke their fears."

I thought about Dumpling's whimpering. But what about the other sailors, like Grebe, who wanted to take a chance at making their fortunes? What about me?

"I understand, sir, but surely in a ship like this one—"

"Say no more about the Harbinger Sea," said Paiyoon firmly. "Trust me, there can only be one reason why it is so dangerous: there are no large bodies of land anywhere nearby to slow down the waves. The currents whip around and around, churning the water into those infamous swells." He huffed out a breath and shook his head. "I understand why people want to believe in the Sunderlands, but the place just doesn't exist."

My conversation with Paiyoon had gone about as badly as possible. If anything, I had probably made him even more resolved that searching for the Sunderlands was a fool's game. My dreams of earning a lineal were vanishing like mist in the heat of the day. But what could I do about it?

Instead of going back to my room, I headed to the galley. I had missed lunch, but I could usually count on Cook to save me something.

"You're in luck," he said, handing me a cold bowl with bits of yellow fat floating on top. "Got some turnip-and-bone stew left over."

"Thanks, Cook," I said, trying to smile. I started to sit at the long wooden table, but he clucked his tongue and shooed me away.

"Just cleaned and polished it and I don't want anything sloshing on it!" he said, spitting onto his apron and rubbing the table with it.

I leaned against the counter near the stove and choked down a bite of bitter turnip. "The galley looks nice," I said, looking around. "It's cleaner down here than when we started our trip."

Cook glanced about to make sure we were alone. "Miss Rian is starting up her card games again tonight," he said in a hush. "I wanted to spiff up the place a bit for her. You know, she's the only one who ever compliments my cooking."

I winced as I swallowed something slimy and tasteless from my bowl. "But won't they get in trouble with the captain for gambling?"

Cook shrugged. "Even the captain's officers know that a ship can't be all work and no play. Besides, Miss Rian don't gamble for much—just a lek or two here and there. There's never been a fight. All the crew loves her, and they wouldn't do anything to cross her."

"Do you think there'll be a lot of people down here tonight?"

"For sure. It's a new moon—too dark to work up on deck. Except for the couple sailors on watch, I bet the whole crew will be in here for the games." He turned to me and patted the newly shined tabletop. "You should come. You been working too hard."

I smiled. "Thanks, Cook. But I have something else I need to do."

CHAPTER TWENTY–ONE

An Even Less Likely Partnership

That night, I swung open the hatch to the hold. I hadn't brought a lantern with me, and the chasm below was pitch-black.

"Psst! Bo!" I whispered. "Come up!"

A moment later, I heard him climbing the ladder. Cautiously, he lifted his head above the hatch. "What's wrong?"

"It's a new moon tonight, so it's dark up top. And most of the crew is playing cards in the galley. I think I can get you on deck if you promise to be very quiet."

Bo's face broke into a wide, dimpled grin. He held up his right hand. "I'll be silent as the rotting bones in a graveyard."

"Gross." I grinned back. "Now, come on!"

Bo was true to his word. He was quieter than a shadow. He slunk around corners, folding his body

into the darkness. Several times we nearly ran into one of the crew, but Bo seemed to have a sixth sense for when someone was watching and when they had turned their back. He floated silently over the dark deck, timing his footsteps with the dip and rise of the ship. I couldn't help thinking that even Mud would be impressed with him.

We climbed up to the forecastle, where Rian and I had had our conversation about the Sunderlands the week before, and I led Bo to the same spot between the stacks of folded canvas. We crouched, silent at first, until we were sure the waves splashing against the hull would drown out our whispers.

I felt guilty huddled inside my wool cloak while Bo wore nothing but thin deck clothes.

"Here." I started to unclasp the cloak from my throat. "You should take this . . ."

"Nah, keep it," he said. "I like the cold air on my skin." He leaned against the canvas cloth and drew his knees to his chest. The breeze blew his tangle of hair off his face. "*Mezores*, that's good," he said with a sigh. "That hold is so nasty that I was starting to wish you'd dropped me overboard."

I leaned back and tilted my head up. With no moon out, there were so many stars; I felt like I could drag my hand through the sky and catch them in my fingers. "I will never get tired of that view," I said. "Back in An Lung, you were lucky if you could see more than a dozen stars."

"What's An Lung like?" asked Bo.

It would take me all night to explain my beautiful, vicious, magnificent, dirty hometown. So I just said, "Rains a lot."

Bo nodded as if that painted the whole picture. "I'm half Mangkon," he said flatly.

I wasn't surprised to hear it. The slender shape of his eyes, the black hair, and the gold-brown skin were familiar for sure. But he had a mix of other features: a narrower nose and face than most people in our Nine Islands. And his eyes were a color you rarely saw in Mangkon: green and brown swirled together, like a fern stem. "And half what else?" I asked.

"I was born in Amnaj."

That explained Bo's hardscrabble life. By the War's end, Amnaj, Mangkon's tiny ally, had been nearly destroyed by Hinmak forces, and anyone left alive had fled in boats.

"So your parents, were they . . . ?"

"Killed in the War? My dad was, yeah."

I felt a flush of shame for having a parent who never even fought at all. Mud had dodged the Navy for years, and then in the last months of the War had broken his leg during a brawl in jail.

"I'm sorry," I said.

Bo shrugged, as if he were talking about strangers. "My mum took off after I was born, so that left me with my old auntie. She got us on a boat to Pitaya Island. She took care of me the best she could, taught me to read, kept a roof over us. But in the end, I was the one taking care of her. Her mind started to go. She'd tell me these wild bedtime stories, but then her stories got mixed up with real life, and she started to live in them. That's when I learned to pick pockets."

"Did you leave her back there on Pitaya Island?"

Bo cleared his throat. "She left me. Died three months ago."

"Tripe. I'm sorry."

"It's fine." Bo looked up at the stars. "I'd been looking for a ship going to Mangkon for a while, but none of the ones that docked at Pitaya were big enough to stow away on. When I saw this one, I thought, *Well, that's perfect. It's enormous and it'll take me back to the place where my people are.* But I guess Fahlin will work for now, and I can make my way to An Lung on some other ship."

I couldn't help feeling sorry for Bo as he spoke about going to Mangkon. He had no idea that he couldn't just stroll in and start a life there. Especially with no lineal, no parents, no connections. I knew exactly where he'd end up. The Fens swallowed people like him and never let them out.

"Mangkon isn't the easiest place to make your way," I said.

He stretched his arms overhead. "I'm not worried about it. Just give me a big, busy town. If I can't find work, I can always pick pockets."

I smiled at him. "Maybe you should practice a little more, then."

Bo gasped, pretending to be offended, and then jabbed me on the shoulder. "About that . . . In all my time picking, no one's ever caught me. How in the world did you—?"

He stopped abruptly and held up one finger. After another moment, I heard it, too: someone walking across the main deck, getting closer.

We both flattened against the packed canvas. I slowly peeked around the side. "It's Master Paiyoon,"

I whispered. He stood at the rail on the port side, looking up at the stars with his eyeglass.

"I thought you said he'd be sleeping," whispered Bo.

"It looks like he's taking a longitude reading," I said. "But that can't be right. You need the sun for that."

Measuring our latitude—how far north or south we were from the equator—was one of my duties because it was fairly simple. But I was still learning how to calculate our longitude, the ship's east-west position. It involved using a whole book's worth of tables, along with the ship's clocks, one of which was always set to the local time in An Lung. And it involved the sun, so what could the old man be up to at this hour of night?

More boots clicked across wooden boards. My eyes followed the sound, and I caught the tall figure of Miss Rian rising from the companionway. My stomach lurched at the thought that the card game was over and the entire crew would be coming up behind her. But the muffled sound of laughter from below told me that Rian must just be taking a break.

When Paiyoon realized that Rian was there, he snapped his eyeglass back into its case and shoved it into his pocket. They began talking to each other, but the wind was too loud for me to hear.

"Stay here," I whispered to Bo. "I want to know what they're saying."

I stayed low and crept back down to the main deck. Tiptoeing around barrels and boxes, I circled close enough to make out their words.

". . . in six weeks at this pace," said Paiyoon.

I guessed he must be talking about when our ship would arrive at the fiftieth parallel.

"I see. That's good news," said Rian.

I peeked around the edge of the box I was hiding behind. I almost wanted to laugh at them. They looked like actors, each playing a part that didn't come naturally to them: Rian was trying very hard to be taken seriously, while the serious Paiyoon leaned against the rail, trying to act casual.

"And have you decided what course we'll take after that?" asked Rian.

Master Paiyoon shrugged, but I could tell from the prickle in his voice that he was annoyed to be questioned. "Nearly. The captain and I will make our final decision after we reach Fahlin."

"I have tried to encourage the captain to plan a route into the Harbinger Sea," said Rian. "From what

I have heard, that part of the world holds promise for all sorts of discoveries."

Paiyoon shook his head, his signal that the argument was settled. "That route is a waste of time. Just empty ocean and rough water."

Rian pressed on. "Sailors have come back from the Harbinger Sea reporting sightings of land. Those sightings line up with our ancient stories about the Sunderlands."

"Ah, you mean the ancient stories of dragons?" Paiyoon laughed gruffly. "Perhaps we can get Lark to catch one in his net, and it will tug us all the way to its homeland?"

"No, of course not, but . . ."

Paiyoon patted Rian's arm. "Someone has been filling your head with nursery tales, Miss Rian. Maybe your fellow card players?" Just then someone burst into laughter belowdecks. "Don't pay too much attention to what you hear from the crew. I have been at this business a long time, and I promise that whatever you've heard about dragons or magical lands is fantasy. You could fill the ocean with sailors' tales and have no more than a thimbleful of truth in the whole thing."

Rian straightened up taller, and I felt a swell of pride that she wouldn't let Paiyoon speak down to her.

"Sir, the captain has told me about the Sunderlands prize. If the place doesn't exist, then why would the Queen offer a prize to find it?"

"The only people on this earth more superstitious than sailors are members of the royal family—as our good captain will agree." Paiyoon's smile was kind but also a little insulting. As if Rian were a toddler who had to be coaxed away from a plate of cookies. "Trust me, Miss Rian. We shall make wonderful discoveries on this voyage. But not if we set our sights on chasing a fairy tale."

Rian started to reply, but one of the crew called her name from the galley below. She bowed reluctantly to Master Paiyoon, then turned to leave, her coattails swirling around her knees. Paiyoon watched her until she was belowdecks. Once she was gone, the old man gave out a big, weary sigh and rubbed the space between his eyes.

I bit my bottom lip in frustration as I watched Paiyoon return to his room. Our chance to do something truly great was crumbling before we could even get started. All because Paiyoon refused to listen to anyone but himself.

"That lineal is as good as gone," I whispered to myself.

"What lineal?"

I whirled around to find Bo crouched directly behind me.

"For tripe's sake!" I hissed. "I told you to wait back there for me!"

"You were taking too long. What are you talking about? And who was that woman your mapmaker was talking to?"

Everything seemed so hopeless that I didn't see the point of keeping it a secret. I quickly ran through what Miss Rian had told me about the Expedition Prize.

"The Dragon Lands?" Bo snorted. "Come on, now, you're joking."

"Yeah, I know," I grumbled. "Everyone says the same thing. I did, too, at first. The minute they hear the name Sunderlands, they think . . ."

"Well?" said Bo, raising his eyebrows. "They think what?"

"He's doing it," I muttered. "Triping tripe, he is doing it!"

Bo leaned back. "What's got into you? Doing what?"

"Paiyoon told me that a mapmaker has to see what's actually there, not what they *expect* to see. But now he's making that very mistake! Paiyoon has already gotten it in his head that the Sunderlands are nonsense. It doesn't matter what anyone tells him; the only thing that will persuade him that the Sunderlands are worth looking for is actual evidence."

"That's the point of the Sunderlands, isn't it?" said Bo. "No one's got any evidence."

"Maybe not . . . or maybe they do, but they haven't fit it together in the right way yet. Paiyoon brought almost the entire contents of his shop with him: every chart of the Southern Hemisphere, copies of ships' logs, captains' journals. He could be overlooking something really important just because he doesn't expect to find it! If I could get hold of those documents and go through them, maybe I could gather enough evidence to make him come around."

"Sounds like a plan. Best of luck to you." Bo yawned and rubbed his eyes with the heels of his hands—his pickpocket hands.

"Best of luck to *us*, you mean."

"Me? What have I got to do with it?"

"Paiyoon would never let me rifle through his papers. I need someone to slip in and get them for me. Someone with world-class thievery skills."

"Why don't you just tell him what you think and go through the stuff together? You told me he trusts you, right?"

I shook my head. "No. If I say anything else about the Sunderlands, he'll shut down again, just like he did with Rian. But if I could work on this on my own, maybe I could make a good case to him. It's like me with my mapmaking—maybe Paiyoon just needs a little taste of success to believe in it."

Bo crossed his arms. "And why should I help you?"

I wanted to shout, *Because you're eating half of my meals and I'm keeping you alive, that's why!* I hesitated before I finally said, "Because if you do and we're awarded the prize, I'll give you one link from my lineal." It hurt to say the words, but I couldn't think of anything else to offer.

"A link from one of those useless pieces of jewelry?" said Bo. "What am I supposed to do with that?"

I rolled my eyes. "I don't care what you do with it. You could melt it down or use it as fish bait. At the least, you could sell it on the shadow market and get some cash to put in your pocket."

Bo fidgeted with his collar as he looked out to sea. He caught me watching him and set his face into a scowl. "This means I'll have to stay with the ship longer. To make sure you don't cheat me out of my payment."

"I'm not the cheat; let's remember that," I said. "And, yes, you'd have to stay with the ship. But you wanted to go to Mangkon, didn't you? That's exactly where we're going to end up."

I could tell Bo was mentally calculating how many picked pockets one golden link was worth. "Fine. But if I've got to stay down in that hold longer, I'm gonna need a proper lantern and more ginger biscuits."

"Fine." I held out my hand.

Bo spat into his palm, and before I could back away, he grabbed my hand. The saliva made a *squirch* between our fingers.

"Ew!"

"Now we've got a deal." Bo grinned. "So? When do we start, partner?"

CHAPTER TWENTY-TWO

The Midnight Mappers

Two weeks later, Bo and I had settled into a routine. During the day, I helped Paiyoon on deck or in his cabin. Working in his room meant that I could get a good look at his bookcase and determine what I wanted. It was a little like window-shopping. I would pick out which books or documents I needed, and later that night they would get delivered right to my doorstep by my own personal pickpocket.

Each night, Bo slipped above deck after the midnight bells, once the crew on watch had settled into their stations or their nightly card game with Rian. Then he'd creep to Paiyoon's cabin and use a sail mender's awl to pick the lock. Working from my shopping list, he'd take the documents we needed and bring them back to me in the hold. He could take only a few items at a time—a ship's log or two, maybe a journal.

If Paiyoon woke in the middle of the night, we didn't want him to notice that something was missing.

"Paiyoon doesn't snore like everyone else on this ship," said Bo, bright-eyed from the excitement and chill of going above deck. He dropped down the ladder and landed silently in front of me. "The old man sleeps like a stone. It's creepy, like sneaking into a tomb and stealing from a corpse."

I frowned as I took the packet of papers from him. "Not stealing, borrowing," I said. "And I don't know about anyone else on this ship, but I don't snore. Not that I even get the chance these days."

My hours were completely filled with work, with only four or five left over for sleeping. But maybe that was a good thing. If I had extra time on my hands, I knew that I would just fall into daydreaming about my new lineal, how I would wear it, and what the look on Tippy's face would be when I walked into the Three Onions and jangled it in front of her. The whole thing was still too much of a long shot to day-dream about. I needed to stay focused.

Bo plunked down beside me on the sailcloth pallet. We had added padding to make it somewhat more comfortable, and I'd brought lemon peels from the galley to try to mask the smell. Our lamp cast lanky shadows on the timbers that wrapped around the hull like massive wooden ribs.

I split a hard ginger cookie in half, checked it for mealworms, then gave one piece to Bo. I began thumbing through the pages of the ship's log he had swiped for me. "Perfect, this is another one!"

"Another what?"

"Another entry from the captain of a Mangkon merchant ship. This one is newer, too, only fifty years old." I ran my finger across the dense script. "They foundered in a storm past Fahlin. The winds blew them due south and west, where they sighted land—or at least they thought they had."

After digging into the documents for the past couple weeks, I was getting used to reading records like this, but the first time, it had come as quite a shock. The fiftieth parallel—that famous barrier that we were striving to break—had apparently been crossed by sailors for centuries. The only difference between their expeditions and ours is that they were lowly whale hunters or merchants, no one that would have counted as a real explorer in the Queen's eyes. Not only had these ships gone beyond the fiftieth parallel, but they had also gone deep into the southern waters, and some had even spotted land.

I set down the ship's log and picked up my chart. Faint lines crisscrossed my paper like a spiderweb where I'd traced possible courses, then rubbed them back out again. Xs marked the instances I'd found of sightings from the logs and journals.

Most of those Xs were best guesses. While I could trust that the sailors knew how far south of the equator they were, I couldn't put much faith in their east-west location. Timepieces that could keep accurate time at sea were relatively new inventions. Anyone sailing more than twenty years ago wouldn't have had one and so wouldn't have been able to measure their longitude accurately.

I used my divider to measure out the distances given by the merchant ship's captain and marked it on the chart.

"From the latitude readings and the amount of time they drifted, I'm almost certain they ended up in the Harbinger Sea," I said. "This captain writes that her lookout in the crow's nest spotted land, but the winds blew them back before she could see it herself."

Bo leaned closer to look over my shoulder. "Does it say how big the land was?"

"Several miles across. That's the best evidence we've got yet!"

"Any spooky dragon stories?" asked Bo with a dimpled grin.

"Not a one, thank goodness."

I marked a table I kept on a separate piece of paper that recorded what documents I had used, the dates, and who wrote them. There was also a column for "believable." Unfortunately, most of the sailors' accounts didn't get a checkmark in this column.

Ships' officers and mapmakers tended to stick to facts: the weather, leagues traveled, bottom depths, that sort of thing. But any mention of the Sunderlands in sailors' diaries was quickly followed by strange sightings and bad feelings:

> We all prayed before the ship's shrine and drank no wine for five days until we lost sight of the beast.

> All the night, strange crooning noises echoed in the hull. Not a one of us slept.

> Two of the crew on watch spotted crests at the horizon. First mate says it's whales, but we all know it's the Slake of the Sea.

Any evidence I gathered from these tales was worthless because I knew Paiyoon wouldn't believe it. Even so, I was able to find enough reliable information to make me think that some mass of land—possibly something big—was hiding just over the southern horizon.

"I can't believe Paiyoon missed all this," I said.

"Can you blame him?" asked Bo. "Everything you've read about the Harbinger Sea talks about storms. It's like the ships get sucked in and can't get out. Anyone in their right mind would be afraid to go there."

I leaned back against the stacked sails. "I don't know. I'm not sure Paiyoon is afraid." I thought of him standing on deck, riding the swells like a pirate. "Mr. Lark and pasty Dr. Pinching, yes, I think they would be afraid. But Paiyoon has seen more of the world than anyone else on board."

I had told Bo that I thought Paiyoon was missing the Sunderlands because he didn't want to see them, because he thought it was all superstition. But now that I'd studied the materials myself, that reasoning didn't feel completely right. He was too good at what he did to make a mistake like that. I had started to get this strange, uneasy feeling under my ribs, like that first day I'd stepped onto the rocking deck.

194

The only thing that steadied me was looking at the chart I'd made. I was proud of it. It was proof of how much I'd learned, how far I'd come since that day I first lifted a scope. I let out a quick breath and sat up, spreading the chart smooth on my lap. "Sunderlands aside, Master Paiyoon's going to be speechless when I show him this."

I expected Bo to have some sarcastic comment, but he sat watching the shadows roll back and forth along the hull, his gaze a hundred miles away. His fingers flicked something at his collar.

"What's that?" I asked. "A necklace?"

He started to tuck it under his shirt but paused and held it up so I could see. It was a shiny white scallop shell the size of a half-lek coin, with a leather cord strung through a hole at the top. A lattice pattern of bloodred marks ran along the shell's rounded edge.

"Pretty," I said.

Bo shrugged. "Not worth anything or I'd have sold it already." He circled the shell with his finger. "You find them all over the beach in Amnaj."

"But when all this is over, you don't want to go back there?"

"Don't think so," said Bo. "I don't have anyone there to go to. Mangkon sounds like as good a place as any to start over." He looked up at me, the lamplight dancing in his eyes. "I know I talked about picking pockets, but I'd rather get a real job. Doing something like what you do, being an Assistant or something decent like that."

I didn't know whether to feel inspired by him or feel sorry for him. Where did he get so much confidence in himself?

"Well, with a lineal link, at least you'll have a better chance."

He smirked and rolled his eyes. "I can't see why any of you put up with all the lineal stuff. No one's going to tell me I'm worth less than some other kid just because they wear a stupid metal bracelet."

"It's not that easy."

"Not that hard, either."

I held my tongue. Bo would find out soon enough how wrong he was. "Well, we've got to find the Sunderlands first." I waved my hand over the blank expanse of the Harbinger Sea on my chart. "We're off to a decent start, but we'll need more than this to convince Paiyoon and the captain." I handed the merchant ship's log to Bo. "You should get this back up where it goes. And be careful."

Bo smiled and slipped my wool cloak over his shoulders. "Will you stop nagging me already? I know how to do my job. It's you we should be worried about. You're the one who's got to face Paiyoon all day."

I slumped back onto the sailcloth. My eyelids felt as heavy as fishing weights. "Don't worry: I haven't let on at all. Paiyoon doesn't suspect anything."

Bo started up the ladder, the log tucked under his arm. "Well, make sure you don't let it out of the bag. It's not easy keeping up a lie day in and day out, you know."

I watched him disappear out the hatch. "It's not that hard, either."

CHAPTER TWENTY-THREE

Miss Rian's Story

Two weeks later, when they rang the bells to alert us that we had arrived at Fahlin, I flew out of my hammock. I'd been salivating over the chance to step on dry land for the first time since Pitaya Island, but as I climbed the steps to the quarterdeck, I saw that it wasn't going to happen.

Instead of happy sailors lined up at the rowboats, our crew was grim and quiet.

Paiyoon stood at the rail, concern woven into his brows.

"What is it, sir?" I asked, taking the scope that he held out to me.

"I'm afraid we won't be going ashore after all," he said. "It isn't safe for us. Take a look."

I surveyed the bay where we had dropped anchor. Fahlin had surrendered to Mangkon early on in the

Longest War without putting up a fight, and it was our flags that flew above the town on the shore. But beneath them flew another banner: yellow with a black spot.

I gasped. "Fever flags?"

Paiyoon nodded. "Listrus fever, if I had to guess. The captain won't let anyone go ashore. They'll have to row barrels of fresh water out to us."

Looking through the scope, I didn't know whether to be disappointed or relieved that we wouldn't be stopping here. I had expected Fahlin to be a green, vibrant place like Pitaya Island, but it couldn't have been more different. From what I could see, Fahlin was made of mud. The streets near the harbor were slick and greasy, and the water was stained brown. The people I could see on the docks moved slowly, as if their feet were clogged in sticky muck. In the distance, the hills that rose above the town looked scraped bare.

"I wish you could have seen the trees of Fahlin," said Paiyoon sadly. "When I was here last, they were as tall as towers, their crowns peeking above the mist in the mornings." He gestured to the sails above us. "It was their height that doomed them. The perfect height for a warship's mast."

My eyes tracked up the mainmast, and I tried to imagine a forest of trees that tall standing guard on the shore of this desolate harbor.

"Fahlin is one of the places you discovered, isn't it, sir?"

Paiyoon's face was a stone. "I was on one of the first Mangkon ships to arrive here, but people have lived here for thousands of years. I made a map of it—that's all."

"Oh, of course. Sorry, sir."

He sighed heavily and drummed his fingers on the railing. "I know that's how everyone talks, Sai. I talked that way, too, once. Our queen is sending ships out in every direction to 'discover' new places. I'll put money on it that every place our ships land was already discovered long ago—just not by us. That won't stop us from planting our flags there, of course. A growing kingdom needs lumber, materials, food. Why pay for it when you can claim it and call it your own?" He waved his hand at the dingy harbor. "Look at Fahlin. They surrendered, and we still took everything they had, down to the stumps." He held still for a moment, then turned to me. "What do you think of all that, hmm?"

200

I looked behind me to see if anyone else was listening to us. "I see your point, sir. But I don't think you should say things like that to anyone else but me."

He smiled and put his hand on my shoulder. "Don't worry, I won't. I trust you not to tell anyone my treasonous thoughts."

I tried to smile back as I handed him the scope. "Since we aren't going ashore, I think I'll go lie down, sir. I haven't been sleeping very well."

As I went to my room, I tried to brush off the guilty feeling that had risen when Paiyoon said he trusted me. I told myself that even though I was making my chart behind his back, it was for a good reason, and I would be coming clean very soon.

Bo and I had now gone through every single document in Paiyoon's cabin. My fingernails were stained with ink, my neck had a cramp from bending over my paper, and my eyes felt sunken and dried out from keeping such late hours. For all that work, I still didn't feel quite sure that what I had was good enough.

I hadn't told Miss Rian what Bo and I had been up to. I didn't want to raise her hopes for nothing. But the time had come to show her my map, whether I was ready or not. Now that Fahlin was off-limits, we would need to stop at the southern outpost of Avens Island for more water and provisions before continuing on. From there, if we set out southeast as Paiyoon had planned, there would be no changing course. If any of my work was going to be useful, we had to share it with Paiyoon and the captain soon.

Late that night, once I could be sure the crew's card game had ended, I knocked on Miss Rian's door.

"Have you brought me a midnight snack?" she joked, opening the door and ushering me inside. She had washed off her eye makeup and wore a simple tunic instead of her usual formal jacket. It made her look much younger. "Do you have good news for me?"

I handed her my chart, and her face instantly brightened. She took it to her desk to examine under the lamplight while I explained what I had been working on. I told her everything but left Bo out of it. I didn't think Rian would care about a stowaway, but something made me want to keep him a secret.

"Sai, my goodness, I had no idea you could do this!" Rian's smile grew bigger with every word. "What a talent you have! Even I can see it, and I know nothing about mapmaking. And these words. They look just like Paiyoon wrote them himself. I couldn't tell the difference between the two if my life depended on it."

"Oh. Thank you, miss." I hadn't copied Paiyoon's handwriting on purpose, but I had been writing in his script for so long that it had become a habit.

I was glad to see Rian so happy with my work, but the map was still incomplete. Yes, it was drawn well, but it was missing the one thing we needed.

She pointed down at the chart, to the blank expanse where the Harbinger Sea was. "You have sketched in some lines here and rubbed them out again."

"Yes, miss. That's the trouble." I sighed and slid my hand down my face. "I've gone through every single document that Master Paiyoon brought with him and read everything twice over. But I can't find any good evidence—anything credible—that shows where land might exist in the Harbinger Sea. There have been faraway glimpses, but those could just be mirages, tricks the light plays on sailors' eyes when they've been too long on a voyage. I know Master Paiyoon, and I know he won't accept such slim evidence as a reason to go looking for the Sunderlands. He'll need some-thing really solid to convince him. And we're running out of time to find that."

"I see. And Paiyoon still thinks we should strike to the southeast from Avens Island?"

"To map the sea ice," I said miserably.

Rian let out a sarcastic laugh. "Well. That would be quite a discovery. A discovery worth exactly zero leks and no lineals."

I pressed the pads of my palms into my eye sockets. I felt like I could sleep for days. "What we need is an account of someone who saw land up close. We need numbers, measurements, a drawing. Something more than just a story." *Preferably without any mention of Slakes or dragons,* I added mentally.

"Without that, we'll be going back to Mangkon with empty pockets," Rian said.

"Well, not *all* of us," I grumbled.

Rian looked up and tilted one perfectly trimmed eyebrow at me.

"I'm sorry, miss," I added quickly. "I didn't mean that. I'm very tired and I—"

Rian smiled and slid my chart across the desk. "It's all right. You didn't offend me." She walked around behind her desk chair, where her jacket hung. Her lineal brooch gleamed softly in the lamplight. "I know what you must see when you look at me. You think this expedition is just a fun excursion for me, don't you?"

I pressed my lips together and looked at the floor.

Rian rested her arms on the back of the chair and leaned forward. "Sai, what I'm about to tell you is a secret that very few people know," she said quietly. "I'm telling you because I trust you. And because I want you to understand me."

I nodded, waiting for her to go on.

"I know everyone on board is wondering how I got a place on this expedition."

"You and the captain are old friends. You saved her life."

"Mm, true, but that's not quite the whole of it." Rian took a deep breath. "Anchalee Sangra is my sister."

I blinked, unsure I had heard her right.

She gave the statement a moment to linger in the air between us before continuing on.

"To be more specific, she's my half sister. We have the same father but different mothers. My mother was a servant on the Sangra estate. Without being vulgar, I'll say that my birth was not exactly welcomed by anyone in the Sangra family." Her easy smile tightened. "Least of all by my own father. After I was born, my mother and I were sent away."

I was speechless. I never would have believed that Rian, who carried herself with enough class to be a princess, was the child of a servant.

"To be fair, Lord Sangra made sure our lives were not difficult," she went on. "He even paid for me to go to school. But it was crystal clear from the beginning that he claimed no part of me and bore no love for me at all."

She caught my shocked look. "Don't feel sorry for me, Sai. I swore early on that I'd never feel sorry for myself. After school, I found my own ways to get by. I've always been good at cards." She winked. "I earned enough at the card table to keep afloat, and then I joined the Navy. I worked my way up through the ranks, always with my eye on my sister. She'd never been told about me, though I knew everything about her. I wanted to be as close to her equal as possible when I revealed myself to her. You understand why?"

I nodded. "You didn't want her to think you were asking her for favors."

"Exactly! Everything I've achieved, even this, I've earned on my own." Rian's fingers tapped the golden lineal on her jacket. "But a few months ago, I finally did ask my sister for a favor. I begged Anchalee to include me on this expedition." She leaned forward and her eyes blazed in the lamplight. "This is a chance to get something more important than money, more important than a whole string of gold lineals—a *name*. Discovering the Sunderlands will vault us straight to the top of Mangkon society! We will be celebrated and sought after, and I'll finally prove that I'm deserving of my father's esteem."

I watched her fingers curl around the lineal brooch. "I do understand you, miss," I said softly. "More than you know."

Rian smiled at me gratefully. "I want to show you something. I should have shared it with you weeks ago."

She reached down into the front panel of her jacket and took out a small paper packet. She unfolded it and held up a white square of fabric.

"I bought this in the Harbor Market before we departed," she said. "Do you know what it is?"

My words were barely a whisper once I got them out. "I know exactly what it is."

It was a fisherman's map, just like the ones Paiyoon had shown me from the trunk in his cabin.

"The woman who sold it to me told me its story" continued Rian. "A hundred years ago, a Pramong ship was found adrift on the edge of the Harbinger Sea. The ship's masts had snapped off, and the hull was taking on water badly. All the crew were gone, except for one man."

Rian's words tumbled out excitedly. "The remaining sailor was near death. He didn't explain why their ship was so far from home, only that they had been caught in a storm and pulled across the Harbinger Sea. In his fevered state, he spoke of a lush continent whose rivers were lined with jade and whose forests were full of trees twice the height of our tallest masts. He said the seas all around were thick with whales and dragons with hides of shimmering gold."

Rian caught my eye. "I know how it sounds. I would feel skeptical if it were not for this. After the sailor died, they found this piece of silk in his jacket. This is a map he made of the Sunderlands!"

She handed the cloth to me. My quickened pulse made my fingers tremble. The map barely covered my palm. Faded lines snaked across the silk, forming the headlands and harbors of a continent that extended past the edges of the fabric.

"I've held this little map against every chart I could get my hands on back home," said Rian. "I haven't been able to find any place in the world that matches."

The silk had a ragged edge, as if the map had been torn or cut. It had no words on it at all, no longitude or latitude. Without those missing pieces of information, there was no way to know for sure where it was made. But the coast had been drawn with such detail. Even in its faded condition, I could tell that whoever had drawn it had really seen this place, and close enough to make a good, solid map of it. Best of all, this was a Pramong chart. Paiyoon respected them more than almost anyone else.

"This is exactly what we need to make our case to Master Paiyoon," I said excitedly. "Once he sees this and hears the story of where you got it, he'll be convinced—I'm sure of it! I'll leave out the part about the dragons, of course." I laughed.

Rian stiffened and reached for the silk map. "Talk to Paiyoon about your own chart first and see what he thinks. If he responds well, you can bring him to my cabin and we'll show him my map together. I'll hold on to it until then."

She folded the map back into its tight square. Her easy smile returned and she tucked her hair behind her ears. "Now, we should both try to get some rest while we can. The crew tells me we're headed for rougher weather."

"This is going to change everything, miss," I said as she closed the door to her cabin behind me.

I headed down to my room and climbed into my hammock. As I rocked side to side, I thought of what Rian had said about earning a name for ourselves, about being celebrated and sought after. I imagined a glittering room packed with important people. In my vision, they stood aside for me, bowed to me, smiled and tried to catch my eye. *This is going to change everything*, I thought as I drifted off to sleep. *Everything*.

CHAPTER TWENTY-FOUR
Up the Maintop

Thoughts about Rian's map made me toss and turn in my hammock. Before dawn, I gave up on sleeping and rushed down to the hold to tell Bo what I'd learned. But when I opened the hatch and swung my lamp inside, he wasn't there.

My feet pounded up the companionway. After everything we had talked about, after all our work together, was he really up top right as day was about to break?

On deck, lanterns threw pools of light onto the slick boards. Most of the crew was still below. I pulled my wool cap over my ears and buttoned my cloak against the wind.

Bo wasn't in our usual spot on the forecastle. I checked all the narrow crevices between the barrels and boxes on the main deck, but I couldn't find him.

Just as I began to climb the quarterdeck stairs, I heard a faint whistle from above. It was hard to see beyond the lanterns' reach, but when I looked up, I recognized the shape of Bo's head. He peered down at me over the lip of the maintop, the circular lookout platform halfway up the mainmast.

"Triping twit," I muttered.

One of the crew jumped down from the quarter-deck steps. I stood aside, pretending to write a note about the weather on an imaginary slip of paper until she had crossed the main deck and gone down the companionway. I could hear other sailors at their stations at the ends of the ship, but the main deck was empty for now.

I took hold of the ratlines and started up. I had never climbed the rigging before, but I'd spent hours watching the sailors do it. The trick was to go up steady and know which ropes to hold on to. If you put your weight on an unsecured line, you could go swinging and fall, which I had no intention of doing. I had a stowaway to throttle.

The horizon had begun to glow dimly by the time I reached the maintop. I used my elbows to drag my belly onto the platform. The waves had kicked up overnight, and this high up the mast, I felt the motion of the ship even more than down on the deck. It was like holding on to the tip of a swinging pendulum.

Bo gripped the lines, the wind whipping through his hair. "I've got a very good explanation for this . . ."

"I should throw you into the water," I said. "You clearly have a death wish anyway!"

Bo kept one hand on the mainmast as he edged back from me. "Don't be mad. I had to get out of that *gowsing* hold! I've been having awful dreams about being squeezed to death by monsters. And I'm hearing things, too. It's all those dragon stories you've been reading. It was still dark, so I thought no one would see. But when I got on deck, I saw someone coming. It was the boy with the scar . . ."

I followed Bo around the mast as if we were circling a temple altar. "Grebe? Do you know what he'd have done if he found you? You'd be jellyfish food right now!"

"I had nowhere else to go, so I came up here."

"You are a selfish, selfish person! Risking both our necks!"

Behind Bo, the lines leading to the crow's nest tightened and vibrated. I had forgotten someone would be up there on lookout duty.

"Hide!" I whispered. "They're coming down!"

Bo slipped behind the thick mainmast. I stood in front of it, hoping that whoever was climbing down wouldn't think to look around the other side.

The sailor swiveled off the ropes and landed in front of me. It was Dumpling.

"What're you doin' up here?" he said, eyeing me warily.

"Master Paiyoon gave me permission to come up," I said. "To see . . . if I could spot anything we should add to our charts."

Dumpling leaned in closer to me. The sailor's life had not been kind to him. His eyes were ringed with dark-purple circles. His formerly plump cheeks sagged loose on the bone. "Has he got you lookin' out for her?" he whispered.

"What are you talking about?"

Dumpling's bloodshot eyes widened. "For the Slake!"

I pressed back against the mast. "Slake? No, of course not . . ."

"She's been followin' us for weeks now. She disappeared when we got to Fahlin, but she's back. She never comes closer than two hundred yards, but she's there." Dumpling pushed his scope into my hands.

214

"That's where I seen her just now," he said, pointing to the east. "Go on, look for yerself."

I held the scope and pointed it where Dumpling instructed me. The sun was almost up, and the sea looked vast and bottomless in the lonely morning light. It took me a moment to get the scope in focus. I watched the dark waves rising and falling in steady rhythm, flicking white spray off their crests. And then I saw it. The shimmer of something solid.

My breath stopped in my throat as a large, dark hump rose out of the water and rolled back down into the coming wave. Another hump, and another, followed in line.

"What in tripe . . . ?" I whispered.

The body disappeared under the surface. And then a sudden stream of water shot straight into the air.

I exhaled with relief and lowered the scope. "Oh, Dumpling! It's only whales."

Dumpling took the scope from me. He looked at me pityingly, as if I were the one talking nonsense. "She uses the whales to hide herself. She's a clever beast. Can hold her breath for an hour. I timed it. And when she does come up, she only shows her head. But she knows I'm watchin'." He pointed two fingers at his eyes, then turned them out at the sea. "She looked straight at me."

I cleared my throat. "Dumpling, have you been eating enough? Maybe I can ask Master Paiyoon to say something to Dr. Pinching about increasing your rations . . ."

"No!" Dumpling gripped my arm. "Don't say anything. To anyone. They'll think I'm makin' up stories and won't let me stay on watch. I have to keep an eye on her, make sure she don't get closer."

I didn't want Dumpling to get grounded. He was a good lookout. So what if he thought he saw the Slake? At least he was being vigilant. I had something more important to worry about at the moment.

"Of course. I won't say a thing," I said with a smile. "But only if you promise that you'll go down before they call the next watch and get some tea."

Dumpling nodded skittishly. His red-rimmed eyes were already trained back on the sea. I waited until he had climbed down and gone belowdecks before giving Bo the all clear.

"That was close," I whispered to him. "Dumpling very nearly jumped on top of you!"

"I would've just told him I was a ghost. He'd believe it, no question."

"He's lost it—that's for sure," I said. "But the rest of the crew hasn't. You've got to get below before they ring the next bells. Here, take this."

I slipped out of my cloak and handed it to him. "And this." I gave him my wool cap as well. "Tuck your hair underneath." I helped him button the cloak and stand the collar up to hide his neck.

"What do you think?" he said, holding out his arms. "Do I look like a fussy map girl?"

"Just walk fast and keep your head down," I said. "If you pass anyone, put your hands over your face like you're throwing up."

Bo got on his belly and slid his legs over the edge of the maintop. I climbed down onto the shrouds after him, my eyes watering from the wind. Halfway between the maintop and the deck, Bo stopped. I nearly put my foot right on his head.

"Shhh!" He clung frozen to the lines. "Someone's standing right under us!"

My pulse raced as I looked down, but I relaxed when I realized who stood below.

"Thank goodness, it's Mr. Lark!" I hissed. "The man wouldn't notice if an elephant stepped on his toe. Here, let me get around you." Bo shifted over while

I carefully climbed past him. "Let me handle him. I'll give you a signal when you can come down."

I hurried down the shrouds as quick as I could and dropped to the deck. I stood up and called out cheerily, "Good morning, Mr. Lark!"

"Oh, Sai! Good morning, child." He returned my bow and tucked a notebook into his jacket pocket. "Goodness, whatever are you doing up here with no coat?"

I strolled up to him, swinging my arms. "I was roasting down below. They've got the galley fires turned up too high." I circled around him awkwardly until I stood between him and the bulwark, forcing him to turn his back to the mast. "Are you working on anything interesting, sir?"

Lark nodded vigorously and tapped the notebook in his pocket. "Something absolutely fascinating, actually! There is a pod of at least twenty fluted whales there, off our port side."

"Really?" I stretched my left arm out and tugged on my earlobe, my sign to Bo that the coast was clear. "That is indeed fascinating."

Lark twirled his long fingers in the whales' direction. "It has always been a mystery where the fluted whale spends its summers. Sighting them here, headed south, lends strength to my hypothesis."

"Oh? Do tell me all about it," I said, trying to keep my teeth from chattering.

Lark looked so grateful for someone taking an interest in his research that I thought he might tear up. Behind him, Bo nimbly climbed the rest of the way down and leaped silently to the deck.

"I believe there is a great surge of nutrients in the southern seas in summertime." Lark swung his arms in big circles, nearly clocking me in the face. "This attracts schools of tiny bait fish, which are fed on by larger fish, which in turn are hunted by even larger fish—"

"Which are hunted by fluted whales?"

"Precisely! If I'm right, we will find the southern waters to be an absolute paradise, full of animals feasting on the bounty that summer brings."

I watched Bo disappear into the shadows of the companionway. Finally! I needed to get down below myself, before I froze to ice.

"Will you excuse me, Mr. Lark?" I asked with a shiver. "I think you're right and I do need to put on a—"

"Heavens, Sai! Do you see that?"

Lark clutched my shoulder and pointed up to the sky off the port side. A small flock of ash-colored birds glided high above us, barely even flapping their broad wings.

"This supports my hypothesis as well!" said Lark, bringing out his notebook and scribbling madly in the pages. "More species headed in our same direction!"

"Right. Good day, then, sir ..." I edged around him and started to leave.

"Perhaps we'll discover where those harbingers nest. Wouldn't that be something!"

I turned. "Harbinger? Is that what the birds are called, sir?"

Lark nodded without looking up from his notebook. "Same name as the sea they will soon fly across. The word means 'omen.'"

"Are they an omen of land?"

"Goodness, no," said Lark with a chuckle. "They can stay on the wing for months without touching down. No one has ever discovered where they nest and raise their chicks. Perhaps we shall!"

The birds hovered like ghosts just above the crow's nest.

"Why do they call them harbingers, then?"

"They're scavengers," said Lark cheerfully. "You see them just before a kill."

CHAPTER TWENTY-FIVE

First Kill

My chance to talk to Master Paiyoon about my Sunderlands chart didn't come that day or the next. As Rian predicted, the weather turned foul, and everyone who wasn't essential crew had to stay below-decks or risk being slung overboard by the waves. I didn't even bring my chart out of my trunk for fear it would get soaked and ruined from the water dripping down from above.

I told myself that I'd get my chance soon, that everything was going according to plan. But the rain and wind didn't clear until we were less than a week from Avens Island.

That morning, the lookout shouted, "Ship ahead! Port side!"

All hands sprang to their posts, and everyone below came up top. After huddling away from the weather, we

were all eager for fresh air. This was the first vessel we'd seen since we left Fahlin. When I spotted Paiyoon on the main deck at the port-side rail, I hurried over to him.

"Sir, I've been meaning to speak with you. I have something—"

"Not now, Sai." Paiyoon pointed at the flag atop the mast: a gold bear's head on a field of violet. "It's a whaling bark. A Rotan ship, from the look of her."

The captain ordered the *Prosperity* closer, then halted us a hundred yards shy of the other ship. A lieutenant stood beside Sangra, communicating to the other crew with flags that she whirled in her hands.

Paiyoon translated the flag code for me. "The whaler says to stay clear. They've caught their target and they don't want us to disrupt them until they've hauled it in." Paiyoon lowered the scope and handed it to me. "Here, Sai," he said grimly. "It looks like you're about to see your first whale kill."

The Rotan ship was a smaller vessel called a bark, about one-fifth the size of the *Prosperity*. Its metal-plated hull and blocky stern gave it the look of a floating sledge-hammer. It was armed to the teeth: guns, harpoons, and great piles of nets crowded the deck. Paiyoon pointed out the brick furnace near the foremast, which the crew used to boil out the oil from whale blubber.

Their crew leaned over the starboard rail, concerned with something in the water that I couldn't see from our vantage point.

Sangra ordered the *Prosperity* to swing around. As we turned and the whaler's starboard side came into view, I saw what the crew had been working on.

They'd caught a small whale and held it trapped in a net hanging from a long beam that extended off the ship's deck. Its slick hide was white as a pigeon's egg. The whale thrashed around, but the net held it just high enough above the waterline to prevent it from swimming out.

Mr. Lark joined us at the rail.

"How extraordinary!" said Lark, peering through his own scope. "I don't recall reading about this type of whale before. We may be witnessing the discovery of a new species!"

Paiyoon scowled. "It's not new to those whalers. They've obviously hunted these animals for years. Your wife's hairpins back home are probably made from the bones of that very species."

Lark wrinkled his nose. "Now, see here, Paiyoon, there's no need to be so—"

A whistle from the Rotan captain cut him off. Their crew stood at the bow, harpoons in hand.

I kept my eyes on the pearly creature in the net. "Are they going to kill it, Master Paiyoon?"

He shook his head. "That whale isn't their target. It's their bait. Watch."

The charcoal sea held still. Then, out past the whaling ship, water sprayed into the air like a cannon shot. An enormous white beast nearly the length of the whaler itself launched out of the water and landed on its side, sending a shower of spray in all directions. The surface of the ocean roiled, then stilled again.

One of the Rotan sailors shouted and pointed past our stern.

The whale breached again, turning as it did so and diving backward down into the deep. It rose and dove again and again, making a wide circle around the *Prosperity* and the whaler.

"That's the mother," said Paiyoon. "It's her baby they've caught in the net."

I swung my scope back to the whaler. The netted infant thrashed more violently, trying hard to get away. The crew held the ropes fast as their ship rocked with the motion.

"They'll kill the mother?" I whispered.

Paiyoon's voice was sorrowful. "Just wait."

One of our crew who stood aloft in the sails cried out, "Starboard!"

A dozen mounds of pearly white rose and fell at the surface as they neared our ships. More whales were coming to join the distraught mother. The crew of the whaling ship let out a cheer.

Paiyoon leaned closer to me. "These whales travel in tight-knit family pods. They think they've come to rescue the calf."

The whaler was swarmed on all sides by the animals. They bumped and bombarded the hull, knocking the ship to and fro. They swam close to the baby, nudging it gently, rubbing the net with their fins. All the while, they called to one another with ghostly whistles and clicks. I gritted my teeth, wishing they would capsize the boat and sink everything in it to the bottom of the sea.

The captain of the whaler shouted an order, and the crack of a harpoon gun echoed across the water. The harpoon lodged into the back of one of the whales with a dull smack. I expected the injured beast to dive, to carry the harpoon and cable down to the bottom with it. But the whale stayed at the surface with the baby and its mother, still rubbing up against the net.

More harpoons were fired into its back. The whales' calls synchronized into one rhythmic, mournful song.

Once, years ago, Mud had gotten himself a job at one of the slaughterhouses on the edge of An Lung. He lasted only a week there. I remember him coming home on his last day with red-rimmed eyes.

I couldn't do it, Sai. They had me pullin' the piglets away from their mothers. I couldn't take the sound of it no more.

At the time, I didn't believe a hard man like him could be moved to tears by baby pigs. I thought it was just one more job he'd gotten fired from. But now I wondered if he had been telling the truth. The sight of the whale flailing hopelessly in its own blood made my insides turn.

"Sir, why don't they swim away?"

"They won't leave the calf," Paiyoon said quietly.

A shrill whistle cut through the air. I looked toward the bow of our ship. Grebe and two of our crew stood barefoot on the railing, holding ropes to steady themselves. They pointed at the Rotan sailors and whooped.

"Lucky fools!" said one sailor. "They won't have to work another day for a whole year."

"That's right," said the other. "I heard each whale's worth five thousand leks, for the bones and oil."

Grebe sneered and lowered his voice, but not by much. "We could have our own fortune, too, if this ship found what it was really after. If some wasn't too scared to go lookin' for it."

I was shocked to hear Grebe refer to the Sunderlands so openly. The three sailors eyed Captain Sangra with barely contained contempt. The captain stood at the top deck, unaware of her crew grumbling about her behind her back.

Beside me, Mr. Lark had started to whimper, his mouth covered with the back of his hand. "Oh, I can't watch . . . It's just monstrous what they're doing to that animal."

"You'll have to get a stronger stomach for blood if you plan to remain on this journey," said Paiyoon.

Lark sniffled. "I'm a scientist, not a butcher. Harming innocent creatures is against my nature."

Paiyoon turned and glared at him. "Are you a *child*? What did you think this trip was about, you fool?"

Lark stepped back, looking livid. "Now, see here—"

Paiyoon pointed to the whales. "You heard the crew. Those animals are worth more than their weight in gold. The southern waters are rumored to be their birthing grounds. Did you really think you were going to just sketch their pictures and that would be the end of the story?"

"I . . . well . . . I . . ."

"Once we pass the fiftieth parallel, and word spreads of what we find, there will be a hundred whaling ships just like that one, right on our heels," said Paiyoon. "And they won't care about how many new and precious species they destroy."

"If you're so upset by it," said Lark, nose in the air, "then what are *you* doing here, sir? It's your map that will make it all possible."

Paiyoon clamped his mouth shut. He stared out at the whales, the wind whipping through the panels of his open coat. Without a word, he left us, pulled open the door leading down to his cabin, and let it bang behind him.

"Well, I never," said Lark to no one in particular. "Just because we're thousands of miles from home doesn't give him the right to abandon his manners!"

As I watched Paiyoon's door swing on its hinges that shaky feeling of doubt that had been swirling inside me for weeks turned to ice.

How could I have missed this?

CHAPTER TWENTY-SIX

The Tail and the Teeth

Before I could follow Paiyoon, my eye caught movement down the companionway. It was Bo, lingering in the shadows halfway up the stair.

I grabbed his arm and pulled him to the bottom of the steps. "What are you doing? The whole crew is up there!"

Bo rubbed the shell pendant at his collar, looking confused. "I thought—but did we run aground?"

"Run aground? We're in the middle of the ocean!"

"I know that, but I heard this awful groaning down in the hull. It sounds like something's scraping against the timbers."

"It's the whales," I said. "You must have heard them crying."

Bo yanked his arm away and glowered at me. "I *know* what whales sound like. Listen!"

A low creaking sound reverberated beneath us. He was right. It did sound like our hull was scraping up against sand or gravel. *Scrape. Scrape. Scrape.* It wasn't a mechanical sort of sound. It was the sound of something alive.

Suddenly, the sound stopped. Overhead, we heard the thump of footsteps and sailors' voices drawing near. The crowd was breaking up.

Bo cursed under his breath. "I can't go back to the hold. Not with that sound!"

"You can hide in my room. There's so much going on, no one will know. Quick, come on!"

Inside my cabin, I opened my trunk and threw the clothes on the floor. "Here, you can hide in this. But don't let the lid snap shut or you'll be in your own coffin."

I thought he'd be cramped in the trunk, but he folded himself up tightly enough that there was plenty of room.

"You've got to be quiet," I whispered. "Stay here. I'll be back soon."

"Where are you going?"

"To find out just how stupid I've been."

I went straight to Paiyoon's cabin and rapped on his door.

"Come in."

He sat at his desk, leaning over the map he'd been working on. The youthfulness brought on by the sea air had vanished from his face. He looked worn, even older than when we'd left An Lung.

I raised my eyes to the books and papers stacked on the shelves along the wall. What a fool I'd been. All those nights working in the hold with Bo, I thought I had found evidence that Paiyoon had missed. But he hadn't missed a single thing. He knew the Sunderlands existed, and he was deliberately steering us away from them.

Paiyoon kept his eyes on his desk as I approached. Without looking up at me, he began speaking. "Thirty years ago, I was aboard the first Mangkon ship to land at Avens Island. We stayed there a month and quickly learned that these seas are home to all kinds of whales. It was incredible. I trekked up and down the shore, making my measurements, sketching my maps, while mother whales and their calves rose out of the water and splashed down all around us." His mouth stretched into a thin line. "If you were to go to that Rotan captain's cabin, you would probably find a copy of the map I drew thirty years ago."

"Sir, you aren't responsible for what's happening out there ..."

"No?" Paiyoon kept his eyes down. "And how about Fahlin? Before I charted the way, no one in Mangkon knew how to navigate its coasts. I don't even recognize the place it has become."

"Yes, but—"

Finally, he looked up at me. "It's far worse than whales, Sai—a thousand, thousand times worse. We didn't land at Fahlin. You didn't see. But I've seen it. Mangkon rules over it now. Do you know what it looks like for one country to take over another? Do you know what happens to the people who live there?"

The question sent a shiver through me. I swallowed and shook my head as Paiyoon stood up slowly and began to pace the room.

"How about Wilna and Dusak, all those faraway places that our Queen has never set foot on but now claims for her own? They have been stripped of their forests, mines have been dug into their mountainsides like open wounds, and their people have been given no choice but to work in them. Mangkon has grown into a bloated beast, devouring all her neighbors. And how does she find her next meal? She uses my maps."

When I finally got my words out, my voice trembled. "But—but that's not your fault! If you hadn't made those maps, someone else would have."

Paiyoon looked straight at me. "But they didn't, Sai. I did. It's my handwriting on those charts, no one else's."

"Those maps are your life's work. They've saved lives. Without them, ships would have been dashed to pieces on rocky shores or missed their targets entirely. You should be proud of yourself!"

Paiyoon's voice was thin and tired. "I want to be, more than you know. That is exactly why I had to join this expedition. Because I resolved that before my life is over, I will do something I can go to my grave being proud of."

I walked to the edge of his desk. Even though I knew the answer, I still had to ask the question. "Master Paiyoon, you believe the Sunderlands exist, don't you?"

Paiyoon stared down at his eyeglass. His fingers shook as he traced the links in his lineal chain. "*The Tail Is the Teeth*," he said quietly. "I have never believed that, have you? That the path behind and the path ahead are one and the same? I cannot change the path behind me, Sai. But I can chart a new course ahead."

"Sir, there are more ships coming along after ours. No matter what you do, all the places are eventually going to be found. So why not let it be us?" I placed my fingers on the edge of the desk and dipped my head to catch his gaze. "Sir? Please."

I stood staring at him, waiting for him to look me in the eyes. But he would not. Finally, he cleared his throat and said, "Please go down and tell Cook not to make supper for me tonight."

I clenched my fingers into my palms. "Yes, sir."

I let the door swing shut behind me. I stood in the narrow hallway a moment, waiting for the heat to go out of my face. I was furiously angry, though if anyone at that moment had asked me at whom, I wouldn't have been able to say.

All I knew was that everything I had been working toward was crumbling beneath my feet.

I wanted to talk to Rian, but when I knocked on her door she didn't answer.

Back on deck, the air smelled metallic, like iron. A few sailors still crowded at the side, looking out at the little Rotan whaling ship. Lark waved me over to him.

I was surprised to see that the whaling crew had stopped their work. The baby whale still struggled in the net, while the whalers crowded around the body of the adult whale they had killed and dragged on board.

It was clear they were arguing about what to do. They shouted at one another, and some looked genuinely panicked. One sailor pointed at the dead whale's body and waved his arms wildly at his comrades. A track of four dark scars ran along the whale's flank, from its head to its tail.

"Will you look at those scratches," said Lark with awe. "Do you suppose those wounds are from a battle with a giant squid?"

"If that's true, then those whalers are deathly afraid of squid," I said.

The Rotan crew had snapped into action. Several whalers were hurriedly freeing the little whale from the net. My heart eased as the baby glided into the water and swam away with its mother. The other whalers used oars to push the scarred whale's body off the ship.

"What? They're leaving?" sneered Grebe. "Look at that! It's like shoving off a solid gold bar and letting it drop straight to the bottom."

The whalers didn't look like they cared. They looked like they wanted to get away from that spot as fast as possible.

Captain Sangra ordered us back on course. I stayed on deck as we sailed south, leaving the whaling bark in our wake. A dozen birds from the flock of harbingers stayed behind, circling in the air above the bloodied water.

But two birds remained with the *Prosperity*, tracking us high above our masts.

CHAPTER TWENTY–SEVEN

Old Business

The next day, my discovery about Paiyoon ceased to matter. In fact, it seemed like our entire expedition might have to be abandoned.

Captain Sangra had taken gravely ill. Whispers spread throughout the ship that she'd contracted Listrus fever, which must have been festering in the fresh water we picked up on Fahlin. Dr. Pinching ordered the rest of the water to be boiled twice over and for Sangra to be isolated in her cabin.

I was on the quarterdeck when the doctor came out of the captain's room. The first lieutenant and Miss Rian stood near, waiting to hear her report.

Pinching pulled off her cotton mask and rubbed her eyes. I could tell by the worry on her face just how serious our situation was.

"Well, Doctor? How is she?" asked the first lieutenant.

Miss Rian's face was pale and drawn. "Do you think it's Listrus?"

Dr. Pinching frowned and wiped her hands on her coat. "She has some of the signs but not all. Her fever is mild, but she is delirious and speaking nonsense. Until I can be sure, I'm afraid I have to assume the worst. Listrus can spread like fire if you aren't careful." The doctor glanced down at the sailors working on the main deck. "I'm sure you are all well aware of how a Listrus outbreak goes. Death is slow, messy, and strikes without reason. It can cut down a crew worse than cannons."

Rian took a deep breath and put her hand on the doctor's arm. "Doctor, you must let me attend to the captain. If you were to catch this illness, our entire ship could be in peril."

Pinching raised her eyebrows. "Do you realize the danger of what you're proposing? As long as she has a fever, she is highly contagious."

"Captain Sangra is my—my oldest friend," said Rian. "I can't let her suffer alone, and we can't afford for you or any other officers to fall ill. I'm the most dispensable person on this ship." She smiled, but it didn't

238

hide the pain on her face. "Please, we both know this is the best decision."

The doctor exchanged a look with the first lieutenant that said she wasn't going to argue about Rian being expendable.

"Your loyalty to her is admirable," said Dr. Pinching. "This will relieve me to attend to others and make sure the water is being properly treated. If you're sure?"

"I insist."

Dr. Pinching handed Rian a clean mask and a little brown bottle. "We can't let the captain's fever run too high. Keep cool rags on her forehead continually. And give her these vitamin drops every few hours. They won't cure her, but they'll help her keep her strength. If she can make it through the next few days, she may pull through."

Rian nodded at the doctor's instructions and put the bottle in her coat pocket.

"From now on, Captain Sangra is under strict quarantine," said Pinching, loud enough so everyone on deck could hear. "No one but Miss Rian may see her. And Rian, if you come down with a fever, you'll be isolated as well."

The first lieutenant stood in the doctor's way as she tried to leave. "But surely I can enter the captain's

239

room?" he said in an irritated tone. "How am I to carry out her orders if I can't even speak with her?"

Rian stepped forward. "Lieutenant, we can't risk you becoming ill as well. Please, let me care for my old friend. I will communicate to you anything she tells me. We know that she wanted to stop over at Avens Island. We should make landfall within a week, is that correct? With luck, she will be on her feet again by the time we put into port."

The lieutenant looked like he might argue, but in the end he nodded at Rian's plan. We watched Rian enter the captain's cabin and shut the door behind her.

The doctor shook her head. "That is a true friend. Not many people would put themselves at risk to catch a disease such as this one."

I was the only one among them who knew that Rian was on the verge of losing not just a friend but her sister.

Three nights later, a quiet knocking woke me. I bolted out of my hammock and fumbled to light a candle. "Just a minute!" I called out.

Bo, who had never returned to the hold, sat up on his pallet next to my trunk, blinking in sleepy confusion. I put a finger to my lips, heart pounding. *Someone's here*, I mouthed, pointing at the door.

He nodded and slid up tight against the trunk. I heaped my clothes and cloak on top of him, then took a breath to steady myself and swung open the door.

To my surprise, it was Rian. Her face was serious.

"Oh, no," I gasped, expecting the worst. "Captain Sangra. Is she . . . ?"

"What? No, no. She's still ill, but I think she'll pull through."

"Thank goodness."

"Can I speak with you a moment, Sai?" I started to edge out into the hallway, but she was already coming in. I lowered my candle to keep Bo in the shadows as much as possible. Luckily, Rian seemed distracted.

"Where do we stand with our plan?" she whispered. "Did you talk to Paiyoon?"

I had tried not to think about my conversation with him. With Captain Sangra's illness, it had seemed like our expedition's fate would be entirely out of anyone's hands, and it wouldn't matter what I had learned about Paiyoon. I didn't want to tell Rian the complete truth: that he was deliberately sabotaging our mission. But I had to tell her something.

"Master Paiyoon is aware of the evidence for the Sunderlands," I said finally. "But I couldn't convince him."

241

"Do you think if I spoke to him, I could change his mind?" asked Rian. "If I showed him my map?"

I shut my eyes and shook my head. "It wouldn't make a difference. Nothing would."

Rian twisted her fingers into her hair. "This is terrible timing. I had nearly convinced the captain to search for the Sunderlands. I was *so* close, and then she fell ill. With the captain in her delicate state, the other officers will rely on Paiyoon to make the navigation decision. He may even advise that we return to An Lung. We can't let that happen. We've come so far—too far to go home empty-handed."

"But what can we do?"

"Sai, if you were the *Prosperity*'s mapmaker, you could advise us to take the course you've charted."

"Me?" I blurted out. "No one would listen to me. I'm just an Assistant!"

"You know almost as much about mapping as Paiyoon does," said Rian. "You've got the skills, and you've read every document that exists about the southern oceans. Most of all, you have the ambition to make this expedition succeed."

"But what about Master Paiyoon?"

"Once we land at Avens Island, he could disembark and sail back to Mangkon on the next whaling vessel. Think about it, Sai. He's old. We're heading into dangerous waters. It's not without risk. I know that you've got the strength to make it, but it will be hard on an old man."

I thought about Paiyoon standing on deck with his sleeves rolled up. I had no doubt that he was at least as hardy as I was.

"He'll never abandon the *Prosperity*," I said. "It would be a disgrace to resign his post."

"He would if the captain ordered it."

"But Captain Sangra wouldn't do such a thing. Even if you convinced her to look for the Sunderlands, she wouldn't do that to Master Paiyoon. Besides, isn't she too ill to understand what you're asking?"

Rian was quiet a moment. "The captain is improving. She's still too weak to go on deck and address her officers. But she's not too weak to write an order. If we had a letter, written in the captain's own hand and signed by her, the crew would have to obey that just as sure as if the order had come from her own lips."

She reached into the pocket of her jacket and pulled out a folded sheet of paper. I could tell from the creases that it had been crumpled and smoothed out again. She held it out for me to see. It was an order from the captain to her first lieutenant, but it wasn't about the Sunderlands. It had been written back when we had docked at Pitaya Island. At the bottom was Sangra's signature.

"I've seen how well you can copy someone else's writing," said Rian. "Do this and you'll change your fortune forever. You'll keep Paiyoon safe, and we'll be heroes. If we can just—" She froze and tilted her head, her eyes roving the room. "Did you hear that?" she whispered.

I swung the candle back toward the door. "It's probably the rats in the storage closet. Sometimes they . . ."

But Rian had begun to step toward my trunk. "No, I heard something. Right here . . ."

Before I could think what to do, she yanked my cloak off the pile and jumped back as Bo sprang to his feet. His fists were ready to fly, but Rian was too fast for him. In one swift motion, she had him by the wrists, twisting them to make his arms form an X over his chest.

"Let me go, you rotten *hoon*," he growled at her.

I was surprised to see Rian hold him so easily. I reminded myself that she was a trained fighter and must be stronger than she looked.

"Who is this, Sai?" she asked, astonished. "A stowaway?"

I stepped in and put my hands over hers. "Yes, but please let me explain . . ."

I rushed through the story of how Bo and I had met, and how I had been hiding him. I told myself not to worry, that Rian would understand, that she would never turn Bo in, but this was the first time I had ever seen her caught off guard. She stared at Bo with a mix of curiosity and confusion on her face. I was relieved when she finally let go of him and took a step back.

When I got to the part in my story about Bo helping me get documents from Paiyoon's cabin, Rian's eyebrows shot up and she turned to him. "How much do you know?" she asked.

"He knows everything," I said. "But he'll keep our secret. I know he will. Won't you, Bo?"

He glared at Rian, and I braced myself for him to start hurling curses at her again. Thankfully, he pinched his lips together and gave a short nod.

"Please, Miss Rian," I said, pressing my palms together and touching my nose to my fingertips. "You won't tell anyone he's here, will you?"

Rian's eyes wandered from Bo's face to the shell pendant that hung from his neck. "Never in a hundred years would I have guessed you'd be hiding a stowaway,

Sai." She smiled. "Of course I won't tell. You know me better than that by now, surely."

I exhaled. "Thank you. I knew we could trust you."

Rian put her hand on my shoulder. I think she meant to do the same to Bo, but he still looked like a dog with its hackles up.

"Trust is the most important thing we have right now," said Rian. "The next part of our work will be the hardest. That's why we must stick together—the three of us. You understand?"

I nodded.

Rian pulled a pen from her pocket and held it out to me. "If we don't find the Sunderlands, someone else will. There are a hundred others back home ready to set sail, ready to claim this prize. They don't have half your knowledge, but who knows? They could get lucky."

I stared down at Rian's outstretched hand. A familiar bitterness had started to fill my mouth. It took me a moment to realize it was the same feeling I'd had that night in the Fens when Mud and Catfish had asked me to forge a letter for them.

Bo stepped close to me and slipped his fingers into mine. "Sai," he whispered, "are you sure about this?"

"The choice is entirely hers," said Rian, speaking to Bo directly. "But if Sai doesn't do this, we'll return to Mangkon with little more than half-leks in our pockets. And all of our lives will be no different from before. Is that what both of you want?"

I swallowed the bitterness down my throat and pulled away from Bo. No, I couldn't have that. I couldn't go back to my old life in the Fens, back to Mud. I'd come too far.

I took the pen.

"Good." Rian produced two sheets of clean paper from her jacket. "There's one more letter I want you to write."

CHAPTER TWENTY–EIGHT

The Edge of the World

The wind had slowed, and the *Prosperity* rocked gently, anchored in the small harbor of Avens Island. Nearer to shore, three stocky whaling barks waited to be scrubbed clean and reloaded with supplies and harpoons. Thousands of tiny yellow flowers clung to the windswept rocks along the beach. It looked like just the sort of rugged place you'd expect to find at the edge of the known world.

I stood on the quarterdeck in the full sun of a glorious southern summer. But even with my cloak buttoned tight at the neck, I couldn't shake my chill. Incense from the ship's shrine filled my nose with sweet smoke. It smelled like a funeral.

Rian stood beside me. She had changed into a jacket cut like a Navy uniform and wore her lineal

pinned at her collar like a military medal. Her hair had been slicked back off her forehead, and she had ringed her eyes with dark liner. Standing tall and straight backed, she was a commanding presence. The ship's bell had just been rung, sounding the call for all hands. From below and aloft, everyone made their way to the main deck.

The first lieutenant strode toward us, his face flushed. "What's the meaning of this, Rian? You know only ship's officers are to ring the bells."

Rian didn't answer. She waited until everyone had settled into place and given her their full attention. She stepped up to the quarterdeck rail and addressed the crew gathered below.

"As you know, Captain Sangra has been ill. These past few days she has neared the brink of death. I am happy to report that she is making a recovery, albeit a slow one."

The crew murmured to one another, but there were no cheers at the news.

"The captain is still too weak to address you," continued Rian. "But she has written out her commands. I ask our first lieutenant to read them now."

The lieutenant seemed very put off and nearly snatched the papers from Rian. I held my breath as he

read them over. By the time he got to the signature at the bottom, the lieutenant's jaw hung open. He raised his eyebrows. "Captain Sangra wrote this?"

"You see it is her signature and handwriting, don't you?" said Rian dismissively.

The lieutenant threw the papers at her feet and stomped to Sangra's door. He knocked on the paneling. "Captain Sangra, I must speak with you!"

I listened. Was that a muffled reply coming from inside or just the creaking of the ship?

"Please, Lieutenant, do go in and ask her yourself," said Rian.

The lieutenant stopped with his hand over the doorknob. Listrus fever was a powerful deterrent. He walked to his quarters instead, slamming the door behind him.

Rian pointed at one of the younger officers. "You. Read these. Unless you want to go against the captain's orders as well."

The young woman started to salute Rian, then stopped, confused. She picked up the letters and read them with an unsteady voice. The first letter thanked the crew for their service thus far and warned of the dangers we would face in the next leg of our expedition. It released anyone who did not wish to continue on with no penalty and no rebuke. At this, Mr. Lark looked extremely relieved. The letter went on to say:

> *This expedition shall press on past*
> *the fiftieth parallel and beyond, to locate*
> *our true quarry: the continent known as the*
> *Sunderlands.*

Shocked whispers rippled through the officers, but the crew smiled. As I'd suspected, word had spread about the Sunderlands prize some time ago, most likely during the late-night card games.

The letter ended with:

> *I shall press on with the expedition*
> *despite my illness. Until I have fully recov-*
> *ered, I pass command of the Prosperity and*
> *all our crew and occupants to my trusted*
> *friend Lieutenant Rian Prasomsap.*

The crew murmured, pleased. Grebe punched his fist in the air and shouted, "Hear, hear!"

The officers stood clustered together, lips curled in disgust. They looked on the verge of seizing Rian. But then their eyes darted to the sailors, who far outnumbered them. The tension in the air was brittle. It was clear that the officers couldn't go against their will, not without violence.

I fought the urge to slink back to my room. I'd wanted to stay below, but Rian insisted I stand beside her. I kept my eyes on the deck boards. I hadn't spotted Paiyoon yet, and I didn't want to see the look on his face when he heard what was coming next.

The lieutenant read out the second letter:

> *Given the perils we shall soon face, and the age and condition of the passenger, I release Master Paiyoon Wongyai from his duties as our mapmaker. May this letter grant him safe passage on the next vessel sailing for An Lung, and serve as recognition of his contributions to the expedition and to his country.*

Lark cried out. "What? Release Paiyoon? But that's preposterous! He's fit as any of the crew to go forth!"

Dr. Pinching also stepped forward. "Rian, what's the meaning of this? Who will guide the ship to her destination? And who will chart it once we arrive—if we ever do?"

Rian put her hand on my elbow and pulled me toward her. "Miss Sodsai Arawan is well skilled in the mapping trade. I have every confidence she will fulfill the duties of her new position."

The crew below grumbled. Even though they were clearly loyal to Rian, they held no such love for me. I felt small and stupid, like a little girl the teacher was forcing everyone to be nice to.

The crew suddenly hushed. I looked out and saw Master Paiyoon making his way to the front of the crowd. He climbed the steps up to the quarterdeck. I expected him to speak to Rian, but he stopped in front of me.

His bushy eyebrows knitted together, and his eyes were dark with concern. "Sai, are you sure this is what you want to do?" he asked quietly.

"Sai sees the great future laid out ahead of her," said Rian. "She's not afraid of going into the unknown. Are you, Sai?"

"I didn't ask you," snapped Paiyoon. "I asked her."

I wanted so badly to look Paiyoon in the eyes, but I couldn't meet his gaze. I had a volley of defenses ready if he should accuse me of plotting against him. I had lists of reasons prepared for why he should go and I should take his place. I'd been saying them to myself all night while I tossed and rolled in my hammock.

But all I could manage to get out were the words "I'm sure."

Paiyoon put a warm hand on my shoulder. He kept his eyes on me, though he spoke to Rian, loud enough so everyone on deck could hear: "Miss Rian, you are right to have confidence in Sai. She has all the skills and experience you will need to complete the expedition. There is no one who could serve you better."

"That's very gracious of you, Paiyoon," said Rian. "I knew you'd see reason."

Paiyoon's eyes swung to her. "I do see the reason. I see it very plainly."

Suddenly, he grabbed both my hands and held them between his dry, crinkly palms. They felt steady holding on to mine. I tried to look into his eyes but couldn't keep my gaze there. I stared at our hands instead.

He spoke quickly, quietly, so no one else could hear. "Sai, I have made many mistakes in my long life, but believing in you was never one of them. I've known for a long time now that you would make a marvelous mapmaker."

"I—sir, I—"

Paiyoon squeezed my hands tight and rushed on. "I should have told you the truth from the very

beginning. I worried it was too great a burden to put on your young shoulders. But now I realize I was wrong. You are more than capable of facing what's to come. Here, I want to give you something."

He reached into his waistcoat pocket and pulled out his eyeglass. He unclipped the lineal chain and held the gold case out to me.

I gasped, too stunned to bow to him. "But, Master Paiyoon, I can't . . ."

"Nonsense. How can you see what you need to see without a good eyeglass?" He took my hand and pressed the case into my palm. "Take care of yourself," he whispered.

Then he stepped back and said, "I'm ready to disembark, Miss Rian. I'll leave most of my things for Sai, so there won't be much packing to do."

Paiyoon turned and descended the steps while Rian began giving her orders to her new crew.

I dropped the eyeglass into my pocket. It weighed heavily against the fabric, like something I had stolen.

CHAPTER TWENTY-NINE

Trust Your Gut

When we set sail from Avens Island, our numbers had dwindled to what the sailors called a skeleton crew. The first lieutenant and the other officers had refused to follow orders from Rian and resigned. Most of the crew were happy with their new leader, but some were too afraid to take the risk. And we lost another twenty sailors who were deemed too unhealthy to continue the voyage. Scurvy, open sores, and weakness had started to take their toll.

Dumpling couldn't get off the ship fast enough. All the other pups had followed him, except for Grebe. I suspected that Dumpling's stories of the Slake had made them too terrified to go on. That left Grebe and me as the youngest on board. Well, and Bo.

I had told Bo that I understood if he wanted to disembark at Avens Island. Rian would have let him

go without any punishment for stowing away, and he could have found work and passage back to An Lung on one of the whaling ships. But when I got back to my cabin that night, I found him swinging in my hammock, eating my ginger cookie rations.

"Couldn't leave," he said, sending cookie crumbs flying from his lips. "Knew you'd bawl your eyes out each night without me."

I tipped him out flat onto his back for that, but I did it with a grateful smile on my face.

Amazingly, we succeeded in keeping Listrus from spreading. No one other than Captain Sangra took ill with the disease. Dr. Pinching stayed with us out of duty to her, but Mr. Lark resigned. He said it was out of solidarity with Master Paiyoon, but most of us suspected that it was because he was too scared to cross the Harbinger Sea.

I didn't blame him. We quickly learned just how well that sea had earned its reputation. Even before we reached those feared waters, the wind picked up fiercely, churning the waves into white-capped peaks. We crossed the fiftieth parallel with little celebration and lots of prayers. We were set on a bigger prize now.

Almost three weeks after we departed Avens Island, I sat at Paiyoon's desk and watched my pen roll from one side to the other. I still slept in my own hammock, but I worked in his cabin to make use of his books and papers. But being at his desk didn't make my task any easier. The chart in front of me had nearly disintegrated from me blotting out my marks and starting over so many times. Even with all the evidence Bo and I had put together, even after seeing Rian's map, I still had doubts about whether I had put us on the best course.

Rian's silk map didn't have a scale, so there was no way to know exactly how big the Great Southern Continent was—assuming it was there at all. We could blow right past our target and we'd never know. If that happened, the fault would be on my head and no one else's.

My fingers wandered to my pocket, where I still kept Paiyoon's eyeglass. I tapped the case through the fabric. I hadn't taken it out since he gave it to me, not even to look at it. When I had to make observations, I used my old scope instead.

"Which way? Which way?" I mumbled to myself.

If Mud were here, he'd tell me to quit thinking so hard.

Listen to your gut, Sai. It's got more sense than your head does.

258

I pressed my palm into the hollow space below my rib cage, then quickly put my hand back on the desk. This was stupid. What would Mud have ever understood about navigation? But as I stared at the open spot on the map in front of me, something kept drawing my eyes to the west.

The other ships I had read about had been swept toward the Sunderlands by accident. We had to figure out how to do it on purpose. If we took a southwesterly course, we'd hug the edge of the Whorls and could use their energy to push us deep into the Harbinger Sea. With luck, we'd end up where the other voyagers had spotted land.

Before I had time to change my mind, I jotted our new heading on a slip of paper. I left the room and hurried up to the quarterdeck to look for Rian.

The wind, gusting hard from the northeast, nearly beat me back down the stairs. I looked up and saw that we were still running with full sails. The *Prosperity* had to be racing near top speed.

Grebe and three of the bigger men on the crew manned the wheel in the center of the quarterdeck. I made my way to them as the ship rolled under my feet. "Where's Miss Rian?" I asked, straining to be heard over the wind.

"Just went below!" answered Grebe, keeping his eyes ahead. I turned to leave, but he reached out and grabbed my cloak. "She should get back up here! We don't like the look of that there."

Grebe nodded to our port side. In the distance, an inky line of clouds hung low to the horizon.

"You think we can outrun it?" I asked, looking from Grebe to the other sailors.

"If any ship could, it's the *Prosperity*," shouted the thick-necked sailor who was now our new quartermaster. "But we gotta be ready to shorten sail if the storm catches us."

"I'll tell Rian!"

Paiyoon had once explained that running with all the sails unfurled during a storm was a disaster waiting to happen. If the wind was too strong, it could put enough strain on the sailcloth to snap the masts. Waiting until a squall hit to send the crew aloft to take in the sails would be a deadly mistake.

I knocked on Rian's door. "It's Sai," I called.

"Yes, enter."

She and I rarely exchanged more than a few sentences these days, other than to check on my progress with our course. She was a different person now. Even though no one called her "Captain," she'd stepped right into the role of our ship's commander. That meant no more socializing with the crew, no more card games. Even toward me, she was more formal and distant than before. I almost would have said that she no longer treated me as an equal, but I didn't like to admit that our friendship had changed.

I shuffled my way to her desk, where she sat leaning her head against two fingers, the picture of cool, as the items in her room rolled back and forth across the floor. Captain Sangra remained quarantined in her own cabin, but all her charts, books, and our ship's log had been brought down one level, to Rian's quarters. This room was now the center of command on the ship.

"Miss Rian, we've got heavy winds from the northeast and a squall line on the horizon. Our quartermaster thinks we can outrun it, but maybe you should order them to reduce the—"

"We'll outrun it," said Rian calmly. "The *Prosperity* hasn't even begun to show her speed. But I will go up in a moment to see for myself."

"Yes, of course," I said, passing her the slip of paper. "At least the winds are favorable for the heading I chose."

"Good. When do you expect we will sight land?"

"I'm working on that now, miss. May I have another look at your silk map?"

Rian looked up at me without that warm smile I was used to. After a long pause, she rose from her chair and walked to where her new jacket hung on a peg near her bed. She took the little map from the inside pocket and handed it to me.

"Thank you. I'll bring it back shortly." I turned to go.

Rian grabbed my sleeve. "Where are you going?"

"To make a copy of this," I said, taken aback. "So I won't have to keep asking you to see it."

"No. No copies. You can look at it here, in my room."

I laughed halfheartedly, trying to lighten the tension between us. "But our mission is to make a map, isn't it? Eventually, once we discover the Sunderlands, the information on this little chart will be copied a thousand times over."

"Suppose we don't discover it this time. This little chart is the only evidence on earth that the Great Southern Continent exists. Anyone with a copy could sell it and make a fortune."

"I wouldn't do that. I'm your—"

I'd started to say "friend." But the anxious way Rian eyed me made the word catch on my tongue.

"Your mapmaker."

Rian smiled, warm once more, but her eyes stayed on the silk square in my hand. "Of course you wouldn't, Sai, of course not."

"It's all right." I handed the map back to her. "I've had a good look. I don't need it anymore."

Instead of putting it back in her jacket pocket, Rian took the silk with her to her desk. When I left the room, she stood swaying with the rocking ship, holding the map close to her chest.

CHAPTER THIRTY
No Return

A splash of cold water on my face woke me. I sputtered and sat up. My hair and shirt collar were soaking wet with the water that had poured down on me from the deck above. I swung myself out of my hammock and grabbed my wool cloak from the floor.

I bent over Bo's pallet and shook his shoulder until he cracked one eye open.

"I'm awake, Auntie . . ." he murmured sleepily.

"I'm going up to check our course," I whispered to him. "You take my hammock."

I buttoned my cloak and left, shutting the door behind me.

Water sloshed down the companionway steps. The ship rocked so hard, I had to brace myself with both hands to keep from falling over. The jerky motion wasn't the rhythmic sway I'd become used to. It felt

like the *Prosperity* was a toy boat held tight in the fist of a child who was shaking us to and fro. I climbed up, into the black night. Rain lashed my face. The lanterns swung above, shining on the rowboats tied to the center of the main deck. I grabbed on to the ropes that secured the boats and used them to pull myself toward the stairs leading up to the quarterdeck.

Lightning pulsed behind the heavy clouds and lit the sea. The squall had caught up to us.

Our ship rolled up and down the faces of waves as tall as our masts. Grebe and four of our strongest sailors stood at the helm in a wide stance, straining against the wheel. They worked to keep us heading into the waves. If we turned and a swell came at us from the side, it could knock us right over. Waves this large would sink us in minutes.

I wanted to run and hide in the safety of my room, but I forced myself to slide toward the helm. The next flicker of lightning allowed me to read the compass mounted near the wheel. We were being blown southwest, right into the heart of the Harbinger Sea. I looked up, horrified to see that all our topsails were still flying and only two of the topgallant sails had been rolled up.

"Why haven't we shortened sail?" I shouted to Grebe.

"Rian wouldn't give the order!" he called back. "The quartermaster overruled her, and they're doing it now!"

I was afraid to ask my next question. "Will we make it?"

Grebe grimaced as he fought against the wheel. "We'll make it! We just got to keep our bow into the waves—that's all!"

"Is there anything I can—?"

"Just get below!" he barked. "And stay outta the way!"

He was right. I was useless. I turned and started for the stairs. As I passed the captain's cabin, the door swung open and a hand shot out, grabbing me by the arm. Sangra stood in the doorway, a wild look in her eyes.

"Captain Sangra!" I gasped. "What are you doing up? You've got to get back to bed!"

Sangra surveyed the storm that raged outside her cabin. With a jerk on my arm, she pulled me into her room and shut the door behind us.

"What's going on?" she rasped. "Where are we?"

I backed away to keep my distance from her. "We're caught in a squall. But it's all right. We're reducing sail and our helmsmen are keeping us running with the wind. We'll ride it out, Captain."

"I said, *where* are we?"

I gulped and tried to make my voice steady. "Two thousand miles southwest of Avens Island, ma'am."

"*Southwest!* You mean the Harbinger Sea? Where is Paiyoon? Bring him to me immediately!"

"He isn't here. He left the ship and stayed on the island."

Sangra shut her eyes. "Then we are truly lost," she whispered.

I backed away another step, thinking of how contagious she was. She looked awful, nothing like the mighty hero I had seen on deck that first day. Dark-purple rings hung underneath her eyes, as if she'd been punched in the face. She was obviously still feverish. Her tangled hair was damp at the temples. "We need to get you lying down again, ma'am. Everything is under control." I spotted the little brown bottle of vitamin drops near her bed and picked it up. "Here, take these. They'll make you feel better."

"Don't touch those!" The captain wrenched the bottle out of my hand and flung it across the room. It shattered against the wall, and the thick liquid dribbled across the sloping floor.

I froze, not sure whether to run or call out for help.

267

Captain Sangra breathed slowly and heavily. "It took me a long time to understand what she had done to them." She smiled grimly. "But I fooled her. I haven't swallowed those vile drops in days. And now my strength is returning."

The captain's fever must have been making her imagine things. "Please, ma'am. Let's get you back to bed. I'm going to go and find Miss Rian—"

"What's your name?"

"Sai, ma'am."

Sangra peered into my eyes. "She's enchanted you, too, hasn't she, Sai? Yes, I can see it. You're completely under her spell."

The ship rocked hard to stern, knocking us both off balance. Sangra staggered to her desk and fell into her chair.

"You're not well, Captain. I'll get you some water."

I used the furniture to steady myself as I crossed the room. Most of the water in the pitcher on the washstand had splashed out. I poured the rest into a glass, took it to Sangra, and backed away again.

She leaned back in her chair and wiped the sweat from her forehead. "Rian charms everyone," she said quietly. "It's extraordinary, really. I've never known someone so able to win people over. Even my crew."

The captain gripped the arms of her chair and grimaced. "Well, I don't need them to love me. I need them to follow my orders. Rian may be charming, but she is no leader."

It was clear that Sangra had no idea what had happened while she'd been ill. She didn't know Rian had taken command of her ship. She also didn't realize just how much the crew had abandoned her. I didn't think there was one among them who would follow her orders over Rian's now.

Sangra took the glass of water and gulped it. Her shirt was buttoned wrong, and one side of her collar gaped open, revealing the gold lineal around her neck. She looked up at me with a vague, amused smile. "Did you know that she's my sister?"

I couldn't hide my shock. I had thought it was a secret I wasn't supposed to tell anyone, but the captain had just blurted it out.

"It's true," said Sangra. "My sister, my blood. A shadow that I can never be rid of."

I bristled at those last words, remembering the story of how the Sangra family had shut Rian out and made her fend for herself. I started toward the cabin door. "Miss Rian has her faults, maybe," I said. "But then again, she hasn't had the advantages of the nobility."

Sangra broke into a laugh. "Is that what she told you? That she didn't have advantages? Yes, I suppose that makes for a much better story."

I stopped at the door. My fingers floated up to that hollow space beneath my rib cage. I told myself I should walk out. The captain was delirious. I didn't have to stay and hear her slander her own sister. Rian wasn't perfect, but she had been kind to me. She wanted me to have a better life. Why, then, did I feel so much doubt gnawing at me?

Slowly, I turned around. "What is the real story, ma'am?"

Sangra looked up. Her face was sunken and pale, but her sharp gaze went right through me. "You don't want to hear it."

I swallowed. "No, I didn't. But I do now."

CHAPTER THIRTY-ONE

A Remarkable Portrait

"From the moment she was born, my father spoiled Rian in every sense of that word," said Captain Sangra. "He gave her the best tutors, the finest clothes, a generous allowance. He set her and her mother up in a nice manor house outside An Lung. Rian and I even went to the University together, though at the time I was told she was a distant cousin, not a half sister. Everything I had, she had. Except for two things: a lineal and our name. I realized long ago that that combination—showering her with gifts while denying her worth—twisted her into the person she is now."

The wild gaze had gone from Sangra's eyes. Her words were calm and measured. "I know how easy it is to be charmed by her, Sai. She charmed all of us at school—teachers and students alike. The day she told me she was my half sister, I felt like the luckiest person

in Mangkon. For years I did anything Rian asked of me. Anything to see her smile. But slowly things changed between us. She has a terrible taste for gambling, and I have given that girl a fortune to pay off her debts. But it was never enough. The more money I gave her, the more she needed. I soon realized that no matter what I did, she would never stop asking me for more."

The captain ran her finger under the links of her necklace. "I begged my father to bestow the Sangra name on Rian. I even offered to give her links from my own lineal! It's just a name, just a stupid piece of jewelry. But he refused. I'm sure he knew that my great-aunt—our beloved Queen—would never allow us to break with tradition."

I held on to a wooden beam in the center of the room to keep my footing against the rolling of the ship. The rocking motion and the captain's slow, steady words made me feel like I was in a dream.

"But what about her Lineal of Honor?" I asked.

Sangra rolled her eyes. "For her 'act of great bravery'? That was Rian's first real battle. Our father had made sure she was under my command so I could keep an eye on her. But that fool wouldn't listen to me! She wanted to be in the thick of things, earn some fame for herself." The captain mimed swinging a sword through the air. "She stepped in the way of one of my own officers, who nearly took her head off. I wrote the report that was sent to the Queen. I made up the story that she had saved my life because I hoped that having a lineal of her own would satisfy her. But my sister will never be satisfied." Sangra looked up at me, her eyes heavy. "She hates me for having what she can never have. She doesn't understand that I'd give it all away if I could."

Sangra went on. "I never wanted Rian on this expedition. I know how reckless she is, how hungry she is to earn a name for herself. I tried everything I could to stop her from coming. But in the end, she found a way to force my hand."

The captain beckoned me to come closer to her desk. I hung back.

She tilted her head at me. "Still afraid I'm contagious? Child, if I had Listrus, I'd be dead by now. Unless you lick that poison off the floor, I promise that you won't catch my illness."

I remembered that day on deck when Rian had insisted on caring for Sangra herself. That would have made it easy for her to slip something into the little brown bottle. The image I held in my mind of Miss

Rian was disintegrating bit by bit, like paper melting into the sea.

I walked slowly to the captain's desk. Sangra unlocked the top drawer and pulled out a little black case. A picture frame.

When she looked down at the portrait, she broke into a wide smile. I had never seen her show a genuine smile before. I noticed for the first time that she had a deep dimple in her left cheek. "We met when I was stationed in Amnaj," she said wistfully. "Just after I had made captain. I loved him from the very start."

She turned the frame around. In the portrait, a young Captain Sangra stood wrapped in the embrace of a handsome man in uniform. His dark curls hung down over his broad shoulders. But it was the bold look in his gaze that made my breath catch.

Light eyes. Bo's eyes.

Captain Sangra coughed and reached up to her collar. "He wanted to marry me, but I wouldn't do it. If anyone found out, I'd be cast out of our family. No, it would never do for the great-niece of the Mangkon Queen to marry a commoner from Amnaj."

I stood so close now that I could see the tiny royal stamps on the thick golden links of her lineal. She leaned to the side and rubbed her neck as if it ached

274

to carry the weight. She unclasped her top button, and I saw that she wore another necklace underneath the lineal: a white shell with dark red markings strung on a piece of twine.

The captain put the picture back in her desk drawer. "We had a child. A little boy. After he was born, I was called back to Mangkon to command the *Prosperity*. It had been easy enough to hide my pregnancy, but I couldn't hide a baby on a warship. I left him with my husband and promised to come back. But the War kept going on and on. And then Amnaj was sacked. My husband and his entire squadron were killed. His aunt took the baby and fled to Pitaya Island. For years I sent her money and kept up with her through letters. I was desperate to get back to my son, but the War always kept me away."

Sangra's words grew more rushed and frantic as her story went on. "I had plans to bring him back to An Lung, where I could keep him close but hide him from my family. A coward's plan, I know," she said bitterly. "I thought this expedition would give me the perfect opportunity to retrieve him, but then, two months before we set sail, the aunt's letters stopped. I searched for both her and my son when we docked at Pitaya, but I couldn't find them. They had disappeared."

I remembered how anxious Captain Sangra had been the morning we dropped anchor at Pitaya Island. I also remembered the devastated look on her face when we departed.

"I had never told the aunt my real name," said Sangra. "I was too afraid that if someone found out, they would use it against me. In the end it didn't matter. Someone found out anyway."

"Rian?" I whispered.

She nodded. "Rian threatened to tell the Queen about my son, and that I was never married. She said that unless I gave her a place on this expedition, she would ruin me and ruin his future. I played her game for so long because I was afraid of what I could lose. But now I see that none of it matters. It's as if I dialed a scope into focus, and for the first time I can see everything clearly." A brief smirk flashed on her lips. "I suppose that's one good thing about being poisoned into a delirious fever."

The ship creaked loudly as it rocked back and forth. Captain Sangra sat still and wooden, and looked up at me with eyes as dark as the sea. "I'm done playing along with Rian. And I don't care what the Queen thinks of me anymore. I have served her all these years without question—and what has it been for? So that

276

we could make Mangkon into a great empire? An empire of cowards and thieves—that's what we are. Sai, I don't care if we are one hundred yards from finding the Sunderlands. I'm turning this ship around to go look for my son. And no one—not Rian, not our Queen—can stop me this time"

My head spun from everything I'd just been told. "Captain, what was your son's name?"

"Amanat," she said softly. "After his father. But I called him Bo."

Shouting erupted outside. The door of the cabin slammed open. It was Dr. Pinching. Black soot covered her face.

"Down below . . . in the galley," she panted. "Fire!"

CHAPTER THIRTY-TWO

The Harbinger Sea

Captain Sangra and I rushed after Pinching onto the quarterdeck, a thick sheet of rain immediately soaking us through. The ship heaved portside, nearly knocking us off our feet. Lightning flashed, illuminating the sea. Mountains of waves roiled around us in every direction. Sailors staggered up the companionway, coughing, followed by thick clouds of smoke.

Sangra's loose hair whipped about her face as she began shouting orders. She pointed aloft to the sailors who were working to reduce our straining sails. "Get them down! There's no time! Just cut the lines! Grebe, turn us starboard!"

Grebe and the men at the wheel looked strained to the point of breaking. "We can't, Captain!" he cried out like a distraught child. "Something's wrong with

the rudder! It's stuck and won't turn! We're heading straight into the worst of it!"

Grebe fell, exhausted, to the deck. Sangra leaped to take his place, throwing herself at the wheel beside the others. "You four there, find the sand buckets," Sangra shouted to the crew standing by the companionway. "Get below and get that fire out! Stay low!"

In Rian's absence, there was no sign of the crew's disdain for Captain Sangra. They snapped to her orders without hesitation. Even Grebe pulled himself to his feet and ran for the sand buckets.

I was scanning the deck anxiously for Bo but didn't spot him. My room was right next to the galley. If he was still sleeping, the smoke would suffocate him.

Covering my face with my sleeve, I followed the sailors with the buckets down the companionway steps. Thick smoke choked me and burned my eyes. I dropped to the floor, crawling along the boards. An orange glow blazed out from the galley. The ship heaved side to side, sending flaming debris sliding over the deck.

I scuttled to my cabin and flung open the door.
"Bo! Bo!"

I rushed to my hammock and swung him out of it. He tried to stand up, but I pulled him back down to the floor.

"What is it?" He coughed. "What's happening?"

"Follow me, but stay down!"

Together we crawled past the sailors throwing sand at the fire. No one saw me take Bo upstairs through the smoke, or if they did, they were too busy trying to save the ship to care.

On the main deck, I filled my grateful lungs with clean air. I didn't have long to savor it, though. The ship pitched, sending us both to our knees. We slid across the deck, knocking into each other as we tried to stop ourselves.

"Over here!" Bo grabbed my arm and pulled me toward the rowboats.

We crouched between the boats, clutching the ropes that held them down. Lightning flashed overhead, and a crack of thunder sounded like the ship was tearing in two. The crew that had been rolling the sails were making their way back down the rigging.

Above us, I heard a low rumble of rushing water. I looked up, and all my courage left me.

We were headed up the face of a wave taller than the Temple of the Nine Islands. The water roared as it broke over the prow.

Bo took the extra ropes tied to the rowboat and wrapped them around and around my arms. He looked straight at me. "Whatever you do, don't let go!"

I gripped the ropes and shut my eyes.

The wave crashed down on us. The force of it wrenched my feet out from under me. The ropes burned my wrists and forearms as I was pulled against them. Everything, everywhere was water. I was sure we had capsized and our whole ship was now beneath the sea. But then my face felt the surface. I gulped in air. With a heaving dip, our ship began sliding down the other side of the wave.

"Bo!"

"I'm here!"

With the next flare of lightning, I saw him, his arms tangled in the ropes. The rowboat beside us was gone, ripped free from the deck. Luckily, the one we clung to still held fast. Above us, half the sailors who'd been climbing down the rigging were nowhere to be seen.

Now the *Prosperity* slid steeply down the backside of the wave. Bo and I had to cling to the ropes to keep from being tossed to the bow of the ship. We couldn't face another swell like the last one. If our rowboat was swept to sea, it would take us with it.

I reached out and found Bo's arm. "We've got to move! We've got to get back belowdecks!"

But now the ship had tipped up again as it began to scale the next wave. To make it to the companionway, we'd have to climb up the slippery deck against gravity. We didn't have time.

"No! This way!"

Bo unwrapped the ropes from around my arms and pulled me astern. We half crawled, half slid toward the cabins at the rear of the main deck. The ship kept tilting up at a steeper and steeper angle.

"Hurry! Faster!"

Straight ahead, the door to Rian's cabin yawned open. The cresting wave thundered above us.

Bo grabbed my hand. "Now! JUMP!"

CHAPTER THIRTY-THREE

Seeing Visions

We slid right through the open cabin door just as thousands of gallons of water crashed behind us.

We tumbled through the room, papers and furniture swirling around us. I flailed my arms and legs uselessly as seawater filled the cabin almost to the ceiling. A hand gripped the back of my collar and pulled my face above water.

"Sai! Here, grab on!"

Bo clung to a post near Rian's bed. I wrapped my arms around the beam, gasping for air. We hung on as the ship rode wave after wave. Water filled and drained out of the cabin again and again. With every swell, I braced myself for the *Prosperity* to be crushed by the force and keel over. But after long, tense minutes, the waves began to weaken.

Bo looked at me. "Do you think we made it through the worst of it?"

"I . . . don't know. I think so."

I let go of the beam. My hands ached from holding on so tight. I suddenly realized I hadn't seen Rian since the storm hit.

"Stay here," I told Bo. "Hide yourself and don't come out until I get you." I splashed through the knee-high water toward the door.

Rain pelted my face as I stepped onto the main deck. I could hear the crew shouting to one another and the voice of Dr. Pinching coming from the decks below. A thin stream of smoke floated up from the companionway.

I cupped my hands to my mouth. "Miss Rian! Captain?"

No one answered.

I made for the quarterdeck stairs, waiting for each pulse of lightning to guide me forward. As I climbed the steps, I looked out to sea. Large waves still battered us, but nothing like the massive peaks we'd just sailed through. Suddenly the ship lurched hard to starboard, throwing me against the rail. I clung tight to it to keep myself from pitching headfirst over the side.

In the water below, lightning reflected off something metallic. I gasped in horror.

A large, smooth *thing* was coiled around our hull. An armored mass of muscle glittered as it slid slowly against the polished planks. In the flicker of lightning, I saw the unmistakable shimmer of scales.

I blinked. When the lightning flashed again, the scaled thing I had seen was gone.

I flew up the steps onto the quarterdeck. Fear rattled my voice as I shouted, "Captain!"

The wheel spun free, unmanned. Whatever had jammed up the rudder was gone now. I could feel it in the loose movement of the ship.

"CAPTAIN! ANYONE!"

A shout rose above the wind. It came from the top deck. I stumbled up the wet steps as the ship swung side to side.

"Someone! Help!" I shouted into the darkness.

Lightning flashed and lit up two figures pressed against the top-deck railing. I started to call out again when I saw one of them reach back and punch the other in the stomach. I gasped when I realized who the two people were.

Sangra and Rian.

Thunder cracked and darkness surrounded me. With the next flash of lightning, I saw Sangra land a hard blow to Rian's jaw. Darkness fell again.

I clutched the stair rail as the ship reeled. The next burst of lightning froze me where I stood. Rian held Sangra by her collar against the railing. The captain was bent backward, her body arched dangerously over the water below.

Darkness returned. The ship rocked hard, knocking me onto my hands and knees. I stayed down and held my breath, listening. But I could hear only rain pelting the deck boards. I waited for what seemed an eternity for the next burst of lightning.

When it came, Sangra was gone. Rian stood with her hands on the rail, looking down. She turned and her eyes, wild as the sea, met mine.

Then the darkness swallowed us both.

CHAPTER THIRTY–FOUR

A Debt Repaid

I stumbled down the steps in the dark as the ship listed side to side. I couldn't catch my breath. What had I just seen? Captain Sangra was gone. But how? Did she fall, or had Rian—?

No. I couldn't even think it. And what had I seen in the water? Was that creature real? Or a hallucination? The more I tried to think calmly, the more my thoughts tangled themselves into knots.

My hands were shaking by the time I opened the door to Rian's cabin.

"Sai?" Bo called from the darkness. Lightning flickered outside the windows. He picked his way through the ruined mess of the cabin and grabbed my hand. "Well? Should I hide?"

Bo was the son of our ship's captain. But the captain

was lost forever now. A voice inside my head said he was in danger. It said we all were.

"Yes, you have to hide," I whispered. "But not here. Come on."

We edged out the door onto the main deck. Lightning flashed in the distance as the storm rolled west, away from us. Every one of the rowboats had been ripped from the deck and tossed into the sea. Our foremast had splintered two-thirds of the way up, covering the deck with a tangled mess of wood, sails, and rope.

The taste of charred wood burned in my throat as we felt our way down the companionway steps. The door to my room had been smashed into jagged pieces by a water barrel, which lay broken on my floor.

Bo started to head for the ladder leading down into the hold, but I held him back.

"That's the first place they'll go," I whispered. "They'll have to get tools and lumber."

"Where, then?"

"Over here."

I led him into the galley. We had to make our way carefully across scattered pans and broken plates. Sand covered the floor. We fumbled to the darkest corner and tucked ourselves behind the cook's counter.

I wrapped my arms around my knees. I hadn't felt this sick since we'd left Mangkon.

"Sai, what's wrong? Won't you tell me?"

I raised my eyes to Bo's. In the dim light, he looked older and so much like the man in the picture Captain Sangra had shown me. But I saw the captain in his face, too. How had I never noticed before?

"Bo, listen," I whispered. "Those wild stories your auntie would tell you—what did she say?"

He shook his head, confused. "I don't know ... She said all sorts of things. Like my mum was a Mangkon princess, stupid stuff like that. Why?"

I shut my eyes. "I . . . I don't know how to say this . . ."

"Shhh!"

Bare feet pounded down the companionway steps, followed by the rough voices of sailors.

Above them all, I could hear Grebe shout, "I'll search this deck while you sweep the hold."

The others grumbled and crawled down the ladder that led to the hold below.

Bo and I crouched motionless in the dark. I tried to breathe as quietly as I could, while we listened to Grebe shuffle around the galley. I could hear him yanking open cupboards and turning over barrels.

"Come on out," he sang softly. "I know you're down here, little miss mapmaker . . ."

My body went to ice. As his footsteps drew closer, Bo slowly reached up to the counter above my head and slid off a heavy iron pan. When Grebe rounded the corner, Bo sprang up, brandishing the pan like a club.

I saw the flash of a jagged blade in Grebe's hand.

"Stop!" I shouted, jumping to my feet before he could hurt Bo.

Grebe didn't lower the knife as he looked to Bo, then back at me. "What's this? A stowaway?"

Bo began spitting curses on all of Grebe's ancestors going back two hundred years.

"You better shut up!" Grebe hissed, keeping the blade out. "If the crew down below hear you, then you're good as dead." He glared at me. "You too."

"Me? For helping a stowaway?"

"No, you idiot," he spat. "Don't you know what's happened? Sangra's gone overboard."

"I know, but—"

"You know how this'll look once we get home? We took control of the ship, then the captain—the Queen's own flesh and blood—goes overboard. We've got the stench of mutiny on us thick. Miss Rian's got

290

fancy friends in high places; she'll find a way out of it. But us crew? We'll swing unless we can convince 'em it was all an accident." Grebe yanked his fist up as if tightening an invisible rope around his throat. "From here on out, every sailor on this ship's gotta row the same direction, tell the same story. The others think there's only one person aboard who wouldn't stick with 'em. Who d'you think that is?"

My throat went dry. All those months of acting the part of the spoiled, snotty girl were now about to seal my fate.

Grebe leaned toward me and sneered. "They're lookin' for you right now."

"They wouldn't do that to Sai," said Bo. "You're talking about murder!"

"You don't know what happens to people's minds when they get this far from home," said Grebe. "The crew's scared to death. They'll carry out their plan quick, while the ship's still in chaos."

We could hear banging and boxes being shoved around in the hold below our feet. My mind raced, trying to think of some way to escape, but there was nowhere to run.

"So what do you want?" I hissed. "Are you helping us? Or turning us over to them?"

Grebe took a step closer to me. "First, I wanna know where you're from. Where you're *really* from."

I hesitated. Would he even believe me? After lying for so long, I had to force the truth past my tongue.

"The Fens," I whispered.

Grebe leaned even closer to me. "What's your name? Your real one."

I shut my eyes. It had been a very long time since I had spoken my real name out loud. "Sodsai Mudawan."

A satisfied look spread over Grebe's face. "I knew it! From that first day we set sail, I knew I seen you before. That night in the Fens, outside the Rooster Room. You was the one I followed." His eyes narrowed. "You do a good job making out like a fancy girl. You had everyone else on the crew fooled. But not me."

Given how dire my situation was, I shouldn't have cared about being found out. But the humiliation still stung, more so since Bo was there to hear it all.

"I'm right, ain't I?" said Grebe.

I nodded.

"You know why I followed you that night in the Fens?"

"No."

"Someone at the Rooster told me you was Mudawan's kid. I thought if I followed you, I'd find Mud. I owed him something."

I held my breath, waiting for Grebe to explain.

"Mud and me was in jail together, about a year ago. I shouldn't have been there. Should've been in the boys' correction home. But they sent me to the men's jail because of my size. One day when we was all out in the yard, one of the guards said I was making trouble even though I wasn't doing nothing. He decided to make me an example. Show all the others who's boss. Had a big club."

Grebe ran his thumb along the length of the scar on his forehead.

"If Mud hadn't stepped in . . ." He winced as if from a blow. "Don't know why he did it, helped me like that. No one else did. He got himself a broken leg for his trouble. And two more months' time for striking a guard."

I shuddered as the memory flooded back to me. I'd had to stay in a girls' home while Mud was in jail. And when he finally got out and came to pick me up, he was on crutches. He'd told me he got in a fight but never said what for.

Don't feel sorry for me, Sai-girl. This way I won't have to go to war. Get to stay with my baby.

Crashing sounds from the hold startled both Grebe and me out of our memories.

Grebe looked at me, and I saw the ghost of a scared boy in his eyes. He whispered hurriedly, "I vowed that one day I'd pay back that man who'd saved my life. Looks like now's the time."

I was speechless. I felt like someone had taken a spoon and swirled it inside my brain, until everything I thought I knew was turned completely upside down.

"I know the crew," said Grebe. "The ones who's left won't let you get off this ship alive. But if we be quick about it, I can help you."

"Him too." I pointed to Bo. "We have to save him, too." With Sangra gone, who would believe me that Bo was her son? I could hardly believe it myself.

"Fine. But we got no time to waste."

Staying low, Grebe crossed the galley and swung open one of the old gunports in the hull. He motioned us over and told us to look outside.

It was a calm, radiant morning. I'd never have guessed there had been a storm at all if it weren't for the debris floating around us. Scraps of torn sail, ropes and rigging, and broken crates and barrels littered the water around the *Prosperity*'s hull.

"You set a good course," said Grebe. "Look."

He pointed to a craggy black island a few hundred yards away. It was so small that I'd mistaken it for a pile of floating rubble. Beyond it lay another slightly larger island, and beyond that hovered the dim shadow of an even larger one.

"We're through the Harbinger Sea. If there really is a continent to find, it has to be close now. We'll be off as soon as they get the repairs made. Everyone up top's busy. Too busy to notice a broken crate floating to that island."

"You want us to swim to that worthless little rock?" said Bo.

Grebe pointed to a wooden crate bobbing upside down in the water directly below us. "I'll lower you down. You can duck under that crate and push it to shore. If you go slow, no one'll see you. I'll tell the others I couldn't find you. They'll think you went overboard in the storm."

"And then what?" said Bo. "We wait for our grandmothers' ghosts to appear and bring us food and water?"

Grebe curled his lip. "You make it to that island, you live another day. You stay here, you don't live another hour."

If we made it at all. I shuddered, thinking of the scaled thing I'd seen in the water. But Grebe was right. What choice did we have?

"All right," I said. "Let's hurry, then."

Grebe fetched a long length of rope from the galley and lowered it out through the gunport. Bo went first, easing himself down, hand over hand.

"Quick, now," Grebe said to me. "Won't take them much longer to finish sweeping the hold."

I climbed out the gunport and braced my bare feet against the hull. Before I started down, I looked up at Grebe. A gust of wind blew his hair forward and covered his scar. In that moment he looked so young, just like any other boy back in An Lung.

He caught me watching him and looked away. "Just paying back something I owe—that's all."

I placed my hand over his rough fists clenched around the rope. They reminded me of Mud's.

"Thank you," I said.

Then I climbed down the rope and left the *Prosperity* behind.

CHAPTER THIRTY-FIVE

The Arrival

I sat at the shoreline and scooped up a handful of sand, letting it sift through my fingers. The grains were as black as jet beads. Overhead, the sky showed off that golden beauty she reserves for after her worst storms. To the southeast, the *Prosperity* was now just a dot on the horizon, headed toward the discovery of a lifetime.

Bo stood shin-deep in the water, watching the ship fade to nothing. I had just finished recounting everything the captain—his mother—had told me. I had described the portrait and shared all of Sangra's stories about Rian. The only thing I held back were the details of Sangra and Rian's fight during the storm.

I still couldn't be sure what I had witnessed. The ship had been rocking so violently. Anyone could have

fallen overboard—I nearly did myself. As much as my image of Rian had been stained, I wouldn't let myself believe that she had pushed her own sister over the side.

Bo hadn't spoken a word the whole time he listened, and now he stood in silence, rubbing the shell necklace between his fingers.

I got up and brushed the sand off my legs. "Bo?" The cold water surged over my ankles as I walked out toward him. "Hey, come on, you're going to freeze standing out there so long."

He stood as still as a boy carved from stone, which made him look even more like Captain Sangra. I shivered as I waded out to him. The wind had died and the air was warm. But the seawater was icy cold, a reminder of how close we were to the southern pole. No one, not even someone as strong as Anchalee Sangra, could live for long in water like this.

"Hey, will you come back now?" I asked him. "Please?"

Bo finally turned his face to mine. His eyes were red, but there were no tears on his cheeks.

When he saw me, the corner of his mouth lifted and that one dimple appeared. He swallowed and it vanished again. "She was coming to look for me," he said quietly.

I nodded. "She was."

I realized then why Bo had wanted to go to Mangkon so badly. He was planning to look for his mother, too.

I tried to think of what to say. What was there to say to someone who got so close to the thing they'd always wanted, then lost it for a second time? I started to put my hand on his shoulder, but he grabbed my arm first.

"Hey. Look at that!" He shaded his eyes with one hand and pointed to a dark object floating fifty yards offshore. "I think it's one of the rowboats!"

"We could shelter under that," I said. "We've just got to wait till it washes ashore."

"It could dash against the rocks and sink first," said Bo. "I'll go get it and bring it in."

"No, don't! Bo, wait!"

He dived into the surf before I could grab him. I ran after him but had to stop when the water reached my waist.

I had told Bo about the shimmering scales I'd seen during the storm, but he hadn't believed me. Even I had to admit that the words sounded absurd coming out of my mouth, like something Dumpling would say.

I watched in terror, then in awe, as he swam out, his arms rising up over the water with each stroke.

I already knew Bo was a good swimmer from our escape from the *Prosperity*. He'd kicked us the entire way to the island while I clung to the crate, useless and petrified.

Just when I felt sure he would never make it, he finally reached the rowboat.

By the time Bo had tugged the boat back to me, my legs ached from standing in the cold water. I grabbed one side and helped him haul the boat onto the sand. We dragged it up the beach all the way to the black rocks in the center of the island.

"Let's turn it over," I said. "It's banged up, but it'll make a good shelter."

"It's a *f-f-f-fooning* m-m-m-mansion," said Bo between chattering teeth.

I grabbed my wool cloak from where I had laid it on the rocks to dry and put it around his shoulders. "You sit down and warm up. I'll fix us up for the night."

With the sun going down, I scoured the beach, scooping up armfuls of fluffy dried seaweed. I piled it all around the rowboat and packed sand on top. Back in the Fens, Mud and I had gone through rough months where we didn't have a roof over our heads. He'd taught me how to make a shelter out of a crate and pack it all around with paper and trash to hold the heat in.

Most people think of food first, I remembered him telling me. *But you can go weeks on a empty belly. Can't go even one night out in the cold.*

When darkness finally descended and the stars came out, I'd managed to get the rowboat completely covered. Bo and I wriggled inside, then packed the entrance tunnel with sand.

The boat kept the breeze off us, and soon the heat from our bodies warmed up the space.

"There, that's not so bad, is it?"

"Cozy as a coffin."

I made myself laugh, though we both knew it was too true to be funny. Even though he was wrapped in my wool cloak, I could hear Bo's teeth chattering.

"Here, lean against me." I scooted beside him and held my arm up, and he huddled close to me. "Go on, try to sleep. I'll take the first watch."

I quickly realized how stupid that sounded. Watch for what?

We were alone in the middle of the ocean, and not a soul on earth was coming to look for us.

CHAPTER THIRTY-SIX

The Discovery of a Lifetime

The island we'd reached was even more misera-ble than it had looked from afar: a jagged rock ringed by a thin strip of sandy beach covered with reeking seaweed. If the season hadn't been on our side, we wouldn't have lasted the night. The day we set foot on that forlorn little spot was the longest day of the year and the height of summer in the Southern Hemisphere. The sun baked our little boat hut during the day, giving it enough heat to keep us warm through the nights.

Even so, Bo couldn't get rid of the chills. He spent most days lying huddled in my cloak, basking on the stones like a lizard. The island's rocks were made of thin black layers pressed together like flaky pastry. Without much effort, we could shear whole chunks of it off with our fingers. Depressions in the rocks had

collected rainwater from the storm, and we slurped up the water with our mouths like dogs.

I spent hours each day combing the shoreline for purple clams the size of a lotus seed. Hundreds burbled out of the sand whenever the waves washed back to sea. But they were so tiny that by the time we'd shelled and eaten them, we were even hungrier than before we started.

More debris from the *Prosperity* floated ashore. I dreaded seeing the washed-up bodies of the crew who had fallen overboard. But thankfully I only found wood scraps. I collected these and gathered them into a pile. We could have made a roaring fire if we'd had anything on hand that wasn't too wet to catch a flame.

We existed like that for three days. On the fourth morning, pale gray clouds drifted over, hiding the sun. Bo stayed inside the boat, out of the wind. He hadn't spoken very much the day before, except to curse the clams. I worried about him. I wasn't sure how water-proof the boat was. If the clouds brought rain and we got drenched, he could get worse. I didn't want to think about what would come next.

Even though I was exhausted, I trudged through the motions of keeping us both fed, watered, and warm. That morning, I tried to keep as busy as I could. But the day was too long, and eventually I found myself pacing the shore, staring at the spot on the horizon where I had seen the *Prosperity* sail away, taking all my golden daydreams with it.

I shut my eyes. I hadn't wanted to think about it, but the date kept flashing behind my eyelids. It was the day before my thirteenth birthday. I'd had some pretty miserable birthdays in my past, but nothing came close to this. I sank to my knees and sat back on my heels. My whole body was chilled and numb, but my thoughts roiled like a pot of boiling water.

What had I done? Sailors had died because of the course I set. I had gotten us stranded on an island that would slowly starve us. I had misjudged so many people: Rian, Grebe, Captain Sangra. My only friend in the world had lost his mother, and now I could very well lose him, too.

I leaned forward and gripped the sand, squeezing the sharp grains in my fists. On top of it all, I had betrayed Master Paiyoon. After everything he had taught me, all the kindness he had shown. He had treated me like his own family, and I had thrown it all away.

I felt the weight of Paiyoon's eyeglass in my pocket. I still hadn't opened it. As the sky darkened overhead, I forced myself to bring it out.

Even under the clouds, the gold case gleamed. My curving reflection stared back at me. I pressed the latch quickly.

It popped open too fast, as if it were spring-loaded. In my surprise, I dropped it on the sand. Something white fell out of the case and fluttered to my feet. I bent down to pick it up.

It was a thin piece of silk, creased from being folded into a tight square. I smoothed it out and recognized it as one of the fishermen's maps from Paiyoon's collection—the one with the slender dragon snaking through the island chain. I picked up the eyeglass and held the lens over the map.

My breath hitched in my throat. Through the lemon-colored glass, I could see words and lines that were too faded to be visible with my eyes alone. There was a scale and a compass rose. And something I had never paid attention to before: the left edge of the silk was ragged and frayed, as if someone had ripped a larger piece of fabric in half.

Blood thumped inside my skull as I ran my fingers over the torn fibers. What if Rian's map had only been half of a chart of the Sunderlands?

What if the silk I held in my hands was the other half?

CHAPTER THIRTY-SEVEN

Two Halves Made Whole

Tiny words dotted the map, only visible when I used Paiyoon's eyeglass. Even then, I couldn't understand them. I recognized only one word written in halting script over the sea: *Alang.*

Alang. I knew I had seen that word before.

I gasped, bolted across the sand, and called under the rowboat.

"Bo, wake up! Come out here, please!"

He mumbled something I couldn't hear.

"Please come out! I've got to show you something!"

The last time I'd seen that word was in Paiyoon's cabin, after we'd left Pitaya Island, after he'd seen the fortune-teller. A *Pramong* fortune teller. Hadn't Paiyoon told me that the Pramong had sailed to the edges of the known world, chasing fish?

Bo slithered out from beneath the boat, squinting against the gray light. "It'd better not be more clams . . ."

"It's not. You're not going to believe this!"

I showed him the silk and explained to him how I had found it. I pointed to the word *Alang*.

"Please tell me you speak Pramong," I said.

"Alang . . . alang." Bo's mouth moved as he thought in silence. Finally he said, "It means a sign from the gods. Like an omen."

I looked out to the ocean in the direction we'd sailed from.

An omen. A harbinger.

"Do you know what this is?" I was nearly shouting. "This is a map of our location! It shows the Harbinger Sea that we just sailed through."

The map in my palm showed a chain of islands that crossed the silk in a diagonal band running northwest to southeast. The smallest island was in the north, and the islands got larger and larger as they marched south. The island at the top of the chain was just a little speck.

I pointed down to it. "That little dot of black has to be the island we're sitting on!"

Bo tilted his head at the map, unimpressed. "What about it? So we know we're on a miserable rat pile in the middle of the sea. That doesn't help us."

I ran my hands through my hair. "I haven't done a good job of explaining." I took a breath and tried to slow down. "The other silk map that Rian showed me—it was made by the same person, I'm sure of it. She told me that the mapper who made it was on a Pramong ship that got swept into the Harbinger Sea. I wanted to show it to Paiyoon, to prove that the Sunderlands were real, but all that time Paiyoon had the other half—*this map*—hidden in his eyeglass case!"

"Where did he get it?"

"Probably the same place Rian got hers. The map seller could have torn it in half so she could make more money on each one." I pointed to the chart in my palm. "This little map is everything. Rian's half gave us hope the Sunderlands might exist, but it didn't tell us how to find it. Paiyoon's half completes the puzzle."

Bo was sitting up straight now, his brows knit together. "Do you remember what was drawn on Rian's half of the map?"

"A continent," I said breathlessly. "And now that I've got this scale, I know it was a massive one."

I lay the silk on the sand and smoothed it out as best I could. I used my finger to sketch what I remembered of the other half.

Bo twisted his chin, studying my sand drawing. "If you're right, that means Rian and the *Prosperity* went in the wrong direction. She went southeast, following the larger islands, but the continent is actually to the west, just over the horizon from—"

"From this miserable rat pile."

"There's something I don't understand," said Bo. "If Paiyoon spent the whole journey keeping this map a secret, why would he give it to you in the end?"

I knew, but I couldn't bring myself to say the words out loud. He gave it to me because despite how badly I'd betrayed him, he still cared for me. He knew how dangerous our journey would be, and he wanted me to have a safe harbor to land in. He never could have guessed that my guilt would have kept me from finding it.

I pressed the eyeglass case between my palms. "If only we could use the two halves together. Without the other map, there's no way to know how close we are to the Sunderlands. Rian would never let me get a good look at it. She's probably clutching it tight in her hand as we speak."

"No, she's not."

I looked up at Bo. "What do you mean?"

"That night of the storm, when you went to look for Rian, you left me alone in her cabin." Bo leaned back so he could reach into his trousers pocket. "I thought while I was there, I might as well pick her pockets."

He pulled out a wad of paper money. Folded in among the bills was a crumpled ball of white fabric.

"Sorry it's so mashed," he said, spreading it out on the sand. "I didn't think it was important."

My grin stretched the length of my face. "Important? This is earth-shattering! Bo, I could kiss you!"

He scooted back faster than if I'd said I had Listrus fever.

"It's all right!" I laughed. "I'm joking!"

I held Paiyoon's eyeglass over the two silk squares. Looking closely, it was so obvious that they were two halves of the same cloth. Rian's map was ripped along the right edge, Paiyoon's along the left. Using my finger against the scale on Paiyoon's half, I measured how far we were from the closest part of the mainland. I sat up again, twisting my fingers in my hair.

"I can't believe it! If this scale is accurate, the Sunderlands are only twenty miles from where we are now."

A breeze blew over us, sweeping Bo's smile away and making him shiver. "Might as well be two hundred. We'll never see it."

I stood up and started pacing the sand. "We could make it there. We've got a boat."

Bo looked skeptically at our shelter. "This thing doesn't have enough wood left in it to make a fire."

"It's battered, but the hull's in decent shape. We can take turns bailing it out if it takes on water."

"And how will we get anywhere? We haven't got oars or a sail."

"I'll lash some oars together with the stuff that's washed ashore. I'll do the rowing. You can sit in the stern and be grumpy."

"Sai, be serious," said Bo weakly.

I knew what he was thinking. I'd just proposed something utterly impossible. If we set out to sea in that wrecked rowboat, our chances of survival were very near zero. The slightest wave would capsize us, and without a quadrant or scope, we'd be sailing on dead reckoning, which wasn't much better than sailing with your eyes shut.

And then there was the matter of the dragon drawn on Paiyoon's map. After what I'd seen during the storm, I knew it wasn't just decoration. But we

311

couldn't stay on this rock. I looked up at the clouds thickening to the north. Now that I knew what the Harbinger Sea was capable of, I knew we'd never survive another storm here.

I knelt in front of Bo. "There's not a soul on earth who could find us now. If we want to get out of here, we'll have to get ourselves out."

He looked at the sea, then turned to me. "All right. But only because I'd rather drown than eat any more of those *bistrid* clams."

I smiled. "Come on, move over. I'm going to flip the boat."

CHAPTER THIRTY–EIGHT

Dead Reckoning

Twenty miles.

We'd sailed thousands of miles over the ocean, crossing vast expanses of the globe, and now our lives depended on the distance I could walk between breakfast and supper.

I sat in the center of the boat, swinging my makeshift oars. I'd lashed them together from the washed-up rigging and broken bits of timber I'd collected on the beach. We had a chipped bottle half-full of water we'd drained off the rocks, extra rope, and a tin cup for bailing. Our rowboat was in better shape than I thought, but it still leaked. Every hour we had to stop to scoop out the water that collected in its hull.

We had started out much later than I wanted, but I was too afraid of getting caught in a storm to wait for

morning. Now that we were on the water, it seemed that my fears were unfounded, at least for now. Sheets of low clouds spread over the sky, but they weren't the fat, rain-carrying sort. The sun wouldn't set until nearly ten o' clock, so at least we had daylight on our side.

We were out of sight of the little rocky island, but I knew we hadn't gone more than a few miles yet. Already, my palms burned from rubbing against the oars. Even though I'd ripped the cuffs off my pants and wrapped them around my hands to protect them, they still blistered up beneath the fabric.

Bo sat on the bench in front of me, wrapped in my cloak, watching the sky nervously.

"Stop doing that," I said.

"My auntie once told me that if you watch the sky, it won't rain."

"If that were true, no one in An Lung would ever look down."

Three inches of water sloshed in a pool beneath his feet. "Time to bail again." He picked up the cup sitting on the bench beside him.

"No, here, let me do that." I set down my oars and took the cup from him. I wanted him to stay as dry as possible. "I like bailing. It gives my shoulders a rest."

314

"I should row for a while." He looked at me worriedly. "You're getting tired."

"Not at all," I chirped. I slung water over the side of the boat. "I could row us halfway back to Mangkon. You lie down and rest. We'll be off again in a minute."

The sky never cleared that whole long day. When the sun finally went down, the moon glowed behind the thin clouds. I could see the waves and our boat, but no stars.

Without the stars, I couldn't tell our heading. The smart thing to do was to stop rowing and wait for the clouds to clear. Otherwise I could be taking us completely off course. I released the oars and set my aching hands, palms up, on the tops of my knees. Even if I knew which way we were going, I couldn't row another stroke. My shoulders and back felt stiff as boards.

Bo lay on his side, his knees drawn up to his chest. He'd been in that position for hours. I was sure he was asleep, but as I reached over to cover him with my cloak, he opened his eyes.

"You should drink some water," he said weakly.

"I just did," I lied. "It's your turn now."

He licked his cracked lips before taking a sip from the bottle. "I've been dreaming about food. Barbecued octopus on a stick, smoky and black from the grill."

I made a face. "You and Master Paiyoon. I'd give my right arm for a bowl of noodles from the Three Onions Café."

"Tell me a story about An Lung," he whispered.

I sat quiet for a long moment. I knew Bo wanted a true story, but I didn't have many good ones to choose from. Maybe it was because birthdays were on my mind that I chose the one I did.

My sixth birthday. My mother was already gone by then, killed by one of those quick diseases that swept through the Fens in winter, leaving it emptier by springtime. Mud never mentioned her, and I couldn't remember much about her other than skirts swishing around me as I played on the floor. And I remembered her frying me duck eggs. I didn't have any early memories of Mud at all. I guess that's because while she was alive he must have been working all the time. But after she died, Mud filled my world.

The year I turned six was hard, with not much to eat most days. Mud couldn't keep a job. We were in and out of friends' houses, sleeping on shop steps and inside boxes stuffed with paper. I spent most of my days begging or searching the trash for thrown-out food.

But then, just as the weather started to get cold, Mud came to me and told me he'd found work. Best of all, he'd found us a place to live. It was a shabby one-room apartment, but it was a palace compared to what we'd been used to. And we had food on a fairly regular basis.

He'd bring me lunch, then be gone the rest of the day. I'd wake up in the middle of the night to find he'd come home and was sleeping on the floor beside the bed.

The morning of my birthday, I woke up to the temple bells. When I looked around the room, I was shocked to see the far wall stacked with piles of wrapped presents. I hopped out of bed and tiptoed over to them—I had never had birthday presents that I could remember. I didn't want to touch them; I was so afraid they would vanish into a dream.

Mud woke up and raised himself onto his elbow. "Happy birthday, Sai-girl."

I ran to him and threw my arms around his thick neck and kissed his cheek. "Really? Mud, are those presents really for me?"

"Every one. Go on, don't you wanna open 'em?"

I tore into the packages. There was a baby doll, and a windup dog, a painted tin elephant, and a set of cups

317

that stacked inside each other. There was a new pair of shoes, much too big for me.

And in the last box, one golden link, shaped like a teardrop, hung from a red silk cord.

I gasped and looked up at him.

He nodded, his eyes gleaming brighter than the present itself. "It's real, Sai. Stamped and everything. We'll keep it till you turn thirteen. I know it's only one, but everyone's got to start somewhere, don't they?"

I squealed and hugged him tight, then jumped as our door slammed open.

Two policemen stomped into the room and grabbed Mud by the arms. He didn't seem surprised to see them and he didn't resist the arrest. As they cuffed his wrists and dragged him out the door, he kept his eyes down and didn't look at me. Not once.

I was wailing and clutching the toy elephant to my stomach. I didn't stop screaming until another officer finally came in and carried me off. He took away the toys and the lineal link and everything else, and dumped me at the girls' home—my first visit there of many.

I had to wait for six months for Mud to be released and come get me. The girls' home headmaster told me that Mud had been pretending to shine shoes outside the palace gates. It was a cover so he could pick all the ministers' pockets, which was how he'd afforded the apartment. The day before my birthday, he'd stolen a gold pocket watch and sold it to buy me the lineal link.

I'll never forget the day he got out of jail and came to sign me out of the home. He didn't hug me or pick me up. He barely even looked at me. And afterward he never mentioned the gifts or my birthday at all. It was like the whole thing had never happened.

I looked at Bo. He had gone back to sleep. I pulled the wool cloak up to cover his shoulders. I sat back down, watching him and watching the sea until I fell asleep too.

I woke with a jolt. The sky had grown lighter, revealing a thick fog that must have formed during the night. I stood up to get to the oars, but my vision went black at the edges, and I stumbled. I put my hands out to brace myself and knocked the best oar into the water.

"No, no!" I cried, grasping for it, too late.

I watched it bob farther and farther out of reach while the fog rolled in more thickly all around us. In desperation, I reached into my pocket and pulled out Paiyoon's eyeglass. I swiveled it from the case and held it up in front of me. For a half second, I imagined it illuminating the way for me like a beacon. But the fog was too thick, and I couldn't see anything.

Even if I'd had the best equipment in the world, I wouldn't have been able to tell our position. But it didn't matter. We should have made landfall hours ago. We were adrift, somewhere far off course.

Tears began rolling down my cheeks. The salt stung my face, but I was too exhausted to wipe the tears away. Every part of me was heavy and stiff as stone. My body begged me to lie down in the boat and sleep my way toward whatever our fate might be.

I lowered the eyeglass. As I brought it down, I caught sight of my own hand through the lens. I waved my fingers beneath it. The angle and the dim light made them look thick and blocky, as though they belonged to someone else.

I shut my eyes.

Ever since that sixth birthday, I'd thought Mud was heartless for not meeting my gaze that day he got out of jail, for never apologizing for what he'd done. Now I understood why he couldn't look at me then. It was the same reason I hadn't been able to look at Paiyoon's face at Avens Island.

Mud had been too ashamed to meet my eyes—not because he didn't care about me, but because he cared too much. He'd disappointed me. He'd disappointed himself. Life had put him to the test, and he'd failed completely. I would never call Mud a good father. But he had wanted me to have a better life. He'd wanted it so badly that he would have done anything to give it to me.

I couldn't see it then, but I could see it now.

I opened my eyes, releasing another stream of tears. I had been trying so hard to run from my past. But the past was like mottlefish ink. Even if it fades, it's still there, and not even the ocean can wash it out. I couldn't change what had come before. But I could change what I did next.

I put the eyeglass back in my pocket and wiped my face on my sleeve. Taking the last oar out of its lock, I climbed up onto the prow of the boat. I lay on my stomach and dipped the oar down on one side, lifted it, then dipped it again on the other. The water felt as thick as honey.

My shoulders were on fire, and my hands shook

with the effort. I raised and lowered my arms, keeping a beat in my head so I wouldn't stop: one side, then the other.

Right side. Left side.

Dawn. Dark.

Truth. Lie.

Friend. Foe.

Father. Daughter.

Tail. Teeth.

On and on.

Go on.

Go on.

When I brought my oar down again, the surface surged up to meet it. I gasped and held the oar still. A spray of salt water shot into the air and rained down on me.

The white backs of a dozen whales flitted past our boat like silent ghosts. I watched them, mesmerized by their white-pearl glow. And then a long, dark shape followed the whales, snaking directly beneath us. I jerked my oar out of the water and sat straight up. I waited, watching the surface as my heart pounded in my ears.

Slowly, a thick, scaled snout rose in front of the prow. Higher, then higher. Nostrils the size of teacups unsealed and exhaled. I staggered back, sloshing into the bilge at the bottom of the boat.

Drops of seawater beaded up and streamed down the Slake's bearded neck as she rose above the surface. Her dark scales shimmered like flagstones after a rain. I held frozen, staring at the beast, as the waves slapped lazily against the boat's hull.

The Slake tilted her slender head, regarding me as though she were a curious bird. She held perfectly still as one translucent golden lens slid down over her gleaming eye.

The haw. The second eyelid.

A dragon haw shows you the true nature of a thing.

The Slake stared at me through her haw. She looked at me the way Master Paiyoon had looked at me all those months ago in the shop. I didn't dare move, didn't dare breathe. The beast blinked once, then slipped back under the water without a splash.

I gasped, filling my lungs with air. I sat still, clutching my oar, wondering if I'd had some strange waking dream. Then I shook my head to clear it.

I scrambled back to my seat. Dumpling had told me that the Slake protected the Sunderlands. I never thought I would find myself listening to Dumpling, but our only chance was to follow this dragon home.

With the last of my strength, I rowed after her, digging the oar deep into the water on either side of me. Finally, our boat pierced the fog. I heard the sudden roar of waves crashing against sand.

And straight ahead loomed the dark, jungle-topped slopes of the Great Southern Continent.

"Bo, wake up," I whispered. "We made it."

CHAPTER THIRTY-NINE

A Noteworthy Neighbor

The crab scuttled sideways across the black sand.

"There he goes!" shouted Bo. "Sai, come on, don't be such a *listrissa*! Pick him up, pick him up!"

I hurried to catch the creature before it reached the shoreline. I grabbed the back of its shell with both hands, careful to keep my fingers away from its front claws, which snapped furiously at me.

"I got him! Tripe, he's a monster! Help me with him!"

Bo rushed in to pin the creature down with the prongs of the "crab spear" he had made from a fallen tree branch. Once he had it secured, I adjusted my grip and lifted it up by its menacing front claws.

"You can just call me the crab master from now on, thank you very much."

Bo nodded approvingly. "Not bad. That's four for you, but we can count him as five, since he's so big. Still doesn't come close to my record."

I held the struggling crab at arm's length as we walked up the beach to our shelter. "True. But when it comes to clams, I've got you beat."

Bo covered his ears and made a gagging face. "The horrors! Do not speak of them!"

When we reached our shelter, I tossed the crab into the pit with the others we'd caught that afternoon. I flopped down onto my mat of dried ferns, tired but happy at the thought of the monstrous dinner we were about to eat.

We had dragged what was left of our sad little rowboat onto the beach and used branches to enclose a leafy sort of hut that looked out to sea. With our fire pit going, it was fairly cozy.

Bo bowed to me and made a flourish with one hand. "How would you like your crab prepared tonight, madam?"

I smoothed my fingers over an imaginary fancy hairdo. "Sautéed with scallions and dipped in fresh chili oil, if you please."

"Hmmm. How about we hold him over an open flame just long enough to stop him from pinching your nose off?"

"Delightful."

While Bo stoked the fire, I tended to the little stone altar we had set up beside the boat. We had put out offerings of fresh water and fruit, and Bo had woven a small garland of flowers. We had no incense, but the smoke from our fire smelled sweet and clean. Surely the spirits here would feel honored. We certainly owed them our thanks for letting us stay in a place like this.

A clear stream of icy fresh water trickled out from the mountain behind us, running down to the shore. Lush trees covered the slopes that cradled our black sandy beach. Some of those trees bore fruit: a green, watery sort of apple and sticky, dark berries that tasted like tamarind candy. Best of all, the beach and tide pools teemed with easy food: shrimp, crab, and octopus, so much that we didn't even have to look at the clams.

That night, we ate until we were ready to burst. I slurped the last of the crabmeat out of its shell and held it out to Bo. "Here you go, all that's left are the brains—your favorite."

When he didn't answer, I looked up and saw that he'd gone down to the edge of the beach. I stood up and walked out to join him. It had been five days since we'd left our rocky island, and Bo had almost fully recovered thanks to the fire and plenty of food and fresh water. The morning he woke up and told me in three languages that I smelled like a goat's backside was the day I knew he was going to pull through. He was now back to his sharp-tongued self, though I often found him gazing out at the sea, watching the horizon for something I could only guess at.

Tonight a full moon cast wavy white beams over the ocean like a lighthouse. When Bo heard me coming across the sand, he turned around.

"I don't think the Sunderlands is the right name for this place," he said. "Sounds too sad."

"Maybe there's a name in Pramong for it."

Bo's dimple sank deeper in his cheek. "We should write the Queen and tell her that she needs to send lineals to those fishermen. They found this place first. Mapped it too."

I tilted my head. "Maybe. But Master Paiyoon told me once that every place he ever went had already been discovered by someone else. So maybe that Pramong mapper wasn't the first either."

I looked out to the headland where I knew the white whales would put on their morning show, leaping into the air and crashing down on their backs. If anyone had ever come to a place this bountiful before, surely they would never have left. I wondered if one morning we would wake up to find people crossing the beach toward us. So far, we seemed to be alone.

Bo shifted his weight, and I could feel him sink lower in the sand, as if he wanted to anchor himself there forever.

The next morning, we woke up early and set out to explore the area around our cove. It was Bo's turn to wear my cloak, and I flapped my arms at my sides to get my blood pumping. The tops of the trees fluttered back in the cold breeze coming off the sea. The summer was fading fast, and a rickety lean-to wasn't going to protect us much longer. We needed to either build or find a proper shelter.

"I'll head up this way, into the trees," called Bo. "Why don't you have a look around that curve and see if we can get over the rocks to the next bay?"

I rolled my eyes at him, since I'd already been planning to do exactly what he described. I picked my way over the boulders near the shore, heading for the cliffs that enclosed our little cove. When I got closer, I realized that the folds in the rock hid the opening to a cave.

A cave could be just what we needed, as long as it was dry and protected from the wind. When I stepped inside, the sound of waves crashing onto the beach hushed to a rhythmic swish. The cave was damp and sandy at the entrance, but dry farther back. The stone ceiling dipped lower there, too. With enough fern padding and a roaring fire, we could make it nice and toasty.

Just as I was ready to get Bo and gloat about my shelter-finding abilities, I felt a gust of cool air blow onto me from the back of the cave. I walked farther in, squinting. At the back of the chamber, I could make out a faint glow of light.

I frowned. The cave might not work for shelter if it was open to the elements on both sides. I continued back, bracing my hands against the rock for balance. The steady roll of the waves grew louder, and a sweet, musky smell filled my nostrils.

I ran my hands along the back wall, feeling for the source of the breeze. The wall curled in on itself, hiding a crack as tall as a man but not quite wide enough for a man to walk through. The flaky rock crunched under my feet as I pressed closer to the crack and put my face to it.

There was another cave, larger than this one, with a wide mouth that opened right over the water on the other side. The rising sun shone straight into the cavernous room, making it sparkle as if the light bounced off a thousand tiny mirrors.

No, not mirrors.

Scales.

My heart thudded in my ears as I registered what I was looking at. The Slake's long body coiled around itself in a tight spiral. This was how I'd seen her that first time during the storm, when she had wrapped herself around our rudder, dooming us to the worst of the squall. My eyes followed her long, muscled body to the center of the spiral. She encircled a clutch of three—no, four—eggs resting on top of a mound of sand and flaky stone.

The Slake's breathing halted and she stirred. I jumped back from the crack. Had she smelled me? But even if she had, she wouldn't be able to get to me through that tiny sliver of space. Cautious, I leaned forward until I could get a clear view of her again.

Her beard dangled limply from her chin as she lifted her head. Pressing her stubby clawed feet against the cave floor, she dragged herself in a tighter circle around her nest. The eggs looked small and out of place beside her hulking body. Each one was about the length of a loaf of bread. The sunlight glowed through their rubbery shells. One of the eggs throbbed twice, then went still again.

Gently, the Slake dug her snout into the crushed rock at the base of the nest, scooping it up higher around the eggs. She did this several times before settling back down. She lay with her head turned out to sea, her great body rising and falling steadily with every breath. Lying in that circular coil, she looked like the emblem for Mangkon's kingdom. *The Tail Is the Teeth*.

I stood very still, just watching her, listening to her sleep. I remembered the stories Dumpling had told me on board the *Prosperity*:

She guards the Sunderlands, devouring any ships that wander near.

The beast I watched had no idea just how many ships were on their way. Soon people would overcome their fear of dragons and come with nets and harpoons. She might sink a score of ships in the meantime, but eventually they'd catch her.

They'd pry off her dark scales, punch a hole through each one, and thread them on strings of leather. Make her haws into truth-telling glasses, just like the one sitting deep in my pocket. They would mount her head in the Queen's new museum. What a prize she would be: the Slake of the Sunderlands.

I leaned my forehead to rest on the cave wall and shut my eyes. And if those things happened, I would have been the person who led them to her.

I watched her one minute more, then withdrew from the crack in the stone. Now that I knew who our neighbor was, we'd have to move out of our cove. I wasn't a fool. The Slake was beautiful, but I knew what she was capable of.

As I stepped out of the cave, I saw Bo jogging toward me across the beach.

"Well?" he called. "What'd you find?"

I couldn't help but smile. "I found out I owe Dumpling an apology."

CHAPTER FORTY

What Is Truly There

After I took Bo into the cave, and after I showed him the Slake, and after his eyes grew wide as oyster shells while I pressed my hand over his mouth to stop him from waking the beast up with a string of curse words, we left our rowboat shelter behind and began hiking up over the next ridge.

Rian's half of the map showed a bay on the other side. We didn't want to go too far inland because we still depended on the ocean for our food, but we hoped we'd find another sandy beach over the ridge, maybe even another cave we could shelter in. One without any nesting Slakes.

"Explain something to me," said Bo, pushing a dark-leaved branch out of his way. "Why didn't the Slake tip our rowboat over when we were adrift? We were easy prey."

"I don't think we are her prey. Remember what I told you? About the whale with the claw marks down its flank? I think the Slake hunts whales. It's just like Lark told me. All these animals come down south in the summer, following the food."

"So why'd she try to sink the *Prosperity*, then? Don't you think she wanted to nibble the bones of some Mangkon sailors?"

I smiled. "Now you sound just like Dumpling. I don't know why the Slake tried to sink us. Mr. Lark is the scientist, not me."

"If that useless old bag were here, it'd be the crabs sucking out his brains and not the other way around."

I actually did have a guess, but it sounded too foolish to say out loud. Dumpling had called the Slake "a clever beast." Maybe he was right. She and her kind had survived all these centuries because no one had found them yet. She couldn't have known that the *Prosperity* was on a mission to make a map of her nesting grounds, but maybe she wasn't taking any chances. Maybe the Harbinger Sea was a graveyard for ships because the Slake made sure of it.

But if that were so, I had no answers for why she hadn't sunk our rowboat. She could have flipped us over with one flick of her tail. I thought of her staring at me through her golden eyelid. What had she seen when she looked at me? Whatever it was, she had decided to let us through. I didn't understand why, but I was grateful.

I glanced over my shoulder at Bo, who was lagging behind, leaning on his crab-hunting spear, which now doubled as a walking stick. Maybe this hike was too much for him. He hadn't gotten his full strength back yet.

"We've almost made it to the top. Let's stop here for a bit and rest."

"I don't . . . need a rest," puffed Bo. He looked around. "But I do need to—"

"Right. Use the facilities."

He blinked at me. "No. I've gotta take a *pisto*."

I rolled my eyes. "Don't let me stop you. I'll walk ahead, just up there. Maybe the trees will clear out a little and I can get a view of where we are."

I hiked through the brush, following the ridge. It sloped up steeply, and the trees thinned away to scrubby fern and then bare rock. The ridge was narrow here, with a section that branched away to my right. I followed along that route until I could go no farther. The rock jutted out hundreds of feet above a wide, circular cove.

The breeze cooled the sweat at my temples as I soaked in the view. I pulled out Paiyoon's eyeglass and held it up before me. The water below was bright, clear teal, just like in the tropics, but through Paiyoon's lens, I could see pockets of dark blue where the bottom plunged out of sight. The cove was shaped just as the Pramong mapper had drawn it: a crescent bay with a narrow opening to the sea. Waves sprayed against a shallow reef that kept the water inside the bay as smooth as a pond. What I wouldn't have given for a sheet of paper and a pen in that moment.

Looking around, I realized this bare spot was the best place to get a view of the entire cove. Maybe with the eyeglass, I could spot somewhere below that we could use for shelter. I took one step forward to get a better look, but the brittle rock crumbled and cleaved off, nearly taking me with it. I wheeled my arms and stumbled back, hearing the faint splashes of stone hitting the water far below.

I didn't need to see a pretty view that badly. We'd just have to climb down and explore the cove on foot.

"Bo!" I called out. "You done yet?"

"Sai?" said a voice behind me. "Is that really you?"

I turned around and stopped cold.

It was Rian.

Her dark hair lay in limp tangles against her cheeks, and her fine suit was tattered and shredded, but her lineal brooch shone bright as ever. An astonished smile formed on her lips as she held out both hands to me.

When she spoke, her words trembled with emotion. "I thought you were dead!" She stepped closer. A gash of dried blood across her cheek pulled tight as she smiled. "What in the world are you doing here? I had the crew search the ship for you after the storm. They told me you drowned!"

I swallowed, unable to speak. Rian's smile was so warm, her voice so sincere, that I couldn't turn away. My heart refused to believe she had ever wanted to hurt anyone. She grasped me by the forearms and held on tight.

"A miracle, an absolute miracle," she said, then tossed her hair back and laughed. "You have no idea how glad I am to find you! After everything we've suffered, this is the good fortune I needed. But tell me: How in the world did you get here?"

"I—I fell overboard," I stammered. "I drifted here in one of the rowboats."

"A miracle," she whispered again. Her bright happiness dimmed as she went on. "We have had nothing but bad luck since that storm. I sailed us in the wrong direction. We hit more bad weather and had to turn back. Two days ago, we finally spotted land. The Sunderlands."

Her eyes glimmered briefly, then darkened again. "But before we could celebrate, we ran aground."

I gasped. "Ran aground? Where?"

Rian put her hand on my arm and turned me to face the sea. Standing at my shoulder, she pointed to the northwest rim of the cove. "You may be able to see the ship from here. Something went wrong with the rudder again. It jammed, and no one could control the wheel. We ran straight onto the reef."

I squinted against the sunlight glancing off the water. One bare mast jutted past the rim of the cove, leaning at a sharp angle. My heart dropped to think of our *Prosperity*, that beautiful ship, lying broken and stranded on the reef.

"It was eerie, losing control like that," said Rian. "The winds were calm, and there was no current. We just slowly ground into the coral, and there was nothing we could do to stop it. The crew say that demons had us on their hooks."

No, not demons, I thought. *A mother with a clutch of eggs about to hatch.*

"Is the hull damaged?" I asked.

339

"Badly. I hiked up here to see if there is any hard-wood we can cut down. With our crew so thin, it will take weeks to make the repairs." Her eyes shone again with that bright ambition I remembered so well. "But we will make them. And then we will return to Mangkon to claim our prize. And now we have a true claim to it! After the storm, I was in despair. My map, the silk chart, was lost, and I thought I had lost my mapmaker as well. But now that you're here, the expedition is saved. We'll repair the ship and have time to chart the coast before winter hits us. You'll make a new map of the Sunderlands to bring back to the Queen."

I looked up at her, aware of the weight of Paiyoon's eyeglass in my palm. I had taken both the silk maps out of the case and had them folded up in my pocket. What would Rian say if she knew her chart wasn't lost at all but was just inches away from her?

She dipped her head to better meet my eyes. "Sai, what's the matter? Do you still doubt yourself? You mustn't! There's no one standing in your way now, not Sangra, not Paiyoon."

Something about hearing their names on her lips sent a cold chill into the space beneath my rib cage.

"You've still got the chance to do something marvelous," said Rian. "To make a new name for yourself . . ."

She went on, describing all the wonderful things that would happen for me when we returned. Accolades, opportunities, fame if I wanted it, solitude if I didn't. She painted my future in colors so vivid I could see it stretching out before me, a glittering, golden vision.

". . . so come." Rian beamed warmly at me. "Let's go back to the ship and get started."

She held her hand out to me. I looked down at her open palm and back up to her face. My fingers rubbed the case of Paiyoon's eyeglass. With one quick motion I could open the case and hold the glass up to my eyes. I could see Rian for who she really was.

"Tell me something," I said.

She tilted her head, smiling curiously. "What?"

"That night of the storm. Did Captain Sangra fall overboard? Or did you push her?"

Rian straightened her shoulders. She looked at me, her eyes true and unblinking. "Sai, I swear to you on my life. She fell."

I slipped the eyeglass into my pocket. I didn't need it.

"I don't believe you," I whispered.

"Sai . . ."

341

"Get out of my way."

As I pushed past her, I watched her mouth curl into a snarl. I planted my foot to run.

I made it two steps before Rian grabbed me. She wrapped both arms around my shoulders and squeezed. My ribs groaned. There was no space left to draw a breath. She leaned back, dragging my feet along the ground. I flailed with my legs, landing useless kicks to her boot-covered shins. I fought with everything I had, but her fingers gripped me like claws and held me fast. She growled with the effort of dragging me backward, toward the edge of the cliff.

Panic flooded my chest. And then I heard Mud's words in my head, as clear as if he stood right beside me.

Just like I showed ya! That's how a small girl brings a big man down.

I pumped my arms like wings. Rian's grip slipped up past my shoulders. My feet touched down. Before she could grab me again, I dropped low. This was all reflex to me now. This move had been drilled into me so many times, not even my own father could escape it.

I reached between my feet and seized Rian's ankle. I sat back against her knee, throwing all my weight, all my force, behind me.

"Ah!" she cried out.

We fell backward and slammed onto the rock.

I rolled away from her and heard a brittle *CRACK!* as the rock beneath my legs broke and fell away. I clung to the edge of the cliff, all my body's weight resting on my forearms, my legs kicking at the air.

Rian was up on her elbows. She spotted me dangling helplessly, and her eyes flashed, determined. Her muscles tensed as she made ready to pounce. And then a sudden burst of motion broke out above us.

Before I could blink, Rian had been pinned down, her cheek flat on the rock. A crab-hunting spear pointed inches from her neck.

Bo stood over her, gripping the spear tight in both hands.

"Hello, Aunt Rian," he said, panting heavily. "So nice to see you again."

CHAPTER FORTY-ONE

A Swift Return

It took me two hours to climb down the ridge while Bo stood sentry over Rian with his crab spear.

Three tries to convince the remaining sailors of the *Prosperity*, with Grebe vouching for my character, of what I had learned about Rian's true nature, and what I had seen her do to our captain during the storm.

Three men to restrain Rian and lock her in the brig, where she would stay until we returned to An Lung.

A little over three weeks to repair the *Prosperity*'s hull.

But when we finally reloaded the ship and pulled up anchor, our departure from the Sunderlands was nearly instant. A steady wind whipped up from the south, filling our sails and pushing us away from the Great

Southern Continent so fast that we barely had time to get one last glimpse before it vanished in the mist. Some on the crew said that the spirits were obviously ready to be rid of us.

I had to smile at that. We rolled back over the steep waves of the Harbinger Sea so swiftly that I wanted to imagine the Slake swimming beneath us, propelling us forward with her mighty tail. But I had seen how tenderly she treated the eggs in her nest, and I knew she had stayed behind.

At night, Bo and I whispered together about the Slake, describing every detail, every scale. We wanted to convince ourselves that we had really seen her, that she wasn't just a product of our imagination. The farther we got from the Sunderlands, the more it seemed like we had made the whole thing up.

It wasn't until months later, back home in rainy An Lung, that we discovered we were not the only ones who had an unbelievable story to tell.

Captain Sangra was alive.

CHAPTER FORTY–TWO

The Importance of Choosing Names

The bell above the door rang timidly, as though whoever pulled it didn't actually want to be heard. I looked up from my drafting table to where Master Paiyoon sat bent over his desk.

He eyed me beneath his bushy eyebrows. "I'm not expecting anything today. It must be for you."

I rose from my table and threaded the narrow pathway through the tall stacks of crates and boxes that we still hadn't unpacked.

"Blast!" I cried as I stubbed my toe. "This shop is a crowded mess!"

"Hmm," mumbled Paiyoon, nodding. "And more packages and orders arriving every day."

I sighed and swung the door open. The delivery boy took off his hat and crumpled it against his chest as he bowed to me.

"Good . . . Good afternoon, miss." His cheeks flushed the color of a raw beet. He thrust a cream-colored envelope at me. "I've a letter for you, miss!"

I smiled. "Don't call me miss. I've told you—it's just Sai."

I took the envelope from him and searched in my pocket for a tip. I could feel his eyes on me.

When I handed him the coin, he whispered, "Is it all true, miss?"

"Is what true?"

"What they say in the papers about you? About what you found on the Sunderlands?"

I leaned closer and nodded gravely. "Every word."

"Tripe," he whispered. His eyes widened. I could tell that his mind was conjuring up images of all sorts of grim horrors.

"Thank you for this." I turned to go back inside and nearly tripped over another stack of boxes near the door. "Hey!" I called after the boy. "Hey, kid, how old are you?"

"Me? Twelve next month, miss."

"We need an Assistant around here. You want the job?"

The boy's mouth fell open. "What? Me? But I . . . I couldn't . . ." He shuffled his feet in a motion I knew well: covering one tattered shoe with the toe of the other. "I don't know how to read," he said quietly.

I waved my hand in the air. "That doesn't matter. I'll teach you. I just need someone who shows up on time and works hard."

"Oh, I am *always* on time!" he shouted, then added more softly, "I mean, I would be on time. And work hard. You could count on me, miss."

"Good. Come tomorrow and we'll get started. But not too early, all right?"

He bowed and took off skipping up Plumeria Lane. I shut the door, chuckling to myself.

"What was that about?" asked Paiyoon.

"Just hired someone."

He nodded. "Hmm, about time. And what's the letter? From the naval secretary again?"

I turned the envelope over. My name was scribbled across the front in blotchy print. "No, sir, it's from Bo."

Paiyoon smiled and raised an eyebrow. "That's your third letter from him this week, isn't it?"

Now I was blushing as much as the delivery boy. "He's just bored—that's all," I said, ripping open the envelope. "Besides, it's good for him to practice his handwriting. It's horrendous." I took the letter back to my desk to read it.

Dear Sai,

Thanks for sending me the book about the pirates. I liked that one. Had lots of gore. Much better than the boring scuzz my tutor makes me read. He told me my language was "uncouth." So I picked his pocket to teach him a lesson. (Don't worry. I gave it all back. Eventually.)

Mum is doing so much better, you wouldn't believe it. We go walking on the beach near the house every day. I'm almost sad to leave. But I'm also really excited for our trip. Mum says she wants you and Paiyoon to come up and stay with us before we sail for An Song. Please say yes. I'll even ask the cook to make you clam stew.

Your Friend,
Bo

P.S. That's Lord Bo to you, vulture turd.

I put the letter with the others in my desk drawer, fighting not to laugh out loud. The thought of Bo being told to watch his language was just too funny.

And it cheered me up to hear how well Captain Sangra was doing. Everything could have turned out so very differently.

I looked up at Master Paiyoon, inspecting my work with his belly pooched out and his chin tucked in. He didn't look much like a seafaring hero, but that's exactly what he was.

After we abandoned Paiyoon on Avens Island, he had immediately chartered one of the little whaling barks to follow us. He knew there was no way to stop Rian, but he also worried we might need help. With just a handful of hardy sailors, he commanded that rusty whaler to the northern edge of the Harbinger Sea. There, they found floating debris tossed from the *Prosperity* during the storm: our snapped mast and shredded sails. As they searched for survivors, they spotted one of our lost rowboats. When they hauled the boat in, they were shocked to find a woman inside, clinging to life. Captain Sangra.

She kept repeating the same impossible story: after Rian had thrown her overboard, a great beast with a hide of glittering armor had pushed the rowboat across the waves toward her with its bearded snout. Sangra had managed to climb inside, and that rowboat had saved her life. The doctors said it was a fever dream, but Sangra stuck to her story: the dragon had watched over her, staring with its golden eye, almost as if it pitied her, as if it understood her.

Shaken by seeing the wreckage of the *Prosperity*, Paiyoon and his crew were convinced that we had perished in the Harbinger Sea, so Paiyoon reluctantly abandoned his search for us in order to bring the captain safely home to Mangkon. When we sailed the *Prosperity* back into Goldhope Harbor, it was a shock to everyone. Bo and Sangra were reunited (with many tears, no matter what Bo denies). And I was reunited with Master Paiyoon (also with many tears, no matter what each of us denies).

With her son finally at her side, Sangra began to recover. True to her word, she was done hiding him. Her family cut her off, but that didn't matter to her or to anyone else. During the nine months of our voyage, Anchalee Sangra's fame had only grown. And after the story of her brush with death on the open sea, she became the most popular public figure in Mangkon. People were touched by her devotion to her son and inspired by their reunion.

Something was changing in our kingdom. A small change, but a change all the same.

Captain Sangra was still a fearless warrior, but she was fighting a new battle now. She had her lineal melted down—something that had once been unimaginable, but now just seemed practical. Who needed to carry around all that extra weight, anyway? Most of her prize money of 150,000 leks for captaining the ship that "discovered" the Sunderlands had been put into a scholarship fund for children in need. She planned to use her prestige to pressure the Queen to make reforms at home and abroad, and she and Bo were leaving soon on a sailing trip through our Nine Islands to spread the word and build support among our people. Rian couldn't hurt them anymore—especially not when she was in custody awaiting trial for mutiny and attempted murder.

As for me, when we returned to An Lung, I had gone to the Fens and found our apartment boarded up and Mud gone. He had left the money tin for me in care of Catfish, who shockingly had spent only half of it. I went to the prisons and the workhouses, but I couldn't find Mud anywhere. Catfish said he'd disappeared from the city about a week after our ship had set sail. I had inquiries out all over An Lung but hadn't found him yet. I didn't know what I would say to him when we did meet again. I knew that it wouldn't be easy. But he was my father, and I didn't want to lose my only link to my past.

As for my future, I had a new place to go home to.

"It's getting late, Sai."

Master Paiyoon reached into his pocket and brought out his new favorite toy: a pocket watch. I had taken the cash prize instead of the Lineal of Honor, and the watch was one of the first things I had bought. Paiyoon's eyeglass hung on the wall in a glass case behind his desk.

He checked his pocket watch proudly, then checked it one more time for good measure. "It's nearly five. Shall we close up the shop and head home for supper? We can stop by the Three Onions and pick up some noodle soup."

"That sounds wonderful, sir. I'm just finishing up here and then I'll be ready."

"Ah, are those the final touches on the Sunderlands map?" Paiyoon rose from his chair and shuffled to my table. "May I take a look?"

I leaned back so he could see.

He stood quietly for a long time, and then a smile crinkled the corners of his eyes.

"My word, Sai," he whispered. "This is extraordinary work. And the names you have chosen couldn't be more perfect."

The Great Southern Continent sprawled across the paper in front of me. While the crew repaired our ship, Bo and I had hiked up and down as much of the coast as we could. I had used my notes and sketches to draw this new map in all its precise detail. We never saw any people or any other dragons. Perhaps the Slake and her young were the only ones of their kind left in the world. I knew that one day not even she could stop people from reaching the Sunderlands. But at least my map could slow them down.

I had chosen the names for every beach, bay, and headland. I'd written each word in my own handwriting this time: Sandflea Beach, Destitution Harbor, Starvation Point, Deathfall Cove. I wanted the names I chose to paint a certain picture of the Sunderlands in the minds of anyone who read the map. To help things along, I gave every newspaper in An Lung detailed accounts of how Bo and I nearly starved to death, baked to a crisp on barren, black-sand beaches while foraging for putrid clams.

It was all true. It just wasn't the whole story.

Of course, the sailors who returned with us painted a different picture, one of a lush, perfect paradise. But no one ever believes sailors' tales.

Paiyoon helped me lift the map off my table and lay it carefully in the glass frame we had made for it. When we were done, we hung it on the wall, next to his many other maps from all over the world.

"There," said Paiyoon, taking a step back. "That is a wonderful start to your career."

We turned out the lights and shut the door behind us. As I locked up, I glanced at the new letters painted on our shop banner:

Paiyoon Wongyai
MASTER MAPMAKER

&

Sodsai Mudawan
MAPMAKER–IN–TRAINING

Acknowledgments

I started writing this novel because I was thinking about mentors and how it often takes us a long time to realize the full weight of their gifts. Becky Jones was my great mentor. She taught me what it means to have strength, how to keep my eyes on the horizon, and how to weather the storms tossed my way. I also owe a great debt to my friend and neighbor, Toshikazu Hamasaki, who came into my life too briefly, but taught me so much. Thank you, Becky and Hama, for shining your light on me.

This book has had such a long journey to make it here. I'm thankful for the friends who read early drafts: Benjamin Polansky, Bradley Wilson, Samantha Clark, and Nikki Loftin (who wisely advised, "More dragon!"). Erin Lee Golden, Sarah Yasutake, Scott Ralph, and all my dear friends from the Writing Barn workshop

cheered me on when all I had was twenty-five pages. And when I was at one of my lowest points, Donna Gephart told me to keep going—not just with this book, but as an author—and it made all the difference.

This is the book that led me to my wonderful agent, Stephanie Fretwell-Hill. Stephanie believed in this story, even when she knew how much work I had ahead of me. Thank you to my brilliant editor, Andrea Tompa, who sees all the details and the big picture all at once. I think she may have a magical eyeglass of her own.

My gratitude to our fearless copyeditors, Betsy Uhrig and Hannah Mahoney, who worked so diligently to make this book shine. Thank you to our designer, Hayley Parker, and our illustrator, Christina Chung, for creating such a beautiful cover and incredible map. Thank you to my smart, imaginative, persevering publicist, Jamie Tan. And thank you so much to our Candlewick School and Library team: Anne Irza-Leggat, Sawako Shirota, Dana Eger, and Kathleen Rourke, for all you do to bring books to libraries and classrooms. My deepest thanks to teachers and librarians, who do the most important work of all. Thank you to Elise Supovitz for your passionate advocacy of my work, and thank you to the intrepid independent booksellers— I owe so much to your support.

I am lucky to have the most wonderful family a human could ask for. Thank you to my cousins Anchalee and Sodsai for being like sisters to me and for giving your beautiful names to our daughters and to the heroines of this story. Thank you to my mom and dad for working so hard all those years and giving me so much. Everything I am, I owe to you. I am so grateful for my daughters, Elowyn and Aven, who inspire me and make me proud every single day.

Finally, I dedicated this book to my husband, Tom, who has steered me true for over half my life. Thank you, Tom. For everything.